DEMON'S ARROW

WORLD WHISPERER BOOK 4

RACHEL DEVENISH FORD

SMALL SEED PRESS

Other Books By Rachel Devenish Ford:

The Eve Tree: A Novel
A Traveler's Guide to Belonging
Trees Tall as Mountains: The Journey Mama Writings- Book One
Oceans Bright With Stars: The Journey Mama Writings- Book Two
A Home as Wide as the Earth: The Journey Mama Writings- Book Three
World Whisperer: World Whisperer Book 1
Guardian of Dawn: World Whisperer Book 2
Shaper's Daughter: World Whisperer Book 3

First published in 2018
Copyright © 2018 Rachel Devenish Ford

ISBN-13: 978-0-9996061-3-1

Small Seed Press LLC
racheldevenishford.com

For Christy, Asha, and Fiona,
the bravest girls I know.

The sun was setting over Dhahara, the Desert City, when Herrith began his walk to King Ikajo's chambers. The colors of the corridors brightened, then faded as the light grew dim. Groups of magicians scurried along, lighting the magical lamps with murmured words. One of the lamps turned on with a loud pop, far too close to Herrith's ear. Inwardly he flinched, but he kept his face absolutely still, pushing his reaction down with the discipline he had honed since he was a small boy in the king's court. Hiding his emotions had always been a matter of life or death.

Herrith was nervous. The king's chambers were increasingly dangerous, with deadly currents gathering force within. Something moved in the king's blood lately. Something changed him. The king was waiting—for what, Herrith didn't know— and his impossible stillness felt like a growing storm.

Something stirred in Herrith's blood as well. He felt as though he was standing on a hilltop, looking down at the moment he had waited and worked for all his life. And now he had to be very, very careful. He could see it, but getting there would be no small thing. Thinking about it, his heart beat faster and he felt ready to meet the king.

At the door to the king's chambers, he stopped to pull his red hood up so that nothing of his face would be visible. He paused for three breaths before raising his hand to knock. His knuckles thudded onto the wood in a pattern that identified him, and the door slave opened the door. Herrith stepped in.

The chamber was large, with tables lining three walls, a dais with a throne, and cushions piled here and there throughout the room. The floor was black and shiny, bare of any rugs. The king paced in an indiscernible pattern. He barely slept these days, and it wreaked havoc on his temper. Slaves were scattered around the room, some involved in the never-ending chore of cleaning the magical black substance under their feet, some guarding the door, and many holding dishes of food for the possibility of the king's hunger.

The king's special female slaves attended him, wiping his bare feet when he paused, or his brow as he worked himself into a temper and sweat trickled out from under his hair and down his face. His women—wives, concubines, and attendants—were always at risk. Closest to the king, they were the first to bear the brunt of his anger. And yet Herrith knew that some of them loved him and longed for him. Some of the slaves were former wives who had angered the king and desired to be reinstated as wives. Some slaves wanted to be lifted up to the coveted position of wife for the first time. Herrith knew that the position of wife wasn't really something to be desired. He felt a twist of pain in his gut as

Amani's face appeared in front of him. She had never wanted to be the king's wife.

Herrith felt sorriest for the women who loved the king. He felt badly about their cloudy thoughts, for the way the king could confuse and tempt with promises he would never keep. But Herrith also felt sorry for the ones like Amani, the ones who were clear-headed but trapped all the same.

He stood waiting, face still hidden in his hood. He was one of only four red robes now. The fifth had perished on the journey back from Maween, when the king's temper was at its worst. It was always dangerous to be close to the king, whether one was a slave or a trusted red robe. Herrith kept his back straight, though his head remained bowed. He had made a promise to himself to never be afraid. Now that he had finally seen her, finally set eyes again on Amani's first-born daughter, he felt so full of joy, he thought he might never be afraid again.

Wherever the king walked, colored lights spread from his feet and swirled across the shiny floor. He was taller than most men and wore no hood or crown, allowing his straight black hair to flow down his back with only a few braids as adornment. He was long, lean, and handsome, radiating power and anger. Herrith had known the king for his entire life, since they were just two cousins playing under palace tables together. But then Ikajo's father had died and he had been made king. There was no more playing, no more friendship. Being the king's cousin meant nothing in this great court.

"Herrith," the king said, his voice a growl. A ripple of unease shuddered along Herrith's skin.

"Yes, Brightness?" Herrith asked, careful to keep his voice at the gentle, quiet level King Ikajo preferred.

"She refused to come."

Herrith sighed, silently. They were going to talk about this again. He kept his voice light.

"I know, Brightness. It was foolish of her."

It was not foolish of her, but the king had summoned Herrith many times to tell him this exact thing. Ikajo was obsessed, not sleeping, barely eating and very, very dangerous.

"I have been thinking," the king said.

He took long strides over the surface of the black floor. Herrith shuffled his feet away from the rays and coils of light that spread from the king's feet. He didn't want the king's magic to touch him.

"She has to come of her own will," the king went on. "She cannot be coerced or kidnapped. We cannot steal her, like my father did with the Maweel queen, because it will decrease her power. But I need her here, Herrith." His dark eyes were trained on Herrith's hood. "I know you understand how important she is to our plan."

His voice was very silky and soft. To Herrith, he felt more dangerous than he ever had before, even after Amani left and they couldn't find her, even after word had come back that the girl was in Maween. Herrith stood with his body like stone, looking back at the king, thinking quickly, thankful the king still could not see him.

"Show your face," Ikajo said.

Herrith sighed another inaudible sigh even as he reached up to pull back his hood. He lifted his head and looked at the king, trying to keep his features as still as possible. The king hated it when his subjects showed emotion.

"I do understand how important she is to our plan, Brilliance," Herrith said. *Of course I do,* he didn't add.

"Good," the king replied. He began pacing again, his feet slapping the floor, barefoot as he always was, reading the depths of the floor as he paced. "She must come here. It is unacceptable that she refused." He was growing agitated again, and Herrith shuddered. A slave approached with a damp, fragrant cloth to wipe the king's face, and with one swift move, the king turned and backhanded her. She fell to the floor and let out a tiny cry.

"Don't make that noise!" the king roared. "I barely touched you, it didn't even hurt!" He looked away from her and up at the ceiling. His face grew darker as he held his breath. Chains of gold and gems hung from the high reaches of the immense room. "I need her!" His voice roared and the chains clanged together, ringing against the crystals as the king's magic strained at its bounds. Herrith stood stock still. It was destructive magic, something that could bring the palace down on them. It could destroy them all.

"Brilliant one," he began, a breeze of fear blowing over him as he spoke. He ignored it. Amani's children were alive, and he could throw himself in harm's way in order to protect the people of the palace. "Surely there is some way we can bring the girl here."

The king stared at him for a long moment. "Do you not think I have looked into every possibility?" he asked, finally.

Herrith bowed his head. He had angered the king, and he needed to tread very, very carefully. "If we cannot kidnap her," he said, "perhaps we can draw her to us with something she loves."

The silence was so complete, all Herrith could hear were slight dings still coming from the leftover motion of the king's magic. After a few moments, Herrith dared to look up. The king was staring, not at Herrith, but at the high ceiling where the hanging gems and crystals continued to shudder and ripple. The gems swayed without anger now, with something like thoughtfulness. Herrith let out a breath.

"Draw her . . ." the king breathed, his voice a low drone. "Draw her . . ."

He looked down at Herrith suddenly, and Herrith was struck suddenly by the resemblance to his own face in his mirror. *Ikajo, my cousin,* he thought. *Is there nothing left to you?* On the floor, the slave the king had struck wiped her eyes and crawled away to a nearby table, where she picked out a fresh, perfumed cloth for the king.

"Wait," the king said, putting out a hand to stop her as she walked back toward him with the fresh cloth. "What's the third one called again?" he asked Herrith.

Herrith's bones froze. He stood very still, electrified by hope, love, grief, and worry in waves.

"The third one, Brilliance?" he asked, his voice so soft, so gentle.

"Don't play stupid with me!" the king roared, slamming a foot down so hard that red lines flew across the black floor, knocking every person in the room off his or her feet, including Herrith, who fell heavily onto one hip. Herrith took a moment to compose himself, rolling onto his hands and knees, then looked up.

"Aria," he said. "Her name is Aria."

Nobody breathed. The word echoed. *Aria. Aria. Aria.*

The king looked around the room, eyes burning, not seeing what was there, but something in his head, something far away.

"Aria," he said, nodding. "That's it. Aria. We bring Aria. We will draw her here, and the girl will have to follow. The warrior-whisperer will be ours, as she is meant to be."

Herrith's skin tingled as he left the king's chamber. He could barely keep his face under control. He kept his head high and walked through the palace, down the corridors his father had walked many times before, his father's father before him. His family had been in this palace since before the emperor had made all languages one. Before the divide and the war that meant they rarely crossed the sea. Before Azariyah, or Maween, became what it was today. Herrith was of warrior blood, like the king, in a line that stretched back into the past as far as anyone could see. But the king prevented most warrior magic from being practiced in his reign. He alone wanted to hold power, so the other warriors practiced in secret, tiny ways that could not be perceived. Herrith was one of these.

He walked quietly, pulling his hood up. He left the palace silently, with a brief nod to the guard on the way out. Then he was outside of the palace grounds, walking into the city, surrounded by an instant rush of noise and crowds. Up on the hill the streets were clean, but as he left the higher streets near the palace and descended into the lower city, they grew dirtier, with shacks and beggars lining the roadways.

Herrith took his red cloak off, bundling it into a harmless shape under one arm. His long black braid swung freely, wrapped with a gold cord. Now that his cloak was off, people occasionally greeted him, touching the fingertips of one hand gently to their foreheads as they passed by. Herrith nodded and touched his forehead in response. At the entrance to the city garden he paused and bowed his head, touching the tops of his eyebrows gently, then walked on, lower and lower into the city. The buildings stretched high on either side of him, homes stacked on top of each other in impossibly precarious positions. Little children ran through narrow alleyways, playing, trying to pick pockets, getting cuffed on the head for getting in the way.

As Herrith descended the narrow streets, he tried not to trip over the beggars sitting in the road, though he was jostled by people behind and ahead of him. His red robe would have cleared the way for him, but he preferred not to wear it here. People were used to seeing him, and some of them possibly knew who he was, but he could count on them not to betray his presence here. There was no love for the king in the lower reaches of the city, and the king did not respect the people here enough to try to gain favor with them. There were no informants.

He stopped at the bottom floor of a many-layered building at a doorway low enough that he would have to duck to get through. The doorway was painted a deep blue and had a barely visible sign of a circle etched into its surface, though the circle had never been finished and was missing a large chunk.

Herrith tapped an intricate pattern on the door, one that he had invented himself, and waited, holding his breath until the door swung open. The woman on the other side of the door was old, her deep black skin creased with the lines of many years. When she saw that it was truly him, she smiled and swung the door open wider so he could see into the dimly lit room. A little group of people sat around a table in the light of a lantern, eating bowls of soup. The smell made his mouth water, and he realized he hadn't eaten all day.

"Come in," the woman said. "There's some for you."

Herrith knew the pair of bricklayers at the table. They nodded to him. He knew the scholar with the wild white hair, who barely looked up from his books. He also knew the tall, startling warrior woman, but she scowled when she saw him.

"He doesn't want your soup," she said to the old woman. "He eats at the palace."

The old woman smiled at the warrior princess. "You don't know him as I do," she said. "Herrith has been eating my soup since he toddled around his mother's legs at my table, eating bites from her spoon."

Herrith felt the muscles in his shoulders relaxing. The old woman's creaky, familiar voice settled his nerves and soothed his fear.

"You have news," the warrior woman said in a flat voice.

He nodded and flicked his braid so that it fell in front of him and they could all see the gold cord wrapped around it.

"I do," he said. He took a deep breath. "It is something for all of us. The king has decided to call Aria."

There was silence as they looked at one another and at him. The old woman drew a shaky breath and put her hand on his arm.

"Will she come?" she asked in a whisper.

Herrith looked at her for a long while, then slowly nodded. "I saw her, back when we were in Azariyah. She bears marks of his poison. She will not be able to withstand his call." He looked around at all of them. "She will be here soon."

They gazed at him in silence. Herrith felt the hand on his arm tighten and looked down to see the old woman's eyes flooded with tears.

"Aria," she breathed, echoing the sound that was in all of their hearts.

Chapter 1

There were knots in Isika's embroidery. She hissed at them, trying to pick the tiny threads apart, her tongue between her teeth. Success. She laid the work in her lap and stretched, sighing, moving her head back and forth to try to relieve the soreness in her neck. She was always sore these days.

The columns in the petitions room stretched up to the ceiling far above her head. She let her eyes travel across the paintings that depicted scenes from Maween's history, all while listening to the person standing in court asking for help with straying cattle.

"They run every day. It must be poison. They always stayed home before."

Isika let her eyes drift to the old cattle herder and smiled at him when his eyes met hers. He nodded slightly.

She knew the elders thought that doing handwork during Petitions was strange. But Isika's foster mother, Auntie Teru, had suggested the work, knowing just how bad Isika's nights had been lately.

"Keeping your hands busy keeps your heart still," she told Isika.

Half a year ago, the Desert King had attacked the sacred city of Azariyah with fire, revealing that Isika was his daughter. She had been bred with warrior and whisperer blood to be some kind of magical weapon for him, Maween's greatest enemy.

It was a bit much. They had defeated him and he went back to whatever hole he had crawled out of. But Isika was still World Whisperer. She still needed to train for her queenship. And the elders had not cast her out. Yet. So she was required to be at Petitions every day, to sit and listen to people who Isika feared thought she was a usurper. Her heart had begun to race during Petitions. She could barely calm herself sometimes. So Auntie taught her to embroider and as she used her hands she found that her heart was more still. She could listen. She could glance up and see that someone was lying by the look on his or her face, and tell Karah, fourth elder, by leaning forward and whispering to her. The handwork had helped her to remain.

These days her time was mostly split between pottery and Petitions, as well as some physical training so she would have the same skills as the seekers. She ran back and forth between the workshop and the palace. She ran up mountain trails with Jabari. He was still faster than her. She sat in Auntie's garden and waited for the sun to go down so she could watch the lights of the insects in the grasses, lie down so the plants reached over her head, smell the night flowers as they released their scent.

Andar had asked her to cease her apprenticeship with the master potter, but Isika had refused. She knew she wouldn't be a good World Whisperer or queen if she dwelled in the realm of the mind. Working with clay kept her aware of order and beauty, which fed her ability to untangle policy and questions. So she kept working at the workshop and ran back and forth all day long.

She looked at the long line of people in front of her and the elders. The day before had been a feast day, and they had not held Petitions, so questions had built up.

The next woman who came forward was a tiny, wizened old woman. She raised gnarled hands in supplication to the elders and began to bow, but Andar spoke gently to her.

"No need for that, Auntie. Don't bow to us. You are here as a child of Nenyi, our equal. What is the matter?"

"They have taken all the fish from my pond," the woman said. "It's my pond and I told a group of men they could have half the fish. I've counted the fish. I can feel them in the water because I have gathering magic." A frown crossed her face. "I could tell that there were twenty, and now there is only one fish left. They say they took only half, but I know they took all of them."

Isika let her mind drift, knowing she wasn't needed in this simple interaction. She smoothed her hand over the story she was stitching with her embroidery. There were purple Keerza, the ancient creatures like gazelle, and a large black bird with red glints in his wings. He was Keethior, another ancient creature called an Othra. He was Isika's own protector, sworn to guard the World Whisperer since the first whisperer had come from Nenyi. Nenyi, the Uncreated One, Shaper of all that existed, was neither male nor female, and could not be contained in a body. He gave his whisperer to help the people. He gave the ancient ones as well, and Keethior was one of those.

Isika had stitched herself, too, just a few lines of brown thread trapped in a green light. It was a grim scene to embroider, she thought, as she looked it over, and the corners of her mouth quirked up. Her embroidery wasn't the flowers and butterflies that Auntie had first taught her.

But she needed to keep the story of what had happened when the Desert King had attacked the city, record it all somehow. Her father was the Desert King. It hurt her every day. She had always wondered who her father truly was and whether he was some majestic, strong person who could come and rescue her, who could justify her existence, her right to be here as future queen. But as it turned out, he was the most dreaded enemy of the Maweel, and even of much of their continent.

Isika could never be glad that he was her father.

Jabari told her it didn't matter. "So many of us are rescued, many of us have parents who have thrown us away," he said, referring to the child sacrifices the Workers made, when children were sent out in boats to die and the Maweel rescued them and adopted them into families.

But Isika knew that wasn't the same as having the Desert King as your father. He was evil, a true enemy, a follower of Mugunta, the evil one. And she was World Whisperer, the one meant to protect Maweel, but it turned out she had a foreign strain of magic that could destroy them all. It was the answer to a puzzle that had long confused the Maweel elders.

When the World Whisperer came back, everything should have been made right again, and yet it hadn't been. In fact, things had grown worse, and now they all knew the reason. It had shaken them all to their very bones and might shake them so hard they wouldn't survive. But what was happening exactly? Where was the poison coming from? Was it because he wanted her? He had tried to get her to come with him. Perhaps he was attacking with poison to get her to move to his side. Or were the problems and fighting and poison because of Isika herself, because of her mixed blood, the warrior strain that tainted her?

She sighed and made another stitch. This was what kept her up at night. She touched the green stitches that represented the light that had captured her and paralyzed her all those months ago. She had been working on it all day, trying to express the way it felt to be trapped under her father's gaze.

"Isika?" Karah hissed. "Are you paying attention? I believe these men are here for you."

Isika looked up, startled, then smiled to see the three Karee men who had asked to remain in the city of Azariyah after the battle with the Desert King. The Karee were a conquered nomadic people, sometimes forced to fight for the king, and these three had been fighters in his force but no longer wanted to be. Isika had advocated to have them brought into the family of the Maweel and the elders had agreed. They looked toward her with soft, hopeful eyes, and all three bowed to her as she nodded at them.

She thought again of how strongly they resembled her friend Abbas, the Karee warrior prince who had helped her escape a prison in the Worker city.

"Honor be on your heads," Andar said. "What is your petition?"

One of the men stepped forward and spoke in the heavy Karee accent. He was tall, with a long black braid that swung to his waist. The Karee had heavy brows, deep set eyes, and high cheekbones. They were tall, wiry, and strong.

"We have recently returned from our journey to find our wives, children, and parents. We brought them back, and though others wanted to come with us, we refused them. But they send a message and a request, which is why we come before you today. People from our village are disappearing, more and more all the time. One will be stolen in the night, from his bed. Two girls will go out to the well to draw water and not come back. They vanish, and we can't find them. Even our great healer can't hear their voices anymore. Their connection with us has been severed. We need help to find them. Will you help us?"

Isika stared at the men with a sinking heart. She had assumed, like a child, that bringing the men into Maween would be a new beginning, that it would be simple for them to come to Maween, become Maweel, and be happy.

But as she looked at the worried faces of the three men, brows furrowed in grief over their missing tribe members, she saw how far the problems stretched in front of her. With each increasing act of mercy, a new one needed to unfold. With each moment of wisdom, more understanding would be required. She could barely breathe.

There was a pause. Then Ivram spoke, his voice gentle. "We will consider your request," he said. "We are busy addressing the problems of our own people, and as a rule, we do not interfere in other lands."

Isika looked at him sharply. She and Ivram had been arguing over this for as long as she had known him. And as she grew more aware of the lands and seas around the little land of Maween, she could see what a small dent they were making in all the trouble, and she started to understand why they kept to themselves and took care of their own lands, because where would it end?

"We will consider your problem," Ivram went on, "and give you our decision. You may come back one week from now and hear our answer."

The men murmured to one another. They bowed their heads and turned to move away.

But at the last moment, one of them looked up at Isika and asked, "Lady, will you help us? Time runs through our hands, and we are losing our people. Will you help us?"

Isika stared at the man, her eyes burning. It seemed that he stood there holding the sorrow of the world out to her in both hands, begging her to intervene. But what could she do? She was only one girl.

She nodded gently. "I must confer with the elders and I will respect their decision, but sir, my heart goes with you and with the people you seek. Please give my love to your wives and children and parents, and let us know if you need anything to settle in."

He nodded, and the three men turned and left, and the gold on their ankles and wrists clinked softly with their steps.

The next person in line came forward suddenly, wearing a dark cloak. She looked up, the cloak fell away from her, and Isika gasped. Her own sister, Aria, stood there in the petitions line like a farmer with a dispute, not a sister to the World Whisperer.

"Aria!" she cried.

She looked at the elders for help and saw that they were

confused too. Aria could come and speak to the elders anytime. Why was she standing in a line? One day she would be sister to the queen of the Maweel.

Aria stared back at Isika, and there was such anger mixed with love and longing in her eyes that Isika felt as though hot, sharp claws were pressing into her skin.

"Aria, what is it?" Karah asked.

And Aria began to speak.

Chapter 2

*A*ria stood in the petitions room, her mind seething, thinking about people and places and feeling secure and knowing you were where you belonged. Every night, she was tormented by dreams. She needed a distraction. She needed to stop feeling sick and useless. She was determined to ask one more time to go on the next seeking mission. She was ready to beg.

Nobody understood her. She knew she was sick. She understood more than anyone else how sick she was. But she couldn't bear to only be the sick one, to not offer anything useful to her land or her people. There were still a few people in line ahead of her and she jiggled her legs to keep them from falling asleep. She pulled the hood of her cloak closer over her face and glanced up at the elders.

Isika sat on the platform that was slightly raised at the front of the petitions room. The four elders were beside her. Isika sat as though she belonged there with them, not even paying attention, playing with something on her lap. Aria felt a jolt of love for her sister, and then, swiftly, hatred so deep she gasped with it. This was her sickness. She switched back and forth between emotions that were opposite and varied, sometimes so quickly she could barely catch her breath. Back and forth in a constant torment. She hardly remembered feeling normal. She wondered if any of the people around her were wounded like her.

Isika was so beautiful. She was staring at something in her lap. Aria wondered what it was and in the next moment she wanted to hit the smug look off her sister's face. The men in front of her were next. They asked something, but Aria couldn't hear because of the ringing in her ears. She paid attention to the men's feet, to the bracelets on their ankles. She tried to bring her attention back. The pillars were smooth and long and reaching into the ceiling. There were paintings on the walls. She had been here in this land far longer than her sister, rescued before her sister ever came here, but look how secure Isika was, sitting up there in her chair barely paying attention. And Aria was not even allowed to go on a simple seeking journey.

She shook her head. They had to listen to her. They had to.

The men bowed to Isika, and Aria thought about all that had happened in the last months and the fact that their father had pursued Isika and rejected Aria. She thought of the fact that she could fight now. She had powers that she hadn't known she had before. She could go out on a seeking mission. She could be of use. She could help. She didn't have to stay in the tents of the healers like an invalid.

Her parents didn't know she was here. They wouldn't approve of her asking to go out on the seeking mission, because they were the ones who had asked the elders to not allow her to go again. She couldn't understand why they didn't understand how important it was for her to go.

The three men were talking and Aria shuddered to know that she would be next under the elders' gaze. The three men seemed to be asking for something and the elders seemed to be willing to give it to them, but maybe not. And her brain was hurting. Her mind kept flipping back and forth between love and hate and love and hate and she was so tired. If only she could run, she would run far and fast on a seeking journey, and drive all this torment away from her.

Isika told the men that she would confer with the elders and consider whether she could help the men. Aria felt a wave of scorn for her sister. Isika was so weak. She should know that as queen she could do whatever she wanted. She could push the elders away. She could take over the whole land. She didn't have to submit to them, she didn't have to make herself so small. In the very next moment, Aria thought about how Isika was arrogant.

She clutched her head, pulling her hood farther down over her face.

It was the arrow inside of her, the arrow that had pierced her all those months ago. It had reached her heart the day she met her father and he rejected her. The healers couldn't get it out, so it dug deeper into her heart with every passing day. The healers weren't sure if she would recover. She knew some of them wondered if the arrow would kill her.

The men left and Aria was next. What was she going to say? She hadn't thought this through. But there she was, at the front of the line and there was no time to come up with something so she stepped forward and threw back her hood.

She looked at all of them, each one in turn—the four elders. Laylit the beautiful, Jabari's mother. Andar the regal, Jabari's father. She didn't know those two very well. They were rather distant, considering themselves above everyone. Not fit to be rulers, Aria thought. But then she shook her head. That was the arrow speaking.

Ivram the wise, Ivy's father. And Karah the brave, Ivy's mother. Karah was pale-skinned with long red hair. She was beautiful in a way so different from Laylit's beauty, they could have been day and night. Karah was the reason that Aria's friend Ivy had tawny skin and long thin legs like a crane.

And then there was Aria's sister. Isika. She sat on her chair with her head up now, fully engaged, her eyes full of compassion for Aria. Questions in her eyes. Aria knew they wouldn't understand why she had come this way. But she needed to show the elders that they had pushed her to this point. She had no other choice because no one would listen to her, no one would let her go on the seeking journey if she did not make it big, come to Petitions, lift her hood and speak.

"Aria, dear, what is it?" Karah asked, but Laylit broke in.

"Surely another place and time would be more appropriate for her question."

Aria frowned. Even now, the elders tried to keep her quiet.

"Don't I have the same rights as the rest of the Maweel? To come to Petitions and offer my questions? Is it because I am rescued that you don't want to hear me? Or because of my father's blood?"

All around, people stirred and murmured to one another. Aria saw Isika's face close down suddenly. The elders shot each other concerned glances. Laylit started to speak, but Andar put up a hand and stopped her.

"You know you are welcome here, young one," he said. "We are simply surprised at the manner in which you have come. Speak. Bring us your question so we may set your heart at ease."

Sorrow and guilt stirred in Aria's heart. She didn't know where those words had come from. The arrow made her think and say things that didn't seem to come from her own heart, but from somewhere or someone else.

"I am sorry, Uncle," she said. "It is the arrow again . . . never mind that, though." She stood as tall as she could. "I am here to ask you to allow me to go on the next seeking journey. I wish to continue my work as a seeker."

There it was. She had made her request and now she would find out whether they were willing to listen. She stood very still.

Their faces were full of pity. Laylit and Andar looked at one another, communicating without words, and then Laylit turned to Aria, holding her hands out, palms up, and Aria knew what she was going to say. A buzzing started in her ears and her limbs felt heavy, so heavy. She could barely hear.

"Dear one, we must say no. You know that you are very ill. Your parents have asked us to keep you home for healing. And we agree with them—in fact, we are full of regret for allowing you to go before. Your injury came from a seeking journey, and you worsened during your last journey. We want you to be well, Aria, child." she said.

It looked as if Laylit would stand and come toward Aria, but in the last moment she remained where she was. "The elders love and respect you, Aria, but we cannot let you go."

Aria waited. Her head buzzed. Her limbs grew even heavier, as though she was pinned down by rage and fear. She waited for Isika to say something, to come to Aria's defense. She stood there looking into Isika's face, but Isika didn't say anything. She only sat and looked back at Aria, and then she shook her head the tiniest bit. Aria knew then that Isika didn't want her to go either. She thought for a moment that maybe Isika was jealous, maybe Isika didn't want Aria to have good things.

The buzzing grew louder until it sounded like a hive of bees inside Aria's head. Then she fell.

It felt as though she fell slowly, like a tree falling in the forest, or a stone falling through water. No one reached out to catch her. No one tried to help her. But Aria saw her sister's face change and then Isika was running toward her, jumping off the platform and in a tiny non-arrow part of Aria's mind, she knew she needed to warn her sister not to touch her. She wasn't sure what the arrow would do.

She started to tell her sister to stay back, but just as Isika reached for her, just as the whole room reacted with concern, she opened her mouth and another sound came out.

Aria hissed a long slow hiss that sounded exactly like the Balota, mud demons that had attacked the city of Azariyah with the Desert King. Horrified, she pulled away from Isika, who stared at her with shock. She jumped up, trying to ignore the stricken faces around her, and as she turned she was already running.

SHE RAN FOR A LONG TIME.

She ran out the palace and tore down the steps, down the

stone pathway, over the bridge alongside the river, and then into the fields. She ran to get rid of the memory of the demon lizard's voice coming out of her mouth. She ran to escape the shame that washed over her again and again. She was coming out of her skin.

While she ran, she threw keep-away thoughts ahead of her, knowing that her brother Benayeem would understand them and leave her alone. She lay in the grass when she was too tired to run, then got back up and ran again.

And at the end of the day when she couldn't run anymore, and she was sore and sick and heart weary beyond recognition, she went home. She opened the door to her house. Her foster parents jumped up and came toward her, and she saw with surprise that they had been crying.

It was her mother who spoke first. Elba had been Aria's mother for six years already, but Aria still did not feel understood by her.

"Do not be angry with us, dear one," she said. "We are doing the best we know. You must rest now, and in the morning we will go back to the healing tent."

Aria shook her head wildly, clenching her fists.

"I don't want to go again!" she said. Her throat was so raw with exhaustion and tears that she could barely get the words out.

"You must," her father said, staring at her with deep, sad eyes. "The healers want you to stay for the next four weeks. Please respect us, Aria," he said.

Aria slumped over, exhausted, feeling the four walls of her home closing in on her.

Chapter 3

The healers had told Gavi that he needed to walk every day as he healed from the enemy sword wound that had cut into his chest and shoulder and nearly killed him, so he walked for miles and worked in the garden. Those were the only two things he did these days, and he was growing bored out of his mind. He was anxious to get back to seeker work.

Spending his days between the kitchen gardens and his room wasn't helping him. Things weren't the same anymore. He couldn't tell if the injury had changed him, or something else. He felt newly aware of his difference. The space Gavi occupied in the world was not the same as the one his brother lived and breathed in, and it made Gavi edgy and confused. He knew Jabari wondered what was wrong with him. Gavi wished he knew.

He wasn't meeting Yab today; Yab was busy training as a ranger. Often he waited for Jabari at the foot of the garden so they could carry baskets of vegetables back to the kitchens together. Jabari would come running up to meet him from the training grounds and try not to appear concerned about the lack of strength in Gavi's left arm.

So Gavi was bringing the baskets of vegetables on his own, ignoring the pain, and trying not to overthink. He missed the simplicity of his old mind.

As he drew near the palace, he spotted Benayeem coming from the training grounds. Ben wanted to be a ranger some-day, so he was training as a seeker—the first step. Ben had the best discernment gift the Maweel had seen in years. Gavi didn't know anyone else who could hear so much of what was going on in others. Ben called it music, and it told him truth from lies, goodwill from malice.

Gavi thought the discernment gift was wasted on being a ranger, but Jabari disagreed.

"We need justice among the rangers," he had said.

Ben hadn't spotted Gavi yet, and Gavi wondered whether he could slip away without being seen, but while he was still thinking, Ben looked up and caught sight of him. His face transformed with a huge smile, and Gavi felt small for not wanting to talk. He shook himself and jogged over to join the younger boy.

"Little brother, your training is starting to show," Gavi said as he fell into step beside Ben.

"What do you mean?" Ben asked.

"Look at your shoulders," Gavi said, reaching out to pat Ben's upper arms, which were wider now, ridged with muscle.

Ben laughed, dodging Gavi and giving him a shove. "You're one to talk," he said.

Gavi grinned. It was true that he had always been

strong— both tall and wide, though he had lost weight since his injury. "Ah," he said, "but when I met you, Ben, you were a tiny thing, like a stick walking along with arms and legs."

Ben laughed and the sound rang out. Gavi felt sorry that he hadn't spent time with Ben lately. Being injured made him feel like hiding. He had always been the easygoing one, these moods were something he had never experienced. Jabari was the one with the stormy temperament. Lately though, he felt as though anything could disappear at any moment, and he only wanted to be around people who understood what it was like to be injured.

He glanced at Ben. Here was someone who might understand. Benayeem had been hurt many times.

"Where are you going?" Ben asked.

Gavi gestured at the basket of tomatoes and peppers that he had picked in the garden. "Heading to the kitchens."

"Ah," Ben said. "You and Ibba should trade secrets. I've never seen someone grow food as well as she does. Even Auntie Teru says she's a wonder."

"What makes you think we haven't?" Gavi asked.

He loved Ben's little sister Ibba. She was uncomplicated, always laughing, in love with gardening. What was not to love? She made him wish he had a little sister. He thought that in Ibba and Kital, he could see what the royal siblings would have been without the abuse that had surrounded their lives for so many years.

Ibba was a sunny, laughing child with powers of her own and a very strong gathering gift. She followed Gavi around like a little duck in the palace gardens, telling him all the things she thought about gardening and critiquing his work, which was disconcerting, since she was nine years old and usually right.

They came close to the palace.

"I'll probably head home," Ben said. "I'm supposed to help Kital with one of his projects, since Uncle is working at the palace today."

"Sounds good. I'll see you," Gavi said, but just then, as they drew close to the stairs, a familiar figure burst out of the front door and ran down the stairs, stumbling as she went. She didn't see them and they weren't fast enough to stop her as she tore down the road.

"Oh no." Gavi said, half to himself. "I was worried about this."

"Aria," Ben breathed. "But what's wrong? Her music sounds distraught."

"She told me she was going to Petitions today to ask again if she could come on another seeking mission." Gavi told him, walking faster, passing the steps and following Aria.

"What?" Ben asked. "Why would she go to Petitions to do that?"

Gavi groaned. "It's a long story." They both watched as Aria ran blindly as if there were mud demons behind her. She stumbled and fell, then got back up and raced away down the stone road.

They exchanged a glance, and without a word they began to run after her, loping along to keep in pace without drawing any nearer. It was clear to Gavi that she needed space. Aria was used to running, but so were they. Gavi settled into a rhythm, readying his muscles for a long run.

"Something's not right with Aria these days," Ben said, only a little out of breath. "Her music is so strange, it's as though someone else has moved into her body. She doesn't sound like herself. It's as though her music weaves in and out of this other music. Strange, horrible music that only reminds me of one other person."

Gavi glanced at him quickly, knowing he didn't even need to ask who the person was. Ben said it anyway.

"The Desert King."

Gavi gritted his teeth. "This arrow is likely to kill her," he said. At Ben's horrified look he went on. "Not now, maybe not soon, but it is eating our little bird from the inside."

Ben still looked terrified. Gavi spoke again, wanting to reassure him.

"It's okay," he said, shrugging away the discomfort he felt. If anyone would understand what he had been thinking and planning since the sword took a chunk out of him, it would be Benayeem, who had thought he was going crazy all his life until he realized the music he was hearing was a gift. A gift from Nenyi herself, not the signs of madness overtaking him.

Ben glanced at him with questions in his eyes.

"I think that I am meant to watch over Aria. To protect her, no matter what happens to her, " Gavi said.

"Wait, what?" Ben asked. Gavi shook his head and pointed.

"Shh, look."

Aria had reached a stream and was bending down to drink. Gavi looked around and found a bend in the stream a little way away. Gavi tried to drink quietly. Ben dunked his head after he took a drink, then straightened to look at Gavi, water running down his face, neck, and shoulders.

"I don't understand what you mean," Ben said. "Who means for you to watch Aria?"

"The Shaper, I think," Gavi said quietly.

"Does Nenyi do such things?" Ben asked. "Give one person the task of watching over another?"

Gavi stiffened. Maybe he had been wrong in thinking that Ben would understand. He wished he hadn't said anything. He shrugged and tried to think of how explain it.

"This is all happening in such a strange way," he said. "You and your sister coming to us at such a time. Every person has some responsibility in the the tapestry of the story. Every person has some thread. I think my thread runs beside Aria's thread. We understand each other, and I feel that Nenyi has asked me to her to watch over Aria. I feel compelled to make sure this arrow does not kill her. She needs to come out of this, Ben. But it will not happen on its own. She needs someone to fight for her. I think I am that person."

Ben shook his head slowly at Gavi, and Gavi watched as a thousand emotions flitted over the younger boy's face.

"I just think you're wrong if you feel that you are the only one who will fight for her," he said, his eyes very serious on Gavi's face. "Isika and I love her and we will not stop fighting for her. But . . . she is lucky to have you." He nodded once, and it felt like acceptance. Gavi knew he didn't have to explain any farther.

They followed Aria all that day as she ran across fields, over plains, and through forests. They saw her fall at the feet of trees, weeping. Many times Gavi wanted to go to her, but Ben held out a hand each time.

"She is crying out to be left alone with her music. I think she is speaking to me, trying to let me know not to follow. Let her have what she needs."

Finally, at the end of the day, they watched as Aria slowly climbed the steps to her house.

Tears leaked out of the corners of Gavi's eyes as he and Ben stood down the road, exhausted, relieved that she was finally home. Gavi knew her journey would go on like this for a long time. The little bird was a long way from being well.

Chapter 4

*J*abari savored the feeling of being on the road as he walked beside Ivy, Brigid, and Chibu. The day was hot and dusty, Jabari could feel dust in his shoes and in his teeth. The rains had been gone for nearly a month now, and the unending sun on the road had everything covered in dust. Chibu was the ranger in charge of training the three seekers who had chosen to go on with their training and become rangers. He was funny and smart, someone Jabari respected.

That morning a messenger had come to the ranger grounds asking for help with poison in a field outside the city. Chibu had jumped to take the work.

"My children need practice," he had said. Jabari scoffed at him.

"Poison in a field? This is seeker stuff."

"Not this poison," the messenger said, but he couldn't tell them more. Just that it was menacing and had been there for a while. Something strange that no one recognized, making noise in the grasses of the field.

Jabari wasn't worried. Since Isika had arrived, there had been plenty of strange poison, and they had taken care of problems well beyond the skill of simple seekers. Chibu cocked an eyebrow at his confidence, but didn't say anything.

The messenger told them the field was near a large stand of Hoona trees. There they would find a well in a field opposite a small white house, and that was where the poison was located. It was troubling the farmer because he couldn't get to his well. So they had quickly gathered their gear and run. After a long run that put dust in their teeth and eyebrows, Chibu told them to slow down.

"I don't think we're in a rush. Let's get our breath back and talk a bit. Where are you kids, anyway? Why so glum?"

"We're not glum," Ivy shot back, laughing. "Well, Brigid and I aren't, anyway. I can't say the same for glum face over there."

Jabari shook his head. He couldn't expect anything else from Ivy. She and Gavi and Jabari had grown up like siblings in the palace, and to be honest, she had gotten them into trouble more times than he could count. She always found trouble and was faster at getting out of it. She knew all the secret passageways, how to get the cook to give them more dessert, and how to disappear when the wrath came, leaving Gavi and Jabari to take the blame.

"I'm fine, Ivy. Thanks for your concern. Just thinking."

"About what? What's on your mind?" Chibu asked.

Jabari felt a flash of alarm. He couldn't tell Chibu what he was really thinking about.

"Plans," he said finally.

Brigid looked surprised.

"I didn't think you spent a lot of time planning," she said. "But I guess I have a lot to learn." Her long brown hair was plaited into a braid like the one Abbas wore. Jabari had noticed that she had started to do her hair like his when he first came to Azariyah. Before that, she had worn it in hundreds of tiny braids like many Maweel women. But her hair was different from Maweel hair, long and straight, and the single braid suited her.

"I do make plans," Jabari told her. "Just not for this day or the next. I make long range plans."

"Thinking about the future," Chibu said, nodding and grinning. "That's good. So what are your plans? Not just you, Jabari, but Ivy and Brigid as well."

Brigid spoke first. "Well," she said, "I'm in this training, and I think I want to be a ranger, but sometimes I wonder if I should join my family as a weaver like them." She smiled. "I'm not worried, though. I'll know what to do when the time comes."

Ivy smiled back at her, then shrugged. "I want to be ranger. That's all," she said. "It's all I've ever wanted to be, and protection is my only gift. I'm a fighter without a scrap of gatherer or builder or justice in me. I guess my plan is to become as strong as humanly possible." She did a back flip and a few impossibly high jumps to illustrate. "And then to protect Maween for all of my life."

They all stopped to watch and laugh at her.

"And what about a partner?" Chibu asked, as they began walking again.

Ivy looked shocked. "What?" she asked.

"You know, a significant other?" Chibu asked again. "Do

you have anyone in mind? All of you? What part do they have in your plans?"

Jabari knew that Chibu was married to another ranger, so their life was very simple. They fought, they often asked for rounds together, though Chibu's wife was staying home more often lately with their infant son.

Ivy shook her head. "I'm not thinking about that yet," she said.

Jabari raised one eyebrow at her, but didn't say anything. He knew he could tease her, but it was very likely that she would tease him right back and her teasing would go straight to the thing he was avoiding.

Brigid turned to him. "And you, Jabari?" she asked. "What about you?"

"It's pretty simple," he said, trying to ignore the heat that was coming from his toes all the way to his face, flooding him in a rush of embarrassment. He didn't dare look at Ivy for very long. She could read him too well. "I just want to be a ranger. I want to protect Maween like Ivy."

Then he pointed at a grove in the distance. "Are those our Hoona trees?" he asked. Thankfully they turned their attention away from him.

It was the second part of his plan that he couldn't tell them, the part that Chibu wanted to know about. Jabari wanted to protect Maween, but beside Isika. He wanted to marry her and work for Maween together. For a thousand other things, he would overcome embarrassment by shouting about his plans. But not this. He knew that he could scare Isika away. She wasn't ready. So he kept his plans to himself.

The stand of trees was indeed their landmark. They jogged toward the tall Hoona trees with their yellow bark and leaves, and soon saw the house and well they were looking for.

Around the well was a kind of haze, drifting along the earth and clinging to the well. Jabari narrowed his eyes, looking at it. What under Nenyi's skies was it? Chibu's face grew serious.

"Silence, kids," he told them. "Keep your hands on your staffs." He had his hand on his sword. Rangers were sword carriers, unlike seekers. Their jobs were more dangerous. They patrolled the borders of Maween and tried to do no harm, but if need be they would fight.

As they approached the well, dry heat soared up at Jabari from the field, pulling at his clothes and sucking the moisture out of his mouth. Cicadas began shrieking from the trees. It was eerie. Jabari rolled his shoulders as pressure settled on him with a heavy hand. What was it?

They drew closer, silently and slowly, all senses alert. Then the ground in front of the well opened up and giant ashy lizards poured out of it, hissing at them. The lizards stood and approached, waving toward them like a mirage of death.

"Mud demons!" Ivy yelled, baring her teeth. Before Chibu could say anything, she leapt toward one of them, slicing through it with her staff, bludgeoning it until it disappeared in a puff of ash and turned back into dust that hissed at them from the ground.

Chibu was not far behind her. He leapt toward the next mud demon, sword flashing. Then ten more sprang up from the dust of the demon Ivy had killed. The Baloto wove and sang in their ashy hissy voices. It was hard to focus on them as they wove back and forth. Though Jabari could not understand their words, the sound sent terror into his bones. Then very suddenly, one of them stood and was still. It turned to look straight at Jabari, and in the clear high voice of Aria, said, "Isika, no! Stay back!"

They froze. The demon dropped back to all fours and joined the others in their eerie sway. Jabari felt spellbound with fear until he shook it off and came to his senses. He ran to join Chibu and they whirled and fought. Then Brigid was there, a tall pale shadow who chopped and swung and stabbed at the Baloto. As they fought together, the lizards disintegrated, and they could not rise up faster than they were killed by four angry Maweel.

They fought for a long time, and then finally, finally the mud demons were gone. The four fighters were covered in sweat and the clinging dust and ashes of the dead Baloto. They stood there, breath heaving, some with hands on their knees. Brigid had just collapsed on the ground. It felt as though they were in a different reality, one where mud demons could come into Maween itself and speak in their voices. This was not right. This was not normal.

"Let's wash up," Chibu said finally, walking over to the well. Jabari followed, but as soon as he got near it, one of his senses came clambering awake.

"Stop!" he said.

Chibu looked back at him. "It's poisoned," Jabari explained.

Chibu looked from him to the well. "Can any of you cleanse it?"

They shook their heads. Isika could have done it, but she was sitting at Petitions, listening to petty quarrels. Jabari scowled. He had argued with his parents that it wasn't the best way to use Isika's gifts, and he knew he was right.

"Okay then," Chibu said. "Let's go find a stream. I need to get this lizard breath off me before it turns me crazy."

After they had found a stream and rolled in it as best as they all could, they sat beside it. Jabari stared off into the distance, in the direction of the desert. How could the Baloto have come so close?

Chibu spoke, his voice wry. "I don't really know how to make this into a lesson, as it is a first."

"Not a first," Jabari said, speaking quietly. Chibu had been away when the Baloto had come the first time. He hadn't seen how they had terrorized the city, but he had heard, surely, that they had come with the Desert King himself, their greatest enemy. For a moment, remembering, Jabari felt his breath constrict. Surely the Desert King wasn't here? No, he couldn't be.

Chibu glanced over at him, his face weary. "No, not a first," he agreed. "But, kids, something is very wrong."

THAT EVENING, back at the palace, Jabari, Gavi, and Ivy met at the bottom of the stairs. They walked into the banquet hall together for the evening meal.

As they gathered plates and began to fill them, Ivy and Jabari told Gavi what had happened that day. He in turn told them what the elders had shared before they arrived. Aria had fallen in Petitions and then hissed in the voice of a mud demon.

Jabari took a step back. At the same time that Aria had

been hissing like a mud demon, the Baloto had risen up out of the ground and spoken with her voice. What was the connection between the two? How could they even be connected like that?

They stared at one another as Ivy told Gavi what the mud demon had said to them out there in the field. Then they took their plates to the corner with the plush cushions to sit with their parents. Jabari could see his own feelings reflected in his parents' faces. They were deeply disturbed by what had happened with Aria during Petitions.

"The Great Waste is trying to poison Maween itself," Ivram said, his brow darkening.

Jabari could not help but agree. And he knew that he didn't even want to tell Isika about the mud demons. He knew how she would take it, how she would blame herself. With a sinking feeling he realized that he would never be able to shield her from things that hurt her. She would always find out and feel the burden for the land she was meant to protect.

Chapter 5

The sky was barely light when Benayeem woke. Through his window, open with a hint of breeze blowing the window cloth, he could see green streaks beginning to shoot out over the mountains, with pink and purple light edging the line of the hills. All around him was the music of the gently waking day, people stirring in their sleep, slowly coming to awareness, looking forward to the morning.

He stretched and smiled at the soothing music. Then he remembered the events of the previous day and frowned. He jumped up and got into his training clothes: soft pants that cinched at the ankles, a short tunic that wouldn't catch on branches, and his ser wrapped around his head. His tall soft leather boots were last.

He padded down the hallway as silently as he could but caught sight of Isika in the kitchen with a tiny cup of hot coffee in her hands. She looked half asleep. He smiled at her, but waved and left, not wanting to be late. He jogged down the hill to the training grounds at the seeker camp and soon found Abbas, the Karee warrior prince. Abbas had been adopted into the Maweel and helped with seeker training because of his skills in foraging and survival.

Abbas looked lively and awake, his dark eyes glinting in his face, his long braid swinging behind him. His music was quick and full of the rhythm of drums. He grinned at Ben.

"Good morning, sleepy head," he said.

Ben groaned. "I'm not sleepy," he said, "I'm totally awake."

"Oh, I can tell," Abbas said, still grinning. "That's why your eyes are half open, and your feet are barely leaving the ground as you walk."

He slung an arm around Benayeem's shoulders and Ben felt a surge of affection for the man who would most likely be related to him some day, though Ben couldn't figure out exactly what the definition of that kind of relative was.

Ben's stepfather, Nirloth, had remarried after Ben's mother had died. Jerutha, Nirloth's new wife, became a sort of stepmother, a dear friend, like an older sister, and after Nirloth had died it was Jerutha who helped Isika and Ben find a way out of the Worker village. Now it was clear that Jerutha and Abbas were falling in love.

"Ready to run?" Abbas asked.

"Always," Ben said.

Ben had changed during the years since he had first come to Maween. He spent half his days running and training now. As he exercised his body, it seemed that his mind grew stronger also. It was easier to ignore the music that flowed from the people and animals around him. He could put it in a room in his mind and close the door easily. He wasn't startled by the changes in music that leapt out at him from passing strangers. Ben had never realized just how strong the link between his mind and body was, but he was glad for it, as his body grew stronger, his mind grew clearer, and the fear that had seemed to imprison him as a child receded.

They ran a few miles and then went to the grounds for strength training: fighting and sparring, pushups, working on muscles and control as they squatted or held their arms out to the side for long stretches of time. By the time they stopped for lunch, Ben was exhausted. He welcomed the exhaustion. His mind quieted when he was tired because he could barely hear the music around him.

They walked into the eating hall for bowls of spicy curry with flatbread and then took their food out to a low hill, where they sat with some of the other seekers. Abbas sat back with a sigh, stretching his legs out in front of him and tearing off a piece of flatbread to dip in his curry. Ben's thoughts turned to his sister.

"Something is wrong with Aria," he told Abbas in a low voice.

Abbas bent his head close, seeming to understand that Ben wouldn't want to be overheard.

"More wrong than before?" he asked. "She's been sick for a long time."

Ben nodded slowly, trying to think of how to explain. He opened his hearing up to see if he could hear her, and was shocked when he found her immediately. She was in the healing tents, though, and he had never heard her from such a distance before. Was training as a seeker also honing his gift? He frowned. Her music was so strange. Parts of it sounded like Aria's song. Her song was soft and timid, easy to drown out, like a flower, but stronger than people believed her to be.

But the new music that wove in and out of Aria's song was spiky, harsh, and horrifying. Ben's stomach turned, listening to it. The poison arrow was becoming part of her. He turned back to Abbas.

"Something is very, very wrong," he said.

Abbas's forehead knit into a frown.

"What is it?" he asked.

"She's being eaten up by the poison of the arrow," Ben told Abbas. "I'm having a hard time finding her song because of so much other noise." He couldn't keep a hitch from his voice. Aria was trying to fight this alone with no healing in sight. The healers had done all they could and she only grew worse. More than anything in the world, Ben wanted his little sister to be healed. But if Isika couldn't do it, who could?

"There must be something we can do," Abbas said. He set his plate to one side and drew up his knees, crossing his arms over them and staring out onto the training grounds.

"It's so strange," Ben went on. "As sisters, she and Isika should be strong and powerful, but the arrow is an affliction they can't remove. It is tormenting one sister while the other sister is powerless to help. And I . . . I am useless."

Abbas sat back as quickly as if Ben had landed one of the sparring punches Abbas had so successfully blocked. He stared at Ben.

"Sisters . . . Ben, there is a prophecy among my people, I remember it only vaguely, like a dim memory I cannot quite grasp. There is something . . . there are sisters in the prophecy," he said, "sisters and a wound that will not heal, and a journey and a sister . . . I can't remember." He frowned and tapped his forehead. "No, I can't remember. Do you know anyone in Azariyah who might know the history and folklore of other tribes, other people?"

Ben wrapped a piece of flatbread around another bite of curry, thinking hard. He shoved the food in his mouth and chewed, staring at his plate, which was still half full. Then it came to him.

"Of course!" he said. "I know the perfect person."

He found Olumi in the library during the sleepy afternoon. He came straight from the morning's training, still dusty and sweaty, so he walked into the library carefully, holding his hands out in front of him so he wouldn't accidentally touch any books. Still, Olumi rushed forward with a look of disgust, his long graying locks brushing the ground. He was only about as tall as Ben's shoulder, with the longest hair Ben had ever seen on a person, tiny, dark-framed glasses perched on his head, and skin like black silk.

"You know better, son of Amani," he creaked. Ben tried to gauge again just how old the librarian was. He was either forty or one hundred—Ben couldn't tell.

Olumi reached behind his desk and pulled out a large duster, brushing it at Ben's shoulders and and face. Ben coughed and laughed.

"Stop, Uncle!" he said. "I won't touch anything!"

Olumi didn't stop. "No, Benayeem," he said. "If you will show up at the library covered in filth like a rat that fell from the roof of a barn, you will be dusted."

Ben snorted with laughter again, and Olumi finally put the duster down, frowning up at him, with his arms crossed.

Ben held his hands up. "I have not come to look at a book. I will not touch anything in your library. I have a question."

"Yes?" Olumi asked, still glaring.

"I was talking to Abbas, the Karee prince, about Isika and Aria," he said. "Well, my question . . ."

"Spit it out, Benayeem," Olumi growled.

Ben took a breath. "Do you know anything about a Karee prophecy regarding two sisters?"

Olumi stared at Ben. And then slowly, so slowly that Ben could see it, it was as though something seem to wake up inside Olumi, whose music had become as old and sleepy as the books around him. The music coming from him changed, growing louder and quicker. Awareness sparked in his eyes and then his face and he gave a little jump before he said, "Of course I know a prophecy, son of Amani. I only wonder that I didn't think of it before."

Chapter 6

*I*sika was in the pottery workshop at the wheel, throwing new vases for the banquet hall. She was on the last of ten when Ben burst through the door, disturbing the quiet. The workshop was too quiet these days in fact, without Jabari. Isika knew Tomas missed Jabari as well, though he would never admit it. Thankfully, Jabari did come to visit every so often, breezing into the large room with tea or snacks for them, often in the last part of the day, when Tomas and Isika were finishing up and everyone else had gone home.

And sometimes Jabari came to help Isika when she worked on the giant storage pots that could fit a man inside of them but usually held rice or water.

It was understandable that she looked up expecting to see Jabari, and she told herself that her heart hadn't sunk a bit when she realized that the guest was only her brother. She sighed. He was in a state, panting and looking around wildly, obsessed with some idea or thought, she supposed.

Tomas looked over at her with one eyebrow raised.

"Are you finished?" he asked.

"This is the last one."

"All right now. Put them in the drying room, wash up, and then go with your brother because he seems ready to explode." Tomas shook his head, a scowl on his face, but Isika knew it was a fake scowl that was really a smile.

"Help me carry these to the drying room," Isika said to her brother as he walked to where she sat at the wheel. "And then we can walk to the market tree and talk there."

Ben nodded and took one of the trays, letting out an oomph as he realized how heavy it was.

"What?" she teased him. "What about all those arm exercises you've been doing?"

"You could have warned me," he muttered, walking over to the drying room.

Isika smiled and cut the last vase off her wheel. She placed it on the second tray and picked it up with a slight oomph herself. Five wet clay vases was heavy, but she had grown strong wedging clay and running and exercising when she found the time. Queens needed to be strong, and she was going to be a queen.

Isika washed up quickly and grabbed a shawl against the chilly air of the evening. The nights had been growing cooler and last night Uncle Dawit had even lit the living room fire. They walked side by side to the market tree. Isika needed it. She was glad that Ben had burst in when he had. Going back and forth from Petitions to the workshop was wearing her out.

When they reached the tree, she leaned her whole body against it, arms reaching out side to side. She felt its life song creep into her muscles, soothing them, calming the aches, bringing restoration to her body. The tree hummed beneath her, and when she closed her eyes she saw lights tingling in its branches. When she felt that she could stand up straight again, she opened her eyes and turned so her back was against the wide tree. Ben sat on the ground not far away, eyes closed. He was probably listening to the changes in her music as the tree gave her its own song.

"What is it that you want to tell me, brother?" she asked, and his eyes flew open.

"Do you know who Olumi is?" he asked.

"The librarian?"

Ben nodded.

"Of course. Well, I've met him once or twice," Isika said. "I've gone for books that Ivram asked me to study. He hasn't talked to me much. He sort of glares from the shadows. He gave me a book called *The Nature and Magic of Caring for Books*."

Ben grinned. "Yes, that's Olumi. Well, he wants to see the two of us together."

"Right now?" Isika leaned her head against the tree. "Can it wait?"

"Today I was training with Abbas," Ben said, "and he told me of a Karee prophecy that might help us find healing for Aria. Olumi knows the prophecy, but he wants to tell us together."

Isika stared at him. A prophecy that would help them know how to heal Aria? What did prophecy have to do with Aria?

"All right," she said. She left the tree, feeling its warm buzz let her go as she lost contact with its bark. "If we must. But brother, honestly. Have you ever heard of bathing?"

THEY REACHED the palace and Isika nodded at the guards as they walked through the front doors and to the stairs that led to the upper floors and the palace library. Jabari sat midway up the stairs, chin in hand, apparently lost in thought, because they got all the way to him before he noticed Isika and Ben. He looked startled when he saw them.

"Jabari," Isika said, "I've never been able to sneak up on you. You must be far away."

Jabari looked flustered, but after a moment, smiled and seemed to recover himself. "Just thinking about a conversation yesterday," he said. "But you two are walking on soft feet. Why are you sneaking around the palace?"

Isika startled to bristle, then saw the teasing light in his eyes.

"You're so funny," she said in a dry voice, then continued. "We're going to see Olumi in the library to hear a prophecy that may help Aria."

Jabari stared up at them with his mouth open. "You're . . . Olumi . . . Hm. Never mind." He slapped his hands to his legs suddenly, then jumped up. "That sounds interesting," he said. "Maybe I'll come along. If that's okay."

"Of course it's okay," Ben said, so the three of them kept walking upstairs, and soon they were at library doors. Olumi swung the doors wide open as they arrived, and peering in, Isika saw a space she had not noticed before at the back of the room on the left. She looked at Ben. He also looked confused.

"Keeper of the books," Jabari said, bowing his head low. "Thank you for welcoming us."

"Stand up straight, son of Andar," Olumi said, brushing his hair behind him. "I don't recall inviting you." Then he sighed and gazed up at the ceiling. After a moment, he shook his head. "I suppose it is good that you are here."

They took off their shoes and Olumi led the way over to the new area that still puzzled Isika. Olumi had pushed some of the towering piles of books back to form a seating area that was several cushions deep. Olumi walked across it to find a place to sit, so Isika followed. It was like walking on a bouncy stack of pillows, and she nearly tipped over but righted herself and found a place to sit, sinking into the cushions. She looked at Jabari with wide eyes and he grinned back at her.

"What are all these books?" Ben asked, gesturing to the tall stacks of books around them.

"These are all the books that concern this topic," Olumi said.

Jabari looked alarmed.

But Olumi went on. "We don't have to read all of them right now," he said. "What do you know of the Karee people?"

"Only what I have learned from Abbas," Isika said, "and a very little from the three men and their families who have come to join us. They are nomadic, and though they are under the power of the Desert King they have historically opposed him. Abbas is in hiding because he led an army of warriors against the king. His father pretends to have no part in this."

"Very good," Olumi said. "There is much more, but that's

a good start. Settle back on your cushions and hear what I have to say."

Isika wiggled around until she was comfortable, and waited. After a dramatic pause, Olumi went on.

"The Karee are an ancient people. They have wandered for most of their existence, though at one point they did have a city. No one knows where that city was, because it was hundreds of years ago and memory of it has been gone for a long time. But they have always had a storyteller, who travels between camps to tell them the news and remind them of the stories. The storytellers are growing more rare, because the Desert King hates them and kills them when he finds them. He has the Karee under his thumb, and though they try to resist, he always shuts them down. There are rumors that the last storytellers have gone into hiding. One of them, a very old man, told a prophecy about two sisters."

Isika shivered.

"It has been passed from tribe to tribe over many years, so I don't know if it has changed, but this is the way I know it. Would you like to hear it?"

Isika hesitated. Now it didn't seem certain that the prophecy was about her and Aria. It could be her and Ibba, or sisters like Karah and Jerutha, or no one they knew at all. She felt prickling in her hands and feet. It seemed like a moment that could tip over the edge into a new kind of understanding. But in a way, how could she not hear it?

"Yes," she said. "Of course. It might have to do with Aria's healing, right? Of course we want to know anything we can. If it will heal Aria, it doesn't matter what it is."

Olumi nodded from his perch of cushions. "Settle back then children, settle back." He began to sing.

"Two sisters, out of the night,
fall into the dirt and the dust.
One lies still, injured and lost.
The other dies to lift her.
Two sisters, a sword, a boat, and a bird,
Hearts broken, lies spoken,
Grip of evil, grip of pain
One must heal the other or death will steal,
One will die for the other's gain
The world cracked open
Out of the night comes the way.
The land cries out, an answer comes."

Isika lay back in the cushions with her eyes closed, looking into the dark night sky, full of stars. As she watched, two stars fell to the earth. Isika saw that one of the stars was her, and she stood and began to run, because the other star was Aria. But Aria's star fell and lay still, and Isika couldn't get her to wake up.

She blinked, back in the library, looking at the concerned faces above her. Everyone was grave, and Ben had tears in his eyes. Isika reached up to find tears on her own cheeks.

After a pause, Olumi spoke. "This is what I have heard of the prophecy," he said. "And I have never known how to interpret it. But I know of a great Karee healer named Asafar who holds the prophecies now that the storytellers cannot be found. I believe he is still alive, though you may ask the Karee warrior who has come to join us. If you find Asafar, he will be able to tell you of the prophecy and whether he knows what it means."

"I don't understand," Isika said. "It didn't seem to say anything about healing Aria."

Jabari looked at her, his face solemn. "It wasn't very practical," he said. "But I think it reveals that somehow Aria's healing is tied up with you."

"Yes," Olumi agreed. "The two of you are linked, and it seems that you cannot be separated. Asafar will know more."

The sun was setting when they came out of the library.

"We should go to the elders," Jabari said, as they walked down the long hallway. "I think we need to travel to the Karee people and find this healer. Perhaps he will have wisdom for us."

The palace corridor was lovely in the late afternoon. Rosy light poured through the windows and played in the white stone alcoves in the walls. Isika ran her hand along the wall lightly. She nodded at Jabari.

"You're right," she said. "Let's do it now."

The eating hall was cozy in the lights of evening, platters of food spread over the tables. Isika realized she was hungry as her mouth watered at the sight of the food. Gavi looked up from his cushion as they walked into the room. He smiled at them.

"Ah, there you are, Jabari," Laylit said, putting her plate down and rising to embrace her son. "Hi, Isika. Hi, Ben," she said.

"We've come from Olumi," Jabari told his mother. "And I invited Isika and Ben to eat with us. We have a question for you."

Laylit nodded and gestured toward the food table. Isika, Ben, and Jabari heaped food onto their plates, then joined Gavi and Ivy on the cushions, near the elders. Sometimes Isika had glimpses of life in the palace for Gavi, Jabari, and Ivy. The palace was beautiful, but Isika preferred her life with Teru and Dawit in their small, simple house. The palace was large, airy, with great echoing rooms, and quarters for the different families. Teru and Dawit's house was small and cozy. One day, when she was queen, Isika would have to live in the palace. She wondered what she would do to make it feel like home.

She looked up from her plate at the sound of Jabari's voice. She had been lost in dreams and Jabari had already finished eating.

"What?" she asked.

Ivy laughed. "Little daydreamer," she said. "Jabari asked if he could share what you know with our parents."

"Oh," Isika said. "Of course."

While she ate, Jabari told the elders what Olumi had shared with them. "And he thinks that the healer, Asafar, will know more about the prophecy. So we are hoping to go visit him."

Ivram ran a hand through his grizzled hair. "I know Asafar," he said. "But from long ago. We have not visited the Karee in many years. Not since Queen Azariyah was taken."

"I don't understand," Laylit said. "Why do you need to know more about this prophecy? It sounds like something that comes from the Great Waste."

"The Karee do not follow Mugunta, beloved," Andar said.

"We need to go because there may be something in it that can help to heal Aria," Isika said. "And also, we may be able to help with the problem the Karee men brought to us."

"The disappearing people," Karah said, nodding her head slowly.

"You can't mean that you want to let them go!" Laylit

broke in.

"Can we have a moment?" Andar asked. The elders moved closer to one another and spoke softly.

Isika took a bite of spicy zita greens and a spoonful of the soft white cheese that sometimes went with the greens. The cheese helped to mellow the sharp taste of the greens. The food was amazing, and she sighed. The palace cooks would help to soften the change of moving to the palace, whenever she did that. The food here was always amazing.

In the corner, Andar was shaking his head, "I don't think it's wise," Isika heard him say, but then Karah spoke, loudly enough for the others to hear her.

"Andar, we must begin to trust the World Whisperer, and Jabari too—your son, and Ben! They have shown that they are trustworthy in their judgement. Why not send them to the Karee people? It would be a good gesture of friendship, as well, after far too long."

"But the Karee are under the rule of Gariah," Andar replied. "It is too dangerous to allow our future queen to go to those lands."

Ivram rubbed at his face, his head tilted to one side as he thought. "It does seem like a journey is necessary. Until we understand what is happening with Aria and the Karee people, we cannot understand how we are being attacked and why there are Balota in our land. This prophecy speaks of the land crying out." He nodded to himself. "I believe we should let the children go. But I feel...Olumi must go with them."

Isika crossed her arms over her chest and waited. After a few more minutes of hushed speaking, the elders turned to the youth.

Andar nodded. "You may go," he said.

Chapter 7

*A*ria opened her eyes and stretched, blinking until the white canvas of the healing tent came into focus. Dark gloom crashed over her. She was here again, still here, always in the healing tent. She had protested, she had told her parents she didn't want to come back, but they hadn't listened and now she was back in this place of sickness. Waves of anger washed over her. She bit the inside of her cheek. There were other patients. In the corner bed was an old woman who had been trapped inside poison walls, and in another corner, a boy who was wasting away of some sickness that she didn't understand. They didn't have an arrow leaking poison into their bodies. They might recover.

She hated it at the healing tents. She wanted to be home with her parents, or better yet, out on a seeking journey, pulling down walls, sleeping under the stars. But no one would let her go. She was losing hope, trapped here because no one knew how to heal her.

After a while, one of the healers came into the tent and

close to Aria's bedside. She gently laid a hand on Aria's head, to feel how she was this morning. Aria knew it wasn't good when the healer bit her lip and smiled, pasting a smile on her face, though tears sprang into her eyes. It wasn't easy for the healers to be with her, since the most skilled ones could feel what Aria felt, and they almost couldn't bear it. Another reason for her to be gone.

"Let me bring you breakfast," the healer, Orie, said, "and then we'll do a session with Sophie. The two of us will find a way to make you feel more comfortable today, Aria."

Aria didn't answer, she just turned and stared up at the ceiling, frustrated. They didn't understand that she didn't feel bad. She didn't feel weak, or sick. She wasn't in pain—most of the time. She just felt angry, and like she needed to run.

The breakfast was tasteless. Sometimes, when the arrow was really strong, Aria couldn't taste food. She lay staring into the moving canvas of the tent until the healers came back. The tents moved at least once each year. The healers sent pain and sickness into the earth, and though it had the ability to absorb great quantities of human pain, it needed time to recover, so they moved around. After they moved, gatherers would come and heal the land itself, planting flowers and trees, putting strength back into the soil.

Orie and Sophie brought hot herbal compresses to draw the arrow farther out of her, though they had never been able to remove it completely. Aria liked the comforting compresses. They smelled good and she liked lying there and pretending that the hands of the healers were the hands of her real mother, Amani, gently wiping the warm cloth over her forehead, her shoulders, her arms.

As they worked, Sophie used the compresses, while Orie put her hands on Aria's head, arms, and legs, drawing the poison out with her gift.

Aria began to feel better. When she opened her eyes, the air looked clearer again, brighter. Before it had been covered with a gray haze. She could think clearly again, and she remembered that Sophie and Orie were helping her, that her parents had sent her here for healing, not to trap her. She didn't hate the tent as much. Then she remembered who she was—that she was Amani's daughter and Isika's sister. She remembered that she was loved and that she loved her siblings and her mother, who had died too young. She also loved Gavi and Jabari, Brigid, and her foster parents.

The healers finished their work and smiled at her. She smiled back and sat up in her bed. Sunshine streamed in through the windows of the tent, lighting up the leaves of the sweet-smelling plants Gavi had brought the day before. She breathed in their smell.

The tent flap opened and there Gavi was. He walked in and sat on the corner of her bed, smiling at her.

"How are you feeling today?" he asked, his voice gentle.

It was an old question, one that Aria was tired of. Sometimes she refused to answer when people asked it, but she felt better after her treatment, so she answered him.

"I'm doing okay," she said. "The herbs and hot compresses felt good today. And your plants are making this tent smell so good."

"Are you up for a walk?" he asked. "Sophie said I could take you up into the gardens, if you want."

Aria thought about it. She saw the shadows of trees dancing in the sunlight, and being outside appealed to her.

She nodded and he jumped up and held a hand out to her, but she pushed it away.

"I'm not an old woman."

He shook his head, smiling. "I know you're not an old woman, Aria."

They walked all the way to the kitchen gardens to see the new peppers Gavi was growing. Gavi went on and on about his plants and Aria listened, allowing her mind to flow along with his words, happy not to wrestle over her problems as they looped through her mind. They fell quiet as they walked among the trees and flowers outside the kitchen gardens.

Aria held her hand out to a tree to see if she could feel the same thing that Isika felt, but it wasn't there and there was nothing except this arrow and the pain. It was strange, when her mind was clear the arrow hurt her more. When it was cloudy, it only made her angry. She stood in front of the tree for a long time, and slowly felt the pain recede, though she didn't think the tree had done anything. She could see that the poison arrow was slowly poisoning the rest of the Maweel as well, including her sister, who might never be the same.

She needed to leave Azariyah. She needed to go, perhaps all the way to the Desert City to find her father. If she stayed, she would poison this entire land and she might even harm her sister. When it was bad, she wanted to hurt her sister, to sink her teeth deep into Isika and make her hurt as much as she did.

"What are you thinking about?" Gavi asked. They stood in a large stand of Hoona trees with warm yellow bark and leaves that flashed with gold.

"I'm thinking about how I need to make this right," Aria said without thinking. She trusted Gavi so much that she sometimes said more to him than she should, but she went on this time, feeling open, like a new flower, like something outside of herself was guiding her. "I need to do something, Gavi. I need to do something. I can't just lie here and let them try to heal me over and over again while it doesn't work."

"What will you do?" Gavi asked. His face was worried, his brows drawn together.

"Something . . . Something. I need to go . . ." She looked at him and suddenly knew that if she told him her idea, he would try to stop her.

He shook his head at her, crossing his arms. His nearly white hair stood up the way it always did and he was growing the beginnings of a slight golden beard on his face. It intrigued Aria as she stared at him.

"You can't go anywhere, Aria," he said. "You need to let us take care of you and wait a little longer. I have heard a rumor that there might be a healer who can help you. Isika and Jabari will go to search for him. Perhaps he can make you well."

Aria stared at him. "What?"

"Well, there is talk," Gavi said. "I don't know what will come of it, but a small group are going to the Karee people to see if they can find a solution for your arrow."

Aria was furious. She felt a sharp pain in her chest. "So that's what you do," she said, "you sit around in your little palace and you talk about me with the heir to the throne, and you mock me and you tell each other that I need to be healed and I need people to rescue me, when I am fully capable of rescuing myself and, in fact, I am more powerful than you could ever know."

Gavi looked hurt. He reached out toward Aria and she

drew back, but he reached out farther and as his hand met her arm she felt the waves of healing coming from him, drawing away the poison. She slumped over and all the power went out of her, and she leaned against him.

"Oh, Aria, I'm so sorry. This is horrible. Please, little bird, please wait. Please don't do anything you can't take back. Please stay here and let us take care of you."

But Aria knew she wouldn't.

It was a dream that night that did it. Flashes of colors came toward her—birds flying, trees that waved. She walked to a tree and put her hand on it. This time she could feel the life song coming from it the way her sister could. A voice spoke to her, and it danced, this voice, and waved, danced and waved, and danced and waved and looked a little like the mud demons. She smiled at the dance, and the voice said, "Aria, I know what can heal you. I have it for you. Come to me. I will help you."

She woke up breathing hard. The sun hadn't yet risen, but the first birds were singing. She knew she needed to leave immediately, before anyone else was up. She needed to go to the voice. Her father, in the Desert City.

She got up quietly and packed the bag that always came with her. She stole into the kitchen and packed as much food as she could, including several small nutrient-rich loaves of bread. She took the flowers and plants that were by her bedside and silently placed them around the beds of the other two patients in the tent. She wrote a short note to the healers saying, "I was homesick, so I went home. I will come back in two days."

She hoped it would work that the healers would think she was at home and that her parents would continue to think she was here.

She stole out into the early dawn, and she ran. She ran first to her home, where she snuck around on silent feet, packing her bedroll, travel gear, and bow and arrows. She changed into her travel clothes, and now she was running out of time, so she left swiftly and started her journey across the fields, toward the road that led to the desert.

She felt as if she knew the way, as if the arrow inside her was turning and pointing home.

GAVI STOOD and watched as a small figure left the tents. He followed as she went home, and sighed with grief when she emerged, fully suited for travel. It was true, then. She really planned to leave them all. As she walked across the fields, he shouldered his own bag and followed her.

Chapter 8

*B*enayeem sat in the garden in the early morning sunlight, checking his arrows. He had fletched them recently, as part of his seeker training. They weren't bad for a first attempt, but they weren't anywhere near what he had seen Jabari make. He smoothed the stiff feathers on the end of one arrow and stretched his awareness out around him, listening for the song of his family in a morning ritual that he had begun when they first moved to Azariyah. For so many years he had lived in a panic, hearing strange music and not knowing where it came from. The music had been full of anger in the Worker village, discordant and angry, so that he thought he was insane. Then he had come to Maween and learned that he had a very rare discernment gift. He could detect feelings, intention, and truth through music that not everyone could hear. Now that he understood the threads of music, he could sort them and put them in their places. It soothed him to know where everyone he loved was.

Recently he had begun playing with sending his awareness out farther and farther, finding the familiar music of friends. Today Ibba wasn't hard to find. He could hear her with his physical ears, singing while she pulled weeds from the garden. Underneath, he could hear her particular music, earthy and fiery, swooping and rising, beautiful in a way that few things were. She had the song of an artist, and he knew that no one really guessed at what the nine-year-old would become.

He found Auntie Teru in the kitchen with Kital. Auntie Teru's song was calming and warm, though run through with tiny notes of anguish. She had lost her son to a poisonous battle and the hurt never went away. But she was strong, and her song remained warm and steady. She was happy with Ben and his siblings near her. Kital's song was sunny and happy, lilting music with very little complication. Kital had always been a sunny boy, and Isika had protected him for most of his life to keep him that way.

He reached out farther. Isika was in her room, her song the way it always was—fierce, longing, tinged with sadness. He and Isika both had songs filled with sadness. They had seen a lot, and they both missed their mother so terribly. Ben always thought that Isika's song was a bit like an anthem. It was purposeful, inspiring. If everyone could hear it, they probably would already have made her queen.

Uncle Dawit was in his workshop. He had the old song of past days. Benayeem could hear songs from the palace. It was harder to isolate the sounds from here, but he knew the palace well. He found Jabari. Gavi must be sleeping, his song too quiet to hear.

He stretched farther and found Aria's family at their house, but he couldn't hear Aria and he frowned, the arrows still in his hands. Then he remembered that Aria was at the healing tents. Ben checked for Aria several times a day lately. Deep worry and concern for her caught his stomach at times, froze him in the middle of routine tasks. She couldn't be so sick that she was lost to them. She couldn't be. Surely they could learn something from this Karee healer that would help her.

He listened at the edges of the healing tents. The pain and worry there made him flinch as he listened to the unfamiliar songs of patients and healers, but he could not hear his sister.

He frowned, staring out into the morning sky, listening hard. Perhaps she was still sleeping. He listened closer, but there was nothing, nothing that sounded even a little like Aria. Usually her music was so easy to hear, as familiar to him as Isika's or his own, even though it was mixed these days. He stood, alarmed now, staring in the direction of the healing tents. Nothing.

He bolted into the house, where the smell of spice tea filled the air and Auntie was making tea-boiled eggs for breakfast. Isika was there now, her face sleepy. She caught sight of the look on his.

"What is it?" she asked.

Auntie Teru was staring at him as well, and Ben realized he probably looked crazy, standing there with a hand full of arrows, body tense. He tried to relax. He shouldn't alarm Auntie or Isika before he really knew something was wrong.

He tried to clear his face of worry. "It's probably nothing," he murmured. "Just music that is louder than normal," he said.

The family stared back at him. Auntie raised one

eyebrow, and he heard her music spike and fall, spike and fall, as she brought herself back from panic. He felt horrible.

"Sorry, Auntie," he said, going to give her a hug. "I didn't mean to alarm you."

"You are the oddest boy," Isika said, pulling an orange from the bowl on the table and peeling it. Ben shrugged, thankful that he wasn't going to be questioned further, hoping that his vagueness would be enough to satisfy their curiosity. And it was, perhaps because he usually didn't have much to hide. Everyone's music calmed and settled into a familiar rhythm in song beginning to blend together into harmony as family rhythms often did.

Ben ate quickly, trying to calm himself as well as he had calmed them. As soon as he was finished and had washed his plate in the washing basins, he put his boots on and ran out the door, calling goodbye, making the excuse that he needed to get to his training early. He headed straight for the healing tents.

When he arrived, Aria was nowhere to found. The healers told him that her parents had come and taken her home. He ran to their house then, taking a short cut over a grassy field near the horse barns. Aria's family raised animals and took care of sick ones. Ben had often thought that their willingness to care for Aria came from their natural compassion. Their music was so soothing and beautiful that he felt himself lulled into it as he ran toward the door. Aria's music was not mixed into theirs, despite what the healers had told him.

He took a few deep breaths while he stood on the doorstep and listened intently. There was no concern woven into their music. They had no idea that Aria was gone. He knocked.

When the door swung open, Aria's foster father, Tal, stood before him. Uncle Tal was wide in the shoulders and impossibly tall, with a gentle soul and soft music. Elba came to join him in the doorway, her face wreathed in smiles as she spotted Ben. He knew from their music that the two of them bore a deep love and ongoing worry for Aria, but they had kept their strong peace despite the stormy ache of her music.

"I came to find Aria," he told them.

Elba looked surprised. "She is at the healing tents," she said. "Didn't you know that?"

Ben shifted from foot to foot, looking up at the sign above the door that proclaimed peace for all who entered. He hated the way people's music changed as they grew sad or worried, and he hated to be the one who caused it. But he knew his gift also came with a desire to keep the peace at the cost of truth, a desire to keep the music good and sweet and whole, not afraid or scary or mad. He always fought this tendency. He looked back at the two of them standing there, questions on their faces.

"She is not at the healing tents," he said, "and I cannot hear her music anywhere."

They didn't get worried as fast as he had, and Benayeem thought that perhaps this was because they didn't trust his gift as much as he did. They didn't realize how far his reach was, that he could have found her anywhere in the city of Azariyah. They weren't afraid the way Ben was, with his palms clammy, his heart racing. At first they thought she was somewhere close by, that perhaps she had just needed to get away. But he knew she was already gone, so he left them as they searched for her. It was time to tell Isika. She would believe him.

She was with Olumi when he found her, in the library going over Karee texts as Isika prepared to leave.

Ben heard them arguing even as he approached the room.

"It's important, Uncle," Isika said, standing with a stack of books in her arms. "It's more important to find a cure for Aria than it is to keep a few books safe. We need to take them on the journey."

Olumi was shaking with barely suppressed anger.

"And what would happen if we lose the books that we have?" he said. "We can never get them back."

"Olumi," Isika began, but then she caught sight of Ben in the doorway. Something on his face made her pause, because she put the books down on a nearby table and moved toward him.

"I can't find Aria anywhere," Ben told her. She stared back at him. "Isika, I can't find Aria anywhere," he said, enunciating more clearly to make sure she understood what he was saying.

Her eyes widened. "How far can you hear?" she asked.

"The farthest fields of Azariyah," Ben said. "She is nowhere within the bounds of the city or the greater areas surrounding the city."

Isika flinched, shaken. "Sorry, Olumi," she said and turned to leave the room. Ben followed swiftly after. He toppled into her as she ran down the hallway and stopped short. He realized that what had stopped her so suddenly was running smack into Jabari, who was on his way to the library. Ben rubbed at his forehead, which had collided with the back of Isika's head.

Ben listened and was surprised by the fearful music coming from Jabari. He must have heard about Aria already. But then Jabari spoke.

"Gavi is gone," he said. "I can't find him anywhere, and I've been searching all day.

"Aria is gone, too," Isika told Jabari. Their eyes were locked on each other.

There were bits of song that Benayeem heard from each of them recently that had nothing to do with fear or anger. Each of them had a song that only appeared when the other was near. It made Ben feel like he was eavesdropping and he tried not to listen, but it was hard when they were locked in a staring contest. He moved to intervene.

"So are they together?" he asked. "What do we do?"

Isika looked at Ben then, breaking her gaze away from Jabari. "Why would Gavi have let her escape?"

Jabari bristled at this, standing taller and looking down at both of them.

"If you think Gavi would do that, you don't know him at all," he said.

Ben could hear Isika's anger beginning to simmer. He sighed.

"None of us know what has happened," he said. "Isika, can you send Keethior to find Aria? Do you think he could do that?"

Isika stared at him. Without a word she turned and walked away. Ben and Jabari shared a glance, then followed. Lately, when Isika was concerned, Ben had noticed she grew imperious. He thought of it as her queen face.

When they caught up with her, she was standing on the steps in front of the palace, her queen face very certainly in place. Ben heard a ripple in her music as she called to the ancient bird who was sworn to serve her. After a few moments, he heard the far-off song of the Othra. Othra song was warm, tender, and invigorating all at once. In the song was the thread of oddness that was Keethior, different from any of the other ancient birds. Despite his worries, Ben smiled.

Keethior came in a rush of wings and feathers and alighted with a cheerful amount of drama onto the space in front of Isika. He was huge. His head reached above Isika's waist.

"You called?" he asked out loud so all of them could hear.

Isika sighed and dropped her head. "Yes, Keethior, I called."

"What do you need, whisperer?" the bird asked, cocking his head to one side.

"Aria is gone," Isika said. "Will you please find her? We need you to bring her home."

The bird departed in another rush of wind and feathers and the three of them stood on the steps. Ben felt powerless and empty, wondering if they would be fast enough to stop the danger that aimed itself at Aria.

Chapter 9

The days of Aria's journey were long. For the first few days, she walked through fields, keeping to the edges, cloaking herself as she walked in the direction she knew she needed to go. She had stopped wrestling with herself over why she was walking in this direction, how she knew exactly which way to go. She only knew, and it was enough.

She had practiced hiding herself for a while, after she realized she could feel Isika wherever Isika was, and that possibly people could do the same with her. She wanted to disappear. She had wanted to disappear for a long time.

She walked every day until she couldn't go farther, ate a bit of the nut-rich bread she had taken, then rolled up in her blanket and slept. The fields grew farther apart. She hid from farmers, and finally she was in the scrubby grasslands with only a few grazing goats. On the fourth day, when she reached the beginning of the long desert, she had grown too tired for cloaking, so she let the magic go, feeling herself exposed. She hoped she was far enough away that no one would find her.

The desert. It stretched on every side, endless sand that seemed to undulate in the distance like an old parchment of paper, golden white bronze in the setting sun. She walked in the early mornings and the late afternoons. Sometimes she walked at night.

She ran out of bread and began to shoot small lizards with her bow, cooking them over a fire during the cold night. She roasted desert plants if she couldn't spot a lizard, and ate them slowly, because there was never enough and she was hungry. Sometimes in the morning she would find more food near the fire, food that hadn't been there the night before. She wondered at this, but concluded that whatever was calling her was also looking after her.

She found she needed to use all her seeker training to remember which plants were edible, how to travel in the cool of day. Or how to keep warm at night when she didn't have enough blankets, hiding behind a bluff, or her pack, to stop the wind. Finding water was one of her biggest problems, but it was there when she needed it most, and this, like everything else, she didn't question.

Something that troubled her was the poison of the arrow, which grew until she could no longer tell the difference between the thoughts the arrow sent her and her own thoughts. She grew angrier, fiercer. She wasn't sure that she remembered the Aria who had existed before the arrow. Sometimes she missed her former self, but she comforted herself, knowing she was going where she belonged. In Maween they couldn't heal her; neither did they want her.

She had scratched seven days of walking into the leather

of her travel bag when the bird came. She knew him. She tried to ignore him at first, but he refused to be ignored, flying in and out of her vision, sending her calm thoughts that battled with the arrow and threatened to bring her back to herself. He tried to speak to her. She ignored him. He flew circles around her, twittering. Finally she turned to glare at him with hands on her hips.

"I know whose you are," she said "so don't even bother trying to convince me that you're here for my good. You're her spy."

"What are you doing, Aria, daughter of Amani? Where are you going?"

"How is that any of your business, bird?"

"Everything in Maween is my business, daughter, and if you weren't poisoned, you would remember that."

"We aren't in Maween," she snorted. "So you can go home now."

He landed at her feet and she frowned down at him. He opened his wings and flapped them back and forth slowly, dazzling her with the red lights within his feathers.

"You are a daughter of Maween, beloved Aria. You are Amani's daughter, Azariyah's granddaughter, daughter of the ancient earth. Where are you going?"

Aria scowled, then walked around him and marched on. He followed, half hopping, half flying.

"I don't have to tell you where I'm going," she spat, "and as for being beloved and a daughter, how would you know any of that? You are nothing but a bird, a slave to the sister who runs the land you speak of. She cares nothing for me."

He gave a low cry and flew away, and Aria told herself she was glad.

That night, there was a dead desert hare at her camping spot when she came back from looking for water. Aria knew the animal came from Keethior, but she was hungry and she hadn't had anything besides lizard in days. She took the hare and dressed it. That night she made a stew in her cooking pot, spicing it with the desert plants and herbs that Abbas had shown them on their last journey.

The taste made her cry as she sat beside the fire.

The bird flew to a nearby dune as the tears ran down her cheeks. He opened and closed his wings in the light of the fire, glittering like red jewels. Hope wafted to her from his wings, and it made her angry because she was gone, she had left. There was no return for her, and how dare he come near with his glimmering hope? She glared at him and sent him dark thoughts.

"Where are you going, daughter?" he asked.

She answered him then, to hurt him and her sister through him.

"I am going to my father, bird. He has called me and I will answer him, unlike my sister, who chooses to ignore the love that he would offer."

"Aria, no," the bird said with deep sorrow, and the sound of his voice cut through Aria's heart and the poison of the arrow.

For one, brief moment she felt horror at what she had chosen to do—to leave Maween and go to the Desert King, enemy of her people. Then, like a shutter, the poison of the arrow closed over her mind and she felt glee at the sorrow she had caused the bird. Perhaps he could take a bit of her own. She wanted him to feel the despair she had felt for so long.

"Daughter, don't do this," the bird said. "He poisoned

you. This arrow that is slowly killing you, turning you against everyone you love, comes from him. It is his poison. Don't go to him."

Aria couldn't think of what to say in response, so she turned her back on him. That night she had a full belly. She wrapped herself in her blanket and lay behind a dune to sleep. She tried to ignore the bird as he sang a mournful song. But that night she dreamed of Isika calling her, saying "Do not leave, sister. Do not leave. Stay with us. Please stay with us."

In the morning, Aria felt refreshed and ready to continue. It was as though the arrow in her was a magnet being led to another magnet. She followed the feeling, as true and strong as anything she had ever felt. She had been lost for so long, but now she had a purpose.

That night she ate stew she cooked from a lizard she shot. She tried to ignore Keethior. He had flown high above her all day, giving her space, but rejoined her while she was cooking her stew over a tiny fire. The stars began to come out and the air grew cold. Aria hunched over her fire for warmth, stirring the stew. Finally she grew angry enough to ask him the question that had been burning in her ever since he had come.

"Why is it, bird, that normally you only help my sister? Speak to *her*? Care for *her*? Why is it that some people are deemed more special than others?" He didn't answer. She shot him a look and poured the stew into a metal bowl, flinching when it burned her. "Why is it that you ignore me?" she went on. "Why does Nenyi ignore me? Why do you choose *her*, the one that gave me up? Why is it that I was sent out, and she remains? Why is that I caught the arrow that was meant for her? Why is it that things are so unequal?" She took a shaky breath and held her face over the hot soup, breathing in. The bird opened and closed his wings.

"You imagine that Nenyi has forgotten you," he said.

"He has," Aria said, shooting him another glare.

"You couldn't be more wrong. Nenyi would never leave his daughter. He is with you, protecting you even now as you betray him."

"He betrayed me!" Aria shouted. "And you didn't answer my question!" She put the bowl down, breathing too hard to eat. "You tell me that Nenyi is with me, but how can it be when I have never in my life felt his touch?"

Keethior waved his wings gently back and forth. Aria crossed her arms over her belly and rocked back and forth.

"Daughter," the bird said. "You feel his touch every day. You feel it in the sun on your skin and the food in your belly and the trees around you lifting their branches to protect you. Now I am here because of his love for you, but you are rejecting his touch because of the pain inside you."

"Everyone feels the sun," Aria said. "I'm talking about the special love that Isika feels. How is that only for her?"

"Maybe you need to understand the simple love that comes to all before this other special love that you want. But even as you betray your people, Nenyi will not leave you. You cannot leave her presence or concern for you. You cannot get rid of it. It is not within your power."

Through the flames of the fire between them, Aria glared at Keethior with all the hatred in her heart. The glow of the fire reflected in the bird's black eyes. She waited for the anger within her to reach its peak force, and then she spit her words at him.

"I am leaving. I am not coming back. I will never come

back to Nenyi or to Maween. I am going to my proper place with my father and I hope you and Isika and all the people who have done me wrong will feel the pain of his rage when I tell him what you have done to me."

With her words, the bird gave a long, keening wail. He flew out into the night in a storm of wind, and Aria fell on her face sobbing. She had never felt so alone.

～

KEETHIOR FLEW BACK to Isika in the brilliant pre-sunset light, and they sat on the porch of her house together, looking over the houses and gardens that tumbled down one hill and up the next. It had been cloudy, and the clouds were lit up by strong light, tinged like copper. The Othra had been sending Isika flashes of what he saw, though he couldn't maintain a connection strong enough over the distance to show her everything.

She had seen pictures, enough to hurt—Aria, hunched, angry, thin, stumbling through sand, looking like a waif in the large bowl of the desert. Her heart ached as she saw flashes of Aria's anger and heard her venomous words. On the porch, Keethior told her the things she hadn't already heard. Aria was going to the Desert King in Dhahara, the far away city of the Gariah people, and Isika could barely hold herself together. She leaned her head on her knees and cried for her sister. She wept for all the pain and anger inside of Aria. She wanted to leave and find her that minute, but she knew it wouldn't be any good for her to run off on her own.

She sat with Keethior in silence, wiping the tears that wouldn't stop. Keethior gently waved his huge wings back and forth, and Isika's heart began to settle into some kind of peace.

"Is she lost to us?" Isika asked the bird.

Keethior cocked his head and clicked his scolding rasp. "Do you have a poison arrow also, my sister?" he asked. "No one is ever lost to us. There is nothing lost that cannot be retrieved. And I didn't tell you the rest," he added, looking at her with one bright black eye. "I found the young son of Andar. Gavi is there following her, watching over her."

Isika's eyes widened. She looked down over the hill with all its gentle people, going about their work, getting ready for the end of the day. She felt the weight of her past and the weight of her future and sighed.

"Well," she said. "That is something."

Chapter 10

$\mathcal{A}$t first, Gavi followed at a distance because he knew Aria wanted to be alone and would not appreciate him witnessing her misery. As she grew more weak, though, he had to offer his help. He watched her go a whole day without looking for water. She ignored so much of her training that he was stunned by how much she had lost, how forgetful she had become.

She knows better, he thought, as Aria walked past a spring without refilling her water flask. He stooped and filled two extra flasks. That night, as she was sleeping, he switched her empty flask with a full one. He began to leave roots and desert plants at her campsite for her to find in the morning.

He tried to watch out for her. One night, he shot a predator that came too near, a large, weasel-like animal that he left in a shadow of a dune, not wanting to risk eating it. The desert stretched in every direction. They wandered beside a tiny stream, just a trickle alongside a line of trees. Aria followed the stream as though she knew exactly where she was going. Gavi wondered about her sense of direction. How was she so sure about where she walked?

Keethior came to him one day and asked him what he was doing.

"What do you think you will accomplish by following Aria, son of Andar?" the Othra called to him.

Gavi wouldn't speak to Keethior. He didn't trust the Othra not to try to sway him. Gavi knew what he needed to do as clearly as if Nenyi had landed in front of him and shouted it. He needed to guard Aria, with his life if needed. His loyalty was to the girl he followed as she stumbled from dune to dune in sand that was deep and difficult to get through. He smiled and waved at Keethior, until the bird scolded him and flew away.

Gavi grinned to himself, knowing that through Keethior, Jabari and Isika would learn where he was. Hopefully the knowledge would keep them from worry.

He did grow frustrated as they walked farther and farther across the desert. He didn't know where Aria was going, but as the days passed and she did not waver, he began to see that they had to be headed straight for the walled city of the desert under the reign of King Ikajo. He worried about what would happen if they entered Dhahara, the Desert City with Aria so weak and deceived. He couldn't be sure, but he knew the Desert King had wanted Isika. Maybe he was calling Aria now, knowing that Isika would never come.

One day, worried and tired of worrying, he decided to approach Aria. He walked toward her over a dune as she trudged through the sand, tottering from step to step. She looked up at him and her eyes were glassy and wild. It took her a long time to recognize him, and he felt despair prick at his stomach. She stared at him, finally seeming to see him.

"I thought you were a vision," she said.

"Have you been having those?" Gavi asked.

"Sometimes," she said.

"You need to drink more water," Gavi said, as he handed her his flask. She took a tiny sip and then handed it back without saying a word. They walked like that for a while longer, stumbling through the scraggy dunes.

"You don't seem to be so well," Gavi said, reaching out to grab her hand briefly and giving it a squeeze.

"I feel fine," Aria said. Her voice was flat.

"You're walking very slowly," Gavi said.

"I am a seeker just like you," Aria spat at him. "I know how to travel across a desert."

"I know that, and I believe you can, but you're so sick, Aria. You're not going very fast and I'm worried that you won't be able to get where you're trying to go. I worry that you will die before you get there."

She didn't deign to answer him, and they kept walking. Every once in a while she would give him an angry look, as though she wanted to be rid of him. But she didn't say anything and they continued to walk. Gavi tried to think about what he could possibly say to get her to come back to Maween with him.

That night he camped beside her. He shot her a desert lizard and helped her prepare food. She seemed very tired that night. She lay on her bedroll, letting him help her. She ate the food he gave her.

She even let him lay a hand on her forehead and try to take some of the arrow's poison. He could feel how little of

Aria was left around the arrow and felt that shiver of despair again. Her sickness was so advanced and they were so alone.

The next morning they ate the rest of the lizard stew over a small fire. They drank cups of coffee that Gavi had made with the supplies in his pack. Aria smiled at him tentatively after she took a sip of coffee.

"I've missed this," she said.

The sun was rising just behind her, and it made the escaped fuzz of her hair glow. Gavi knew that he had to speak.

"You are so sick, Aria," he said. "Please come back to Maween with me."

She stared at him, her smile disappearing, replaced with fear and rage in her eyes. She stood up, ran toward him, and shoved him so that he fell backward over the log he was sitting on, splashing hot coffee over himself. She slapped him then, and the shock of violence from a friend hurt much more than her little slap. He held up a hand to stop her when it seemed that she would hit him again. She took a step back, and he slowly got up, shaking coffee off his shirt.

The sun swung suddenly above the horizon, and he could see the lines of anger in her face, in every muscle as she stood facing him, fists clenched. If she would hit him, she was farther gone than he had known.

"I will not be turned back," she hissed, and her voice changed until it sounded like a mud demon. Gavi faced her, keeping his face calm, though terror for his friend raged inside of him. "I know where I am going and you cannot change my mind, so don't bother trying. Leave me alone, Maweel brat. You are no longer my friend, no longer my brother. I am going to my father and my true people."

Poison oozed from her words, driving fear and despair into him. He watched as she rolled her things and set out. He sat on a rock for a long while, but the conviction to guard her didn't budge, so he stood to follow, weary and sore of body and heart.

He followed at a distance again, watching over her. At some point every day, he would turn up and smile at her to let her know he was there. But then he would retreat so her anger couldn't find a place to land, so he wouldn't feed the demon that was trying to take her over. His days were filled with boredom and a heavy heart as he simply followed. He listened and walked carefully, offering her help when she needed it, heaping sand to shelter her from the wind when there was no shelter. He filled her flask. He shot desert lizards or rabbits when she forgot about food, and some days he felt so lonely, he wished he could go back, but his conviction never wavered, so he followed.

Chapter 11

*I*sika left Petitions one afternoon and found Jabari sitting on the steps in front of the palace. She watched him for a moment as he sat with his chin in his hands, gazing out across the town and the stone road to the valley below.

He glanced up. "Hey," he said. "I was just thinking about you."

Isika felt heat come to her face. "Aren't you always?" she asked, sitting next to him.

He laughed. "I meant more than usual," he said. "I was thinking about how tired you must be, going back and forth from pottery where I know Tomas bosses you without mercy, to Petitions, where my parents make you sit for hours. Aren't you exhausted?"

Isika felt tears prick behind her eyes at the unexpected sympathy.

"Well," she said, composing herself. "I did come from a Worker village, so I understand work. I think they're trying to prepare me for being queen. Unceasing work," she said, at the same time as Jabari. He grinned at her.

"Ivram?" he asked.

"Of course," she said. "You've heard it." She was quiet for a moment, then laid her forehead on her hand. "The exhausting thing . . ." she broke off and Jabari finished the sentence for her.

". . . is worrying about Aria," he said.

She looked at him. "You knew."

"Because I'm tired of worrying about Gavi," he said. "And Aria."

It was late afternoon and all around birds were beginning their evening calls. The trees whispered in the tiniest of breezes. The season had been hot, hotter than usual. Isika felt ready for the coolness to begin, the rains to come first and then cool air to wake them up in the mornings with light touches on their faces.

She looked out over what would one day be her realm and sought pride or excitement. But she was discouraged. Had she found Aria only to lose her? Jabari elbowed her.

"I know what you need," he said, his mouth lifting at the corners. "Let's go to the market tree."

Isika smiled.

The market was teeming with life, with everybody there to buy food to prepare for the evening meal. The stalls were busy, the vegetables ripe. Women with colorful headscarves haggled over prices, cloth sellers called out to one another. Isika saw giant piles of tomatoes, greens, the golden yellow of ripe mangos. The tree that spread over the market was the oldest and largest tree in Azariyah, with huge smooth branches that twisted over one another, and large bright green leaves.

As soon as Isika reached the tree, she leaned against it and spread her arms across the wide trunk. She sighed, her spine tingling with happiness as the tree's lifesong found her. It was like falling into a warm bath or slipping into the cool waters of a lake.

She climbed up the tree and into its branches, vaguely aware of Jabari climbing after her. She found her favorite wide branch and lay down like a cat, her arms on either side, eyes closed, her cheek resting on the warm wood.

Visions flickered behind her eyelids as they often did in the tree. A city, a garden, and a red-robed man who was familiar to her. He had been with her father when the Desert King had tried to burn her city down.

In the vision the red-robed man was smiling, and Isika felt her heart reach out to him with happiness as he stretched his hand to her.

She blinked and came out of the vision. Jabari was sitting on another branch, not far away. His back rested against the gray trunk of the tree. His eyes were closed.

"I saw the red-robed man from your dreams," she said.

Jabari looked at her, startled. "I've been dreaming about him every night," he said.

"Do you feel happy when you see him?" she asked.

He nodded.

"That's how I felt just now," she said. "What does it mean?"

He shook his head. "Did you see any big cats?" he asked.

"Big cats?"

"I've been dreaming about large silver cats."

"Do they exist?"

"In legend. But the legends seem to be coming to life lately."

Isika sat up on her branch, reaching her arms up to the one above her.

"Jabari," she said. Isika wanted to go after Aria. It was obvious, as soon as she saw Jabari's face, that he didn't think she should go. He looked as though he knew what she was going to say, and a muscle flexed in his jaw. She crossed her arms, balancing on the branch easily.

"I want to go find Aria," she said. "I know I said I would go to the Karee people, but I need to go to Aria, and Keethior says she's going to Dhahara." It didn't matter what he said, she knew she was the one who had to go and find her sister. It was her fault that Aria had been pierced by a poison arrow, her fault that Aria was sick and had gone to their father. Isika felt a familiar flash of panic at the thought of her little sister wandering into the Desert City.

Jabari was shaking his head before she even finished. "I should have known I would have to talk sense into you," he said.

"I have plenty of sense, thank you!" Isika snapped, her temper beginning to boil.

He lifted his hands, seeing the look on her face. "Hear me out," he said.

He rubbed his hair with one long hand, distracting Isika from her anger. He was keeping it longer these days, little spiky tendrils of curl that Isika liked. She pulled her eyes back to his face and scowled.

"I'm listening," she said, her voice flat.

"Her gift tells her where you are. We don't know yet

what she will do. She could betray you to your father if she knew you were there."

"She would never . . ."

"You don't know what she will do!" Jabari's voice cracked a little and Isika sat straighter. He was upset. She hadn't seen it. She had thought they were just wandering back into a typical Isika and Jabari argument. "She's not herself, Isika. From this point on we have to treat her as though we don't know her. She's dangerous like this, especially near King Ikajo. I would've said that she would never leave us and go to the Desert King," he went on. "I would've said that my brother would never leave without telling me goodbye. It seems to be a time of impossible things. People do things we never would've dreamed they would do. People try to set fire to our city and people can heal rivers that we thought were poisoned, and our friends run away," his voice broke again and his hair was completely mussed. "We can't say what Aria will do. We can't say whether she will betray you. It's too dangerous. You can't go. Until you can learn to block her, you can't go."

Isika watched his face and softened. He was hurt that Gavi had left and was worried about her.

"Block her?" she asked. "Do you think I could learn to do that?"

"You should be able to," he responded. "People can usually learn to block any kind of magic, especially if it's malicious. You should be able to learn how to keep yourself hidden from her, otherwise anyone who had that gift could find you at any time. You need to work on that."

Isika hadn't thought of it that way. Yes, if people could tell where she was just by seeking for her, it was a weakness.

Jabari was still speaking. ". . . for now we should divide into two groups. You take some people to the Karee camp. And the rest of us should go to the Dhahara and try to find Gavi and Aria."

"So you can go and I can't?" Isika shot at him, but her voice wasn't really angry.

"You know why."

Isika did. Other than her, he was the most gifted. He would be the best to find Gavi and Aria. She let her eyes drift shut as she softened into the buzz of the tree.

"Could we meet, maybe at the Karee tribe?" she asked. "Could we find each other in the wilderness so that I can know right away if she's okay?"

"You always seem to forget that you have Keethior," he said.

"Who would you take?"

Jabari thought for a moment. "I think Ivy, and Deto, and Brigid. We work well together. And you should have Benay-eem, and Abbas, because Abbas is our key to the Karee tribe. I would tell you Gavi, but he's not with us."

Isika felt a sudden pang of jealousy when he listed Ivy so quickly. She frowned down at her hands, annoyed with herself. They had grown up together. But Ivy wasn't related to Jabari and their parents could have plans for them to marry that Jabari just didn't know about.

"What's wrong?" Jabari asked. Isika looked up at him.

"What do you mean?"

"You're staring at your hands like you want to kill some-thing," Jabari said, grinning at her.

His face transformed when he smiled like that, going from a very handsome face to a face that you only looked at if you wanted to be blinded. Isika could barely look at him. She scowled again.

"You aren't going to tell me?" he said. "Not fair."

"It's just . . . never mind."

"It's okay, Isika," Jabari said. "We'll find her. If anyone can find her, Ivy can. Her gift with attracting and finding people is amazing. She's incredible."

Isika stared at him in disbelief. She shook her head in a sudden blaze of anger at him, at the world, at her sister. She left the tree, swinging from branch to branch until she could jump the rest of the way. Jabari scrambled down after her, landing like a cat. He put a hand on her shoulder, but let her go quickly when their magic sparked.

"We're going to have to work on that," he said, frowning. "I need to be able to give you a hug if I want to."

Isika felt heat rise to her face. She couldn't take any more —her insides were a mess of knots, so she just gave him a little wave and turned to walk away.

"Where are you going?" he shouted at her as she left.

"Sounds like we have a plan," she called over her shoulder. "I have to get ready." And she began to run, as if she could get away from it all—the jealousy, confusion, and especially the brilliance of his smile.

Chapter 12

*I*n the week before the journey, Jabari dreamed every night. The days seemed to drift by in a fog, but the nights were alive with color because of the dreams. Jabari was exhausted from sleep that didn't feel like sleep, and he could see by the lines on Isika's face that she was tired, too. They decided to visit Lake Ayo first, with Ivram and Karah, and spend some time in the life-giving waters.

Ben's voice was more haunting than usual during the leaving ceremony, and Jabari noticed that he sang with his eyes closed. They were all shaken. Their siblings had left without saying goodbye, and the ceremony was tearful, the goodbyes lingering and frustrating. Auntie was there, and Dawit had to remind her three times to let go of Isika when the time came. Abbas stooped and kissed Jerutha on the forehead, and Jabari couldn't stop his eyes from darting to Isika's face, but she was watching the Worker and the warrior who had fallen in love. She didn't see him watching her.

Abbas was the only one who seemed cheerful as they

walked down the stone road. Jabari assumed it was because he was going to see his family, without even having to leave Isika. The rest of them walked with their heads down. They needed the time at the lake. Jabari thought he understood why. It was one thing to feel like there was hard work ahead of you, hard work of seeking and pulling down walls. It was another to feel that you were going after people who shouldn't have left in the first place, wondering if you would be betrayed.

Jabari felt that he understood Aria, who was sick and poisoned by that stupid arrow. But he couldn't understand his brother's choices. He would never betray the Maweel, but why did he leave without saying anything? Jabari ran the problem through his head, going over what he knew about Gavi. His mind had been circling around this for weeks, but he didn't get any closer to an answer.

In the early afternoon, they reached the lake. The shimmering waters of Lake Ayo glimmered and Jabari felt his heart leap up. He had been coming here with his brother since he was a small boy. He remembered being small enough that his father could throw them into the water, back when his parents were happier, before there was so much conflict and so many questions.

"Jump in, everyone!" he shouted, laughing. "You need cheering up!" He received several dark looks in response. "Jump in, or I will push you in!"

He peeled off his outer clothes and ran into the water in his shorts. The cool, silvery waters rushed around him, and he ducked beneath the surface, feeling the rush of healing that came from the lake. He floated on his back and gazed at the sky, the silverwood trees fringing the lake like needles. His whole body relaxed and he felt blissfully happy.

Abbas cried out in wonder as he stepped into the lake, and Jabari stood up.

"You've never been here?" he asked.

Abbas shook his head, his eyes wide. "It feels like the water is going right into me, washing out everything that has been hurting."

"The waters of Lake Ayo find all your sadness and send it away. They help you join with the light of life," Jabari said.

"We have a stream like this running through a grove of trees not far from our village," Abbas said, his voice thoughtful. "It must come from here. It is only a trickle, and the most we can do is wash our hands in it. When I was a small child I used to try to lie down in it to get the feeling deep inside me. But it was never like this." He was quiet for a moment, cupping his hands and letting water run through them. "Most of our marriages take place near the stream so the couple can bathe their hands and faces in it afterward," he said.

On the other side of Jabari, Olumi had wrapped his long locks around his head and begun walking into the water slowly, a tiny bit at a time. He glared at Jabari as if he was reading his mind.

"Don't you even think about it, son of Andar."

Jabari held his hands up, all innocence, and swam away.

Ivram swam with Ivy and Karah, and they splashed each other, laughing. He grinned at them, a little in awe of how easy their relationship was. His with his parents hadn't been like that in a long while. Isika swam up beside him, then, but when she saw where he was looking, she turned and swam away.

Something occurred to Jabari just then, a little nudge. He thought about their conversation at the tree, and his mouth fell open as he watched Isika swim away. He could barely keep his eyes on her. She was too beautiful. He had to look away. How could she not know how he felt?

Ivy? Ivy was like a sister to him. Never, never in a thousand years would Jabari ever end up with Ivy. His parents had tried to make it happen, of course. But the thing was impossible. They had grown up together like siblings, hiding under the same tables, racing down the palace corridors, getting the same punishments, teasing Gavi mercilessly. Ivy would always be Jabari's sister, but she would never be the woman for him.

He felt a bit desperate. There was no time now. They would separate, and Isika had this strange idea in her head. Jabari didn't know what to do without showing too much of how he felt right before they parted ways. He wished there was some sort of ranger training for love, something that would help him understand what to do.

They swam all that afternoon, taking breaks on the shore. At one point he found himself swimming next to Isika again. He still couldn't look at her full in the face, her braids flowing down her back, water running off her brow and cheeks. She looked like a queen. She looked like the night sky if it were to become a person; the stars were in her smile and her eyes.

He shook his head at himself. He had it bad.

He turned and shoved Benayeem under the water and before long there was a mass of wrestling bodies splashing water everywhere, until everyone crawled up onto the shore and Abbas started a fire. Karah roasted fish and they ate until they were full.

The fire leapt and crackled. The stars were brilliant against the night sky, the silverwood trees gleaming, when Ivram spoke.

"This has been long in coming," he said. "But I believe it is time."

He reached down and picked up Queen Azariyah's staff from the ground beside him. He held it for a long moment, then held the queen's staff out for Isika to take.

She stared at Ivram with large eyes, her face full of fear. Benayeem put his arm around her and Isika exchanged a look with her brother, then reached out slowly with both hands and took the staff.

As soon as it passed from Ivram's hand to hers, the stone glowed silver in a brief, blinding flash, letting out a keening song that raised goosebumps on Jabari's arms and legs. It settled into a hum as the light from the staff traveled up Isika's arm and right through her until it lit up the circlet on her head.

It was a moment Jabari knew he would never forget: Isika receiving her staff and the staff responding to its true queen. It seemed to him that the staff was crying with joy. Isika shut her eyes and tears ran down her cheeks. Impulsively, Jabari went to her and put his hand on her shoulder. There was the usual spark of magic but he didn't move away and the spark died.

Jabari felt the magic that was coursing through her and it called to the magic within him, and he felt a lightning quick inkling of what it could mean for them to fight together, to not be separated anymore. She turned and looked up at him, tears in her eyes, but it was like she couldn't see him. She looked past him, at the stars, the staff glowing silver in her hands. They all sat in silence—Ben with his arm around Isika, Jabari standing with his hand on Isika's shoulder and the others quiet around the fire, watching them. They stayed like that until the fire died down and they crept off to find their bedrolls.

Before he drifted off to sleep, Jabari spoke to Isika, only a little way away in her bedroll.

"I wanted to tell you something," he said.

"Mmm?" she replied, nearly asleep.

Jabari could see her fingers draped over the staff as though she never wanted to let it go. He thought of all the things he actually wanted to say to her. He wanted to tell her that if he had his choice of anyone, he would take her with him to the Desert City. That he wished they could fight together and never be separated again, but he couldn't say it. He told her something else instead.

"I've been dreaming of the red-robed man every night," he said. "He's always walking through a city, and at some point he takes his hood off so I can his hair—a long black braid with a gold cord tied around it. The cord beckons to me and I want to catch up to him. I walk faster and faster, but I can never quite reach him. I dream of Aria walking in the desert and I see how weary she is but she keeps going. I dream of the man again as he walks through the city. I dream of a black sky with red lights through it and then the sky is actually the floor and there are people falling over it. I have all these dreams and I don't know what they mean."

Isika watched him in the darkness. Slowly she reached out her hand and he reached out too and touched just the ends of her fingers. They fell asleep like that and Jabari dreamed of water and trees and Isika's laughter.

Chapter 13

"We'll split up at the Hadem village," Jabari announced the next morning, poring over his crumbling map. It was late in the morning, after the tears and blessing of farewell with Ivram and Karah, after they and the rangers that had accompanied them left to return to the city.

"Hadem?" Isika asked. "Why is your map so old, anyway? Don't you have one in better condition than that?"

He glanced up at her. "No," he said. "This is my traveling map. It is well traveled."

"It looks like you use it for a blanket," Ivy chimed in. Deto snorted.

"Why the hostility?" Jabari asked. "Is it because I mentioned the fact that we have to split up again? You will be deprived of my company, Isika. I'm sorry about that. I truly am."

"Please deprive me also," Ivy said. "I want to be deprived!"

Deto stood and stretched, smiling down at Ivy. She was

taller than him by an inch or so, but since she was sitting, Jabari saw, Deto could look down at her fondly. He shot a glance at Isika to see if she noticed the looks the two were giving each other, and was startled to find that she was standing right next to him. He jumped and she looked puzzled.

"What?" she said.

"You move like a cat," he said.

"I completely stomped over here," she said. "You're just too involved in being nosy about Ivy and Deto."

"Well, she is like my sister," Jabari said, watching her. She smiled and looked away. Good. Jabari hoped he had put that fear to rest.

He wished he could figure out how Deto had managed to convince Ivy that they should be more than friends. The last he knew, Ivy had pledged to live her whole life as an unmarried ranger.

Deto walked over to join them at the map. His hair was long and black like Abbas's, but where Abbas's was slightly curly and braided in many braids, with feathers and beads wrapped in it, Deto's was straight as silk and in one long braid. His long eyes glinted as he looked at Jabari.

"What?" he asked.

"We need to talk, my friend," Jabari told him. "But anyhow. We're all getting distracted. Abbas and Olumi have agreed . . ." He glanced up at them and Abbas nodded. Olumi wasn't paying attention but staring off into the distance. He always looked a bit squinty outside the library. Jabari still wasn't sure about the wisdom of bringing the old librarian with them, but he'd been doing fairly well so far. ". . . they have agreed that the Hadem village is an excellent place for us to stop for a rest, as well as the last possible place that we can separate without making either of our journeys too much longer." He pointed at the village on the map. "And," he added, "we can see if they have heard anything about these Karee disappearances."

"Who are the Hadem again?" Isika asked.

"They look like me," Brigid said, in her soft voice. "Like Workers. But they are our allies."

"Where do they come from?" Isika asked. "How did they get to be our allies?"

Olumi hopped on one foot and gave an odd little bark of laughter. "This is a long story and I can tell you all about it. But it will take time. Shall we walk and talk? My bones are tired from standing still."

"Can you talk loudly enough that we can all hear?" Jabari asked, rolling up the map and tying it.

"Of course," Olumi said. "Have you never read the book on projecting your voice?"

"I can't say that I have," Jabari said. "But I'll take your word for it. Let's pack up and go," he said. "We have two more days of walking. Hopefully that will be enough time for your stories."

"It might be," Olumi said cryptically.

Jabari rolled his belongings into his pack and tightened the ties. He muttered a few words over the fire to douse it, and looked around. Their group was big and clumsy and he knew he should have separated them before now, especially since they really needed to find Aria and Gavi. He knew the reason he hadn't was because of Isika, and he didn't even really feel that badly about it, but they needed to make good time today. He swung his pack onto his shoulders, wrapped his ser around his head to protect it from the sun, and with a nod at the others, began to walk down the nearby path.

They were still in the fields of Maween, not yet having reached the scrubby landscape that came before the desert. They would follow the river to the Hadem, and then head northeast into the great desert.

The path was wide and they fell into an easy formation. Olumi walked at the back because he said it was easier to project that way, but it was hard for them to reach a consistent pace. Olumi was the shortest among them by far and had trouble keeping up. Abbas was the tallest, then Jabari, a few fingers width shorter than Abbas. Olumi didn't really walk, either. He ran-walked a few steps, then hopped. Jabari had to hide a smile when he watched the unlikely traveler. He preferred for Olumi to walk ahead of them, so they could adjust their pace for him.

Ah, he wanted to run. His muscles were itching for it. When they separated, he and Deto and Ivy would run and he could shake off the tension that had been following him for weeks.

Isika walked ahead with Brigid and Abbas. Jabari noticed the graceful bend of her neck for what felt like the thousandth time. He would never have guessed that he would find necks so interesting. Had he ever seen a beautiful person before he saw Isika? Everyone else seemed covered with a dusty film, just eyes and teeth and ears, where on her, everything came together into perfection.

"If everyone is listening, we will begin," Olumi said.

Jabari saw Deto trying to stifle a laugh. He felt such a sudden pang of missing Gavi that he winced. He tried to shrug it off, but there was a faint sting of betrayal in there. *Don't be silly,* he told himself. *Gavi would never betray us.*

"Long, long ago, back when there was no Maween, no Workers, no desert, no continent, all the people were one. Nenyi took care of them all, and they took care of each other. They didn't know one another well between the distant lands, but Nenyi helped to unite them. The Uncreated One gave them lifework: the dancers to dance, the gatherers to gather, the warriors to train and grow great strength, the worshipers to offer devotion. He sang to the singers (that was us, the beginnings of the Maweel), to teach them his songs. He offered knowledge of the earth and of gathering, how to care for the vulnerable beings, to respect the ancient ones, to placate the hard earth. He was everywhere and nowhere.

And then Mugunta came. We don't know where Mugunta came from, or if he was always there. Some think he came from another place, from the spilled future of pain. When Mugunta came, we were vulnerable to his lies."

"You keep saying 'we.' Were you alive for all of this?" Brigid asked.

There was a shocked silence.

"Daughter of weavers, I said long, long ago. This is before recorded history."

Brigid turned bright red. "I skipped over a lot in school," she said. "I just wanted to weave. Sorry."

Jabari turned to catch a glimpse of Olumi staring at the back of Brigid's head with horror in his eyes. He recovered himself and continued.

"As I was saying, when Mugunta came, the poison came.

Mugunta lived in one place, spilling all his evil and greed into the land around him, and that land became the Great Waste. When Nenyi saw how dangerous this poison was, saw people falling into the Great Waste, he picked it up and threw it, far, far, across the ocean, under the earth. But still we feel it, and poison seeps up from the Great Waste. Some people gave themselves to the poison. It was then that the emperor took over the land from across the continent, making the languages one, it was then that the priests began to worship Mugunta in the shapes of the four goddesses. The warrior line became tainted, as one of their kings drank the power of the evil one. The World Whisperer was born to care for the earth and sing so the songs would not be forgotten. Nenyi retreated, because he could not work in the same way, with poison thick in the air. He began to work through the World Whisperer, coaxing life back into the people through the one who could heal, who taught the old songs.

"As time went on, though, the people grew more separate even as they moved closer together. The singers isolated themselves, staying close to Nenyi, and the World Whisperer cared for them. They found a fertile land and named it Maween. The warriors were much divided. Many among them looked into the old ways and found Nenyi's footsteps everywhere. They longed for strength, as in the olden days, and so became separate and kept to deserts and tents, so they could focus on strength and not become blinded by the acquisition of things or places. Their homelessness made them vulnerable, and the Gariah, who came from the first warrior ever to betray Nenyi, attacked them again and again. The land was filled with contradiction and strife. The nomadic warriors became the Karee, ever trying to be free of the evil of the Desert King. And the dancers moved to the plains to make their dances easier. Many of the dancers were captured and poisoned, and these ones became the Workers. The ones who remained free were few in number, like the Karee. But they continued to dance, and they dance their steps all along the plains, to this day. They are the Hadem, the ones we are going to visit now."

There was a thick silence. Jabari felt as though he couldn't breathe. He had never heard it all laid out like this in a story. How had it happened that the World Whisperer only protected the Maweel? He felt creaky stirrings in his heart that were not comfortable.

"And my people?" Deto asked. "We are not warriors, or singers, or dancers. What are we?"

Jabari thought of the one time he had glimpsed a large group of people who looked like Deto, high in the mountains in the north. His father had taken him and Gavi on a long trek that included a visit to the people of the mountains. Light brown skin, eyes that crinkled to lines when they smiled, wide cheekbones, long limbs.

"Your people were the worshipers, with flowers and bells, honoring the Shaper without ceasing. Now some worshipers remain, but they are a gentle people, caught often by the Desert King, and their children are enslaved by him. Many have retreated out of his reach, far away in the mountains, in the ice and snow. Many have turned to worship the mountains and have forgotten the Shaper."

Deto looked at Olumi for a long moment. Jabari realized then that they had stopped walking and were standing in a loose group.

"Let's get some water from that stream, at least," he said,

"if we're going to stand around like a bunch of slack-jawed priests."

They all burst out laughing. "What?" Ivy asked. "What under Nenyi's skies, Jabari?"

"It was all getting a little too serious."

One touch from Isika purified the water so they could drink it.

"Such a good trick you have," Jabari said.

"I could have called us a stream," she replied, raising her eyebrows at him.

He pretended to swoon. "Don't look at me like that," he said.

She smiled and turned away.

"Can we take a rest?" Olumi asked. "Remember, I'm an old librarian."

So they lay back in the needles of the Hoona trees that lined the stream, and Jabari stared up at the blue patches of sky he could see, acutely aware of Isika near him. If he stretched, he could touch her elbow. He didn't.

"How come Nenyi made us all different? And separated us by the way we look?" Deto asked. "Didn't she want us to blend together? To know each other well?"

"The books say that it was out of her pleasure in making things, and that she intended us to blend, truly, like dye colors in the water, dancing and changing each other. Until Mugunta came, no one had thought to be angry about differences, or hate because of them."

"What I want to know," Isika said, "is how under Nenyi's skies people became Workers from dancers? Workers don't dance. I can't imagine them dancing! They would look like puppets if they tried to move their arms and legs to dance."

They all laughed. Jabari smiled to hear Isika joking about the Workers. She had been serious about them for a long time.

Olumi sighed, though. "It is strange how people become poisoned, how they turn dance into rigid rules, strength into slaving and killing."

"Some people say," Abbas started, speaking for the first time since Olumi had started his story, "that there is a strain of warrior still true to Nenyi inside the city of the Gariah. I don't know if I believe it. I have been to the Desert City, and I didn't see anyone who seemed true to Nenyi."

"Maybe they are in hiding," Ben said.

"If there were warriors true to Nenyi in that city, they would have to be in hiding."

"Right under the king's nose. That would be amazing," Isika said.

And Jabari thought of his dream of the man with the gold cord, and wished, simply because of the wonder in her voice, that it was true.

Chapter 14

The arrow made everything sharper for Aria. The wide, dry waves of the desert, the pounding of her heart, her breath in her ears. She could feel Gavi beside her acutely, hear his short breaths and little sighs. He didn't give her distance anymore and she had stopped fighting him.

Sometimes, if she was feeling particularly powerful, she shot him a triumphant look. He had thought she couldn't do this. He had been so wrong. His only reaction to her looks was to hand her the flask of water, over and over again. It was getting so boring. All he cared about was water, rest, the food he thought she should eat. She tried to ignore him.

Aria's father was calling her, and she was going to him. She finally knew what she needed to do and the knowledge filled her with power. It hummed under her skin, even while she slept.

Even if Gavi was getting boring, Aria had to admit that she would be lonely if he wasn't there, so she let him walk with her.

He would only walk in the early hours of the morning and the late afternoon and evening, saying something about the sun being too hot. It was weak of him, but she allowed it. And though she felt so much power coursing through her that she didn't need to eat, she permitted him to catch food for her. There was a river of power within her. Often, she barely slept before she felt the arrow picking her back up, setting her on her path.

"I'm so glad the healers weren't able to take the arrow out," she confided on one of those nights, as Gavi, yawning, scrambled to catch up with her, hauling both their packs. "I never realized it was in me for a purpose. Imagine—we thought it was sent to hurt me. We were so wrong, Gavi, so deceived."

His face twisted with some emotion. She couldn't read it.

"It's just good that I've finally stopped fighting it. And I'm glad it found me and not Isika." She shook her head. "That would have been a tragedy. She's always gotten everything she wanted. It would be horrible if she had the arrow too."

"Can you speak more clearly?" Gavi asked. "I'm having trouble hearing you. Are you speaking words?"

She stared at him. "Poor Gavi, the sun must be getting to you."

He stared at her for a moment, then handed her the water flask. She tried to brush it away, but he insisted, so she took a small sip, missing her mouth at first and wiping at her face as water cascaded down her chin. Her hands were shaking with power.

"It's okay, little bird," Gavi said, gently touching her

shoulder. "It's going to be okay. We're going to find someone in the Desert City who can help."

His eyes were rimmed in red, with deep shadows under them. His hand on her shoulder made her feel weak and shaky, questioning her own power, so she shook it off. For a moment she wondered whether he was just slowing her down. Should she leave him? Shake him off for real? But then she remembered that he had been a friend of hers once.

"Perhaps there are healing tents in the Desert City," she said to him. "And you can take a rest there, get better after the journey. I'll ask them to treat you nicely."

He stared at her as though he couldn't understand her. Oh, he was really not doing well. She picked up the pace.

They saw a smudge in the distance and Gavi looked at it for a long moment before saying, "I think that's a village, Aria. Maybe we should stop in and ask them about the king and what he's been up to lately."

"He'll tell me if I ask him," she said, smiling up at Gavi. "Don't worry."

There was a familiar rush of air, and the mad bird was back. Aria scowled at him and kept walking, but Gavi made a strange, choked sound and stopped walking.

"Now you are ready to talk?" the bird asked.

"Don't talk to him, Gavi. He's a betrayer," Aria shouted over her shoulder without slowing her pace.

The bird stared at her, then whistled.

"What did she say?" he asked Gavi.

"I don't know. She's been doing this for a couple of days. She talks and talks, but I don't understand the words, and she seems to think she's speaking normally."

Aria broke into a run. She didn't need their nonsense.

"What's she doing now?" the bird asked behind her.

"I don't know. I think she believes she's moving quickly, but we are barely getting anywhere."

"That could be good. Jabari is on his way."

Gavi heaved a huge sigh that turned into a sob. "I'm so glad. What do I do, Keethior? This is beyond me."

"Stay with her. The poison has reached her heart. I think it would have killed her already, but he wants her, so he's keeping her alive. Isika is with the Karee, searching for a cure. But we could still lose her. You will have to prepare yourself for that."

"What will happen if we lose her?"

"If she doesn't die in the desert? She will turn, son of Andar, as others have before her."

"Never. I won't allow it."

"You're not looking so good yourself."

"Well, what else would you imagine? I've been walking in the desert for weeks."

Gavi and the bird weren't nearly as far in the distance as Aria had hoped as she tried to lose them. She could still hear them quite clearly, going on and on about who knew what. But what was that, up ahead?

"Gavi," she said. "What is that?"

"Aria? Keethior, did you hear her?"

After a moment, Gavi and the bird were beside her. She pointed, and Gavi let out a slow breath.

"It looks like a dromed and a cart," Gavi said.

She smiled. "My ride is here."

~

AS THE CART DREW UP, Gavi felt his muscles tensing. He wanted to be far from here, but there was no way he could leave Aria. The driver of the cart wore a long white robe. He jumped down from the cart and bowed to Aria, pressing his face into the ground. Keethior squawked and flew away, leaving Gavi glaring at the empty sky. What could he do? *Stay with Aria*, the Othra had said. Okay, Gavi would stay with her. But who was this man and why was he bowing to Aria?

Aria swayed and Gavi reached out to grasp her elbow. The sand, stretching in every direction, radiated heat. Gavi's eyes longed for a bit of green.

"I am here to take you to your father's palace," the driver said, not meeting their eyes.

Aria smiled a beatific smile. It would have been more convincing if her eyes weren't half closed and her head wasn't drooping like a cut flower on its stalk. Gavi felt himself raging again, as he had many times already, over a man who would do this to his own daughter. He had never been a violent person, but he hoped that he would have the chance to kill the Desert King.

"Nenyi, forgive me," he whispered, "but I hate him."

He knew that Ikajo was only using Aria to get to Isika. The king had said as much last year when he was trying to burn Isika out. But Aria didn't believe him when he tried to tell her. How could any man do this to his daughter? He ground his teeth. He was in far over his head, and he didn't know if either of them would get out of this alive.

The white robed man rose and held out a hand to Aria. She took it without even a glance at Gavi and the man helped her into the cart. Gavi's heart sank.

"And me?" Gavi asked. "I need to go with her."

The man looked at Gavi. He didn't look like a bad person. His eyes were wide and gentle, though proud. He looked like a cross between Abbas and Andar, both in looks and expression.

"This cart has room for one passenger and one driver," the man said. "But you are welcome to follow."

"Aria," Gavi said, knowing it was no use. "We're doing fine on our own. Don't go with him."

She smiled at him through half-open eyes and said nothing. The driver turned the cart to face the road and rapped the dromed to get it to walk. Very well, Gavi would follow. He could walk fast and all those trips with Jabari would allow him to run, if he needed to. Maybe it was better for Aria to ride. She needed good food, water, shelter, healers. The dromed fell into a lumbering trot and Gavi began to run silently behind the cart as it rattled along the road.

The man took breaks at various wells, and Gavi was thankful, because he needed the breaks. He was exhausted, but he didn't begrudge the swift pace of the cart. He grew increasingly worried about Aria, who seemed almost half asleep now. They drove through villages deeper in the desert than Gavi had ever been. The villagers emerged from their houses and bowed their faces to the ground as Aria passed by. Gavi tried to look invisible as he jogged after the cart. This went okay for a while, until they came to something that was more like a town, and along the road a big man stuck his staff out to trip Gavi.

Taken unawares, Gavi tumbled face first onto the hard track of the road.

"What's this?" the man sneered. "A runaway Worker slave?"

Gavi put his hand to his face and pulled it away to stare at the blood that had come from his split lip. He felt shock as he realized what he looked like. He was used to being one of the Maweel—not just one of the Maweel, but the son of the first and second elders—and he hadn't considered how he would appear to the Gariah. He had vaguely wondered whether they would be suspicious of a young Maweel man in their city. Of course, he looked like a Worker, and unwashed and exhausted, he looked like a slave.

He got to his feet, only to be knocked down again by the man's fist to his face. Gavi tucked his knees up to his chest and raised a hand to protect his head, holding his bleeding nose. He needed to get back to Aria.

"I serve her," he said, gesturing to the cart still making its way along the road.

The man laughed in a harsh voice. "Sure you do. You serve the princess."

Gavi felt despair, but then he heard her voice, ringing out, more clear than it had been in weeks.

"Leave him alone! He is with me."

The man looked up, startled, and bowed suddenly with his face against the sandy hard earth. Gavi looked up to see Aria standing in the cart, holding her thin arms out.

"Come, Gavi," she said imperiously, "there is room for you in this cart after all. I need you with me."

Gavi stood up and brushed himself off, picking up his pack and using his ser to stop the bleeding from his nose and mouth. He didn't meet the eyes of any of the silent people who watched the interaction. Alone and afraid, he still felt a surprising lift in his heart, a foolish and hopeful thought. Aria had helped him. There was still a little of her left in there. All was not lost.

Chapter 15

*B*en didn't know for sure what he had expected from the Hadem, but it wasn't this. He had grown up in the tyranny of the pale-skinned Workers, who were forbidden to dance, sing, or look one another in the eye. They were forbidden to enter the home of someone who wasn't family. Next, he had gone to the Worker city with Isika, and they had been captured, imprisoned, and beaten by the pale-skinned Worker priests.

He had assumed that all pale-skinned people were like the Workers. Well, he knew that Brigid, Karah, and Jerutha were different. Of course, Gavi, too. But mostly. As a whole. Today he saw how unfair that was.

They walked into a wonderland slowly, as if in a dream. Of the group, only Ivy and Jabari had visited the Hadem village before. As they walked under the archway that led into the village, Ben saw Jabari looking over at him and Isika again and again.

"That's the fortieth time you've looked at me since we got

close to this village," Isika said, her voice dry but full of awe. "Do you need something?"

"Me?" Jabari asked, innocently. "Nothing. Just wondered if you've ever seen anything like this."

She looked at him sideways. "You know I haven't. You're pleased with yourself, aren't you?" But she smiled at him with real warmth.

Jabari sighed, and Ben felt a sigh slipping out of his own throat. "I just like coming here," Jabari said. "And I don't get to very often."

Ben couldn't blame him. He had never seen anything like it. They were near the water, at the last bay before they left the coast and walked into the desert, and the boulders were bleached pure white. Thousands of tiny carvings had been etched into the stones, making them look multilayered and alive. The entrance to the village was under a stone archway draped with climbing flowers in brilliant shades of pink and red. Inside, everything was carved out of the same stone in colors that ranged from white to deep pink, giving the place a bleached, pale look that echoed the skin of the people. What the buildings lacked in color, though, the people made up for with the wildest clothing Ben had ever seen.

"Olumi, you're sure these people are of the same strain as Workers?" Isika whispered loudly as the people stood nearby, watching on the edges of the pathway while their procession passed.

"It doesn't take many generations for lies and evil to take hold once they start, daughter," Olumi replied. "The Hadem dancers have retained the joy that the Workers traded for obligation and fear."

The Hadem were dressed from head to toe in bright

colors, with ribbons that wound around their arms and legs and wove through their hair. The women wore bright skirts that reached to their knees, embroidered with chips of metal and orange, green, and purple thread. Over simple shirts they wore long sweeping cloaks of every color. They had paint on their faces in patterns of dots and lines that were different from person to person. The men had long hair and beards with ribbons and yarn woven into them, and wore flowing pants and the same cloaks as the women. They all jingled as they walked. There were bells on some of the ribbons around their ankles, and bells on their cloaks.

"Are there a lot of people like this in the world?" Isika asked. "Why don't we ever see them?"

"This is the last village," Abbas said in his low voice. "And if the Desert King captures them, he won't allow them to dress like this. This is the only place you will see them in their own clothing, for they dress in dark colors to protect themselves if they travel. The Desert King hates them even more than he hates the Karee. I've never been here before, but my father has spoken of this place. He admires the Hadem for holding their village against the Desert King."

A very old woman walked close to him then, and she had heard the last thing Abbas said, and answered him.

"That is something we could not have done without the Maweel," she said. "They protect our borders, and the Naia, the ancient dolfina who live in the ocean, help us keep the sea against the attackers who would take us. But here," she murmured, looking at Isika, "here is a Naia friend. Welcome, child, we have been wondering when you would visit."

Isika stared at the woman, and Ben watched as understanding lit her face. "You are the people the Naia love," she said. "They told me about you. But I didn't know what they meant."

"We are blessed," the old woman said. "We have always had their love."

Ben was distracted by the music from the old woman. It was jangling, wild, drumming, free. It was catchy, he thought, something he could dance to. She turned her gaze on him next.

"And who is this, who is listening to me?" she asked. "How can you hear the music?"

"He can hear all the music, honored elder," Jabari said, "not only the music of the Hadem. He discerns all music, everywhere. In people and animals too."

Ben was surprised that Jabari was speaking for him, but when he looked at the older boy, he saw that his eyes were intent on the elder's face, who was still gazing at Ben. Her eyes were very blue, her hair a pale white, woven with orange ribbons. Her face, tan from the sun, was seamed over with what seemed like a thousand lines. Ben realized it was an unfamiliar sight because the Workers stayed indoors or under shade coverings, and while their skin grew old and sagged, it didn't look like this woman's face, scarred and touched by sun.

She wore thousands of colorful bracelets. Her cloak billowed in a slight breeze and bells on her legs tinkled as she stepped back and shook herself slightly. She turned to Jabari.

"I am sorry, son of Andar. I have been surprised for the first time in what feels like forever. I did not know that what you describe is possible. A child who hears all music." She shook her head, looking dazed. "Please follow me, the day's heat has not yet fled to the sea. We will find a cool place to sit and talk. Will you stay for the night?"

"Yes, honored elder," Jabari said, bowing. "But only one night. Our errand needs us to be quick."

"I'm sure it does," the old woman said. "Your brother is not here." Jabari's eyes widened.

Ben fell into step beside Jabari as they followed the woman.

"It's scary when she does that," Jabari said. "She sees too much."

"What did she mean about the music?" Ben asked.

"Hadem can hear each other's music, as part of their gift for dance. But she says she has never heard of anyone who can hear all people's music."

"Yeah, I caught that part," muttered Ben. He was deeply intrigued, but a little put off by being a freak again. And he wanted to know how the woman could tell that he was listening to her.

THEY WERE LED into a cavern within the white stone. Ben and his companions stood for a moment with mouths open. Every inch of the cavern was carved in intricate designs, not scenes of history in murals like the ones in the Maweel palace, but designs of suns, flowers, stars, circles, lines, all of them moving and flowing over the cavern walls in a—well —a dance.

"Come and sit," the elder said, and as she gestured with one graceful hand, quiet people came close, setting stools and cushions on the ground. There were cups of a cool drink that tasted of cinnamon and mint, and the servants handed them cold cloths for their faces. Ben sighed with relief. He was tired already and he knew they had many days of travel ahead of them. It was good to be in a cool place and rest.

"So," the old woman said. "Do I get introductions, Jabari, son of Andar?"

Jabari made an embarrassed face. "Of course, Vitalkar Auntie," he said. "Honored elder, these are my friends and travel companions. This is Abbas, from the Karee." Abbas touched his fingers to his forehead. "This is Olumi, our honored keeper of truth." Jabari turned a hand toward Olumi, who stood, bowed very low, and shuffled backward on his feet with tiny hops.

The old woman laughed. "Oh my! A truth keeper who knows our customs."

Ben frowned. Truth keeper. They had always heard Olumi described as a librarian or a keeper of the books. He exchanged a look with Isika. They got their information piecemeal, and it was never easy to tell when more would come leaking their way. He frowned, then looked up and wiped the look from his face in time to be introduced.

"This is Isika, our World Whisperer, and Benayeem her brother. They have come back to us recently. You remember Ivy, daughter of Ivram, third elder? And Deto, and Brigid, children of Maween, seekers and friends."

"That was an excellent introduction," the old woman said. "I didn't know you had it in you!" She cackled and Jabari smiled. "Last time you were here you caused a ruckus in the dance."

"Well, I was eleven."

"You can all call me Vita. So tell me, where are you going? Where is your brother?"

Jabari filled her in, and Ben zoned out listening intently to the music. The Hadem had such harmonious music, so close in sound and song to one another, with very slight variations that seemed to shift for personality and age. It was wild music, full of joy and passion. He thought he would like to stay here for a long time, listening. Their music quieted his mind, but when he shifted his attention back to his companions, he felt anxious again because of their troubled thoughts, the worried shifts and notes in their music. How did the Hadem keep their songs so in tune with one another?

There was a change in the music and he began paying attention to the conversation again.

"I am honored to meet you, prince of the Karee," Vita said. "And I can affirm the disappearances your tribe members have told you about. We have gone near to try to understand the sadness we have felt from the tribe to the north, and have been much disturbed by the tales we have heard from them."

"Thank you," Abbas replied. "I am honored to meet you, also. And please, tell me about what else you have heard. I am anxious to get back to my tribe."

"I have only heard tales of people being stolen, and I know that your people are still moving often, bent under the Gariah, and trying to avoid their full weight."

"We were one once, you know," Abbas said, his face shadowed with pain, "the Gariah and the Karee. Olumi knows. Before the Desert King decided to follow Mugunta."

"Yes," Vita said. "And if you know that, you must know our own history."

Silence fell on the little group. They were all thinking of the Workers, endlessly enslaved to the four goddesses who demanded the sacrifice of their children. In comparison, this last village of dancers seemed tiny.

"I want Jerutha to come here," Isika said suddenly. "My stepmother," she said, at the elder's inquiring look. "She comes from the Worker village but she is not a Worker in her heart. I wish she could meet you and know about you."

"She is welcome to come and visit," Vita said. "But we don't take anyone in to live with us the way you Maweel do."

Ben frowned. Jabari stirred beside him, and Ben heard frustration from him.

"We don't need to go into that old argument," Vita said. "You heard enough about that when you were eleven, I would venture to say. But to help the rest of you understand, we cannot keep our music pure if we open our village."

Now Isika was frowning as well. She began to speak, but the elder held up a hand, the bells along her arms jingling.

"Enough. We need food and beds. And before beds, we will show you our dance. We haven't had visitors in a while and my people are excited."

They ate food that was spicy and sour—a journey in flavor—then moved out under the stars and sat among clusters of people, waiting for the dance. It took some time for everything to be ready, then it began.

A large circle of Hadem people moved and swayed together, and the music the musicians played echoed the music Ben heard coming from the people. It was played on stringed instruments, with deep drums and one flute that soared above everything else. They didn't sing and the dance was wordless but complete.

The dancers moved as one, and then apart. Their feet hit the ground hard, or very soft. They lay on the ground, they moved in a circle and a line. There seemed to be nothing they couldn't do with their bodies. Vita sat with the group of travelers, openly watching their faces, but at the end she got up and joined the last dance. Ben thought that when she was younger she must have been a dancer beyond compare. She flowed and moved toward their little group, stomping her feet so her whole body rattled with the clacking wood pieces and bells she had on her arms and legs. At the end, though she was out of breath, the dancers turned as one and lifted her to the stars.

When the music stopped, Ben looked around to see that Isika, Ivy, and Olumi openly wept, and Jabari dashed the back of his hand against his eyes. Ben felt tears on his own cheeks. He carried the feeling of the dance with him all the way to sleep, and when he dreamed, it was of motion, bright colored clothes and limbs moving. He dreamed of their music.

Chapter 16

*M*orning dawned in the village of white stone. Isika sat with her arms around her knees, watching the light change in the eastern sky. It was time to leave the village and and split the group, to journey in their different directions. Isika leaned over and bent with her face to the ground, trying to find the strength for this. When she heard her friends talking nearby, she stood and took a deep breath. *Now.*

They all hugged one another, clasping arms and gripping in farewell. Isika hugged Deto, Ivy, and finally found herself face to face with her friend, Jabari.

He looked serious.

What's wrong? she asked in her mind.

Who will I be competitive with, if we are always split up on journeys? He gave her a tiny wink. Heat rushed into her face. This was getting ridiculous. She could be normal around him. She could. But she also saw worry in his eyes.

"No, but really," she said. "What's going on?"

He was silent for a long moment, looking at the ground. Then he looked at her again. "This is not like before, you know."

"What's not like before?" Isika asked.

"It's not a child's game. This is serious. The Desert King has ways of convincing people. He's full of dark magic, more power than you've ever seen. Don't imagine you can walk up to him like you did with the walls, back when we first met, and pull him down with no effort at all."

"I don't think that," Isika said, stung.

He caught her elbow. "Isika, he has Aria. Aria. Why do you think she's going to him?"

"Because of the arrow," she said immediately.

"Because he is using the arrow to draw her. Because he knows you'll go after her."

"You can't know that he's drawing her," Isika said, shaking her head slowly. "And if he was, he could be doing it for her sake. Maybe he wants her with him."

"You are so stubborn, still. You haven't spent your life studying the Desert Kings, the ways they have tried to defeat us all these years. He has a plan for you." His voice cracked again, and Isika stared at him, reaching out a hand to touch him. She pulled back at the spark that cracked between them.

"We just found you," he said. "You're our World Whisperer, not his warrior. He can't have you. I don't—"

Isika felt like he had slapped her. "That's what this is about? Ownership of the World Whisperer? You don't want him to win?"

"That's not what I said, Isika. Don't just hear whatever bad thing you want to hear from me." He looked up at the sky for a moment and Isika stared at the side of his face. He was about half a head above her. "Of course I don't want Maween to collapse because he has you again. But I'm afraid for you, too, Isika. I don't want him to hurt you."

He looked at her as he said it, and she felt her eyes grow very wide at the look on his face. Suddenly she wanted to be very, very far away, not because she was angry but because this was all a bit much and Aria was gone and they were splitting up. She put her hand on a rock and leaned on it a bit, feeling the earth beneath it, the long song of the dirt and rocks longing for the Shaper.

"Thank you," she said finally. "I'll be careful, Jabari. I promise. And I won't be on my own with him. I'll have you." She smiled at him and gave him a hug, readying herself for sparks, but they didn't come. They clasped each other just below the elbows in the farewell hug, and still there were no sparks. Isika backed away without meeting Jabari's eyes, surprised and pleased.

Remember that you can always talk to me, Jabari said in her mind. *You can even try doing it from far away.*

"Don't worry so much," she said aloud. "You're doing the dangerous part."

His face split with a white grin. "That's true," he said. "I am, aren't I? Well don't worry, I'm sure there will be some adventure for you too."

"I'm sure there will be," she said wryly, and he frowned.

"Not too much, though," he said, and she laughed. His answering grin was white and perfect.

Isika's group headed straight north from the village, while

Jabari's turned east, toward the Dhahara. Isika was thankful for Abbas, as she immediately felt Jabari's absence. She had a lot of gift in her, but Jabari still had more experience as a seeker.

"Are you nervous?" Ben asked, as they scrambled up boulders of gritty stone.

"Are you listening to me again?" Isika said, her teeth gritted against the dust that blew constantly as they walked.

"Only your music. And it is very nervous. What are you worried about? Don't you remember our trek across the desert to reach Batta? We've done more difficult things than going to visit a tribe, accompanied by their very own prince."

Isika squinted into the distance, noting that Abbas, comfortable in the travels, had traveled a long way ahead of them. Olumi and Brigid, however, were falling behind. She whistled and Abbas turned back toward her at once. She stopped walking to let the others catch up.

"We were younger then. I don't think we really understood how dangerous things were. Besides, you know what happened when we reached Batta." She took a long drink from her flask, then passed it to Ben.

He looked uneasy as he took it from her. For a moment, he held it without moving, then seemed to shake himself. He took a drink. They had both been imprisoned and beaten in Batta.

"But we're only going to the Karee," he said.

"Ben, there is no way this is going to end without me going to the Dhahara. I know it, I can feel it, and I am daily working on cloaking myself so Aria can't see me."

"I can hear her," Ben said. Isika looked at him, shocked.

"From here? Can you tell where she is?"

"No. Only that she is very, very far away. I can hear the arrow, too."

Isika felt cold dread settle in her stomach like a stone. "The arrow? It has music? Like it's a person?"

"Yes," Ben said. His face was worried. "And the arrow's music is getting stronger while Aria's is getting weaker."

"We have to get there," Isika said, and she began walking again, her soft boots slipping on the stones in the path. "We have to find this healer and save her."

"Well, we're not going to get there if you break your neck first," Ben said. "Slow down, big sister."

"Okay, okay, little brother," Isika muttered, but she tossed a smile at him over her shoulder.

"How long has it been since you have been back in a Karee village?" Isika asked Abbas, as she drew up to him and they walked side by side.

"Remember we have camps, not villages, but it has been nearly two years."

"Two years!"

He nodded. "I was making trouble around the Desert City when Ikajo trapped me and some of my men. He sent them off to the mines, but he wanted to humiliate me, so he sent me to the tiny Worker city to live as a slave. Stupid of him."

"Yes, it was," Isika agreed, remembering the day Ben's gift had told them to trust Abbas, and how he had saved them and helped them escape. "I'm glad he did, though." Something occurred to her then. "Wait!" she said. "You shouldn't go to the city if we go . . . if he finds you, he'll capture you again."

For a moment, Abbas was silent, and then he broke out in a huge laugh. "Do you really think you're safe there, Isika? Or that I'm a bigger prize to him than you are? No, it makes no sense for any of us to go there. No sense at all. Like everything you've done since I first met you. And yet somehow you continue on, making no sense. It is incredible."

"Some things I do make sense," Isika muttered, feeling slightly hurt.

"Not many do," Brigid said in her soft voice. "You're like this wind. Sometimes shaking trees, sometimes blowing dust. But Nenyi works that way sometimes."

Isika tilted her head to one side, thinking about this. She smiled at her friend.

"Well, our fighting hasn't stopped him," Abbas said, "even after all these years, though we wear him down. Perhaps it will be Isika who will finally stop him."

Isika stumbled on a rock. "I only want to get Aria back," she said. "I never said anything about *stopping* him." *But was getting Aria back enough?* The question seemed to hang in the air, heavy and round. She wasn't sure anymore, after meeting the Hadem, after hearing Olumi's stories.

Olumi and Ben were trailing behind, deep in conversation. It made Isika think of something.

"Olumi," she called back to him, "what did Jabari mean when he called you the keeper of truth?"

Olumi grimaced. "It's just another way to say librarian."

Brigid laughed. "No it's not," she said. "Uncle! You know that's not true. Olumi is keeper of truth," she told Isika, Abbas, and Ben. "Have you never heard of that before?"

"No," Isika said. "Big surprise, something that the elders neglected to tell us." Brigid regarded her out of wide, gentle eyes.

"Okay, I'm steering clear of that particular piece of bitterness," she said. "The truth keeper holds the stories and rulings from the ages, making sure the books are available to everyone, making sure the stories are remembered. It is a very high position. My father told me past truth keepers have been very pompous, wearing fancy clothes and presiding with elders and monarchs over all the tables and feasts."

Olumi snorted. "Silly men, silly heads are we, to ignore true wisdom and pay attention to greed!" he sang. "I wrote that. I have no use for such things."

Isika couldn't look at Brigid or she would laugh.

"But the daughter of weavers is right," Olumi went on. "The position is important. It goes back to the first World Whisperer. Nenyi didn't want to give so much power to one person so she made sure there wasn't only one who knew all. Always a gifted relative of the king or queen holds the knowledge."

"Relative of the king or queen?" Ben asked.

"Yes, I am a distant cousin of your grandmother's. Did you not know that?"

"Nope," Isika said, narrowing her eyes at Brigid.

"It's not my fault," Brigid said. "Don't look at me!"

"Well, it's nice to meet you, cousin," Isika said. "I don't think we have any other cousins."

Olumi stopped short in his tracks, his nose quivering. He hopped on one foot three times. "Of course you do, you ninny."

Isika stared at him.

"Excuse me, but what are you thinking?" He pointed at Brigid. "Her parents—her adopted parents—are distant cousins, for one, and the head gardener also."

They were all standing still now.

"How come one of them isn't queen or king?" Ben asked.

"Because it can only pass down the direct line. The World Whisperer gift as well. Not my gift, though. My gift can pass to any relative of the queen. I'm still waiting for Nenyi to reveal who the next will be." He looked around, his eyes landing on Ben.

"Don't look at me!" Ben said, taking a step back.

Isika felt like she was going to laugh again, so she turned to catch up to Abbas, who was waiting impatiently for them ahead. Ben looked terrified of being anything like the odd old librarian. But Isika didn't stop thinking about the conversation for a long time. She had relatives! Blood relatives. No one could be more like family than Teru and Dawit, but it was interesting to find that she wasn't alone in the world. And then with a sudden pang she wondered why none of them had come to find her.

The sun was setting when they stopped for the night.

"Tomorrow," Abbas said. "Tomorrow we will arrive."

Something had been bothering Isika for a while. Something different at the edges of her senses, which seemed to be sharper lately. What was it? She paced while Ben cooked, and washed her dishes restlessly after dinner.

"Where is that bird?" she asked, as she set her bedroll out. "What is the use of having a protector if he's never around?" She knew she sounded petulant when Benayeem gave her an odd look, but Keethior had never been away from her for this long.

"What does he say when you try to call him?" Ben asked.

"He's ignoring me. He checks in, asks if I'm okay, but then when I ask where he is or if he's coming, he doesn't answer."

"How did he get the job of protector?" Abbas asked, his laugh a rumble in his chest. "He's not very good at it."

"He is good at it in Othra terms," Olumi said. "They value mystery and independence. They don't want their strength to undermine the strength of the World Whisperer, so they keep their distance. Frankly, I've been surprised by how often they are near you. Keethior seems to be particularly fond of you."

Isika snorted and Ben laughed out loud.

"I can't believe that," she said. "But maybe they know I need all the help I can get."

They settled down to sleep, and in the dark, Isika nudged Ben.

"Do you hear anything odd lately?" she whispered. "I feel strange, like something new is around."

"I hear it," Ben answered. "But whatever it is, it seems friendly."

Isika sighed. *What are you?*

"Get some sleep," he said. "Tomorrow we will probably hear a lot of histories and we can't fall asleep in the middle." Isika smiled at him and closed her eyes. Right before she went to sleep, though, she reached out softly and tentatively.

You all right? she asked.

It was a moment before she heard something. The lightest touch, like a hand on her cheek.

Sandy and tired but fine. Jabari's voice was very faint in her head. *There's no water to wash and we're drinking cactus juice. You?*

We're fine too. She hesitated. *Goodnight, my friend.*

She could barely hear him. *Goodnight, lovely one.* Her

eyes jerked open, then she realized she must have misheard, and she smiled and went to sleep.

It was before dawn when she woke and had her answer about the strange presence. There was weight pressed against her back and legs. She lifted her head, very slowly and came face to face with a large cat. Lying down, it was nearly as long as she was, and she thought its head might be twice as large as her own. She looked around in the bright moonlight and saw that she was surrounded by four of the cats, all looking at her.

"Olumi?" she whispered, but it came out strangled and hoarse. "Abbas?"

Don't worry, daughter, said the closest cat in animal speech. Her fur was silver, and in a non-panicked part of her mind, Isika thought she must be blinding in the sun. Her eyes were gold, with black pupils, and she had a few markings around her ears and paws. Isika could barely breathe.

"*Olumi!*" she said, her voice louder.

Across the fire pit, he sat up, fumbled for his glasses, and put them on to peer at her. His jaw dropped, then he smiled, his face as bright and innocent as a sunrise.

"Palipa," he breathed. "Our great, ancient cats. They have not been seen in my time. Oh my dear, you are . . . what have they said? Have they spoken to you?"

"Only to tell me not to be scared," Isika said through clenched teeth as the nearest cat stretched and rolled closer to her, pushing her head under Isika's chin. Her fur was so, so soft. "Are they safe?"

Olumi frowned, looking slightly dazed. "Well, I suppose that depends on who you are asking."

Safe? The cat under Isika's chin asked. It sounded like

she was laughing. *Safe is a strange question. We are yours. We will come with you.*

Oh. Isika said. *Good?*

A stirring and flapping and Keethior flew into the camp, bringing his immense feeling of calm with him. Isika relaxed slightly.

"Oh," Keethior said aloud, so they could all hear him. "That's all it is. I felt a lot of fear from you . . . it's just the Palipa. Come on, can't you see you're scaring her? Give her a little space. Humans generally need time before they get comfortable with cuddling. And Othra never cuddle with cats, so please try to remember that this time."

Isika narrowed her eyes at Keethior as the cats grumbled and drew away, padding down to the spring Isika had called out of the earth the night before, bending their heads to drink.

"Thanks," she said, scowling. "But Keethior, really? Where have you been?"

He ruffled his feathers, annoyed with her. "I don't answer to you," he said.

"Actually, you do," Olumi said, standing now to look over at the cats.

"Oh, well, I don't want to tell you then."

"Fine," Isika muttered. "Who are they?"

"They are ancient creatures, like us, like the Keerza. Creatures from before people were here."

"Are there any more creatures I should be aware of?"

"There are many creatures. But many of them haven't been seen in hundreds of years. Thousands." He cocked his head to one side and whistled suddenly. "Palipa haven't been seen in a hundred."

Two hundred, the large cat corrected, blinking slowly at them from a distance. Isika felt the skin on her arms turn to goosebumps.

"This is a little different from Keerza or Othra," she whispered loudly to Keethior. "Look at the size of them. Keerza and Othra don't eat meat."

"True, but they seem to like you," Keethior said. Isika huffed a sigh and gave up on going back to sleep. Her companions began to stir. She gingerly walked to get water from the spring, taking care to give the cats a wide berth. The smallest one, still much larger than Isika, chose to ignore Keethior and came and rubbed at Isika's arm with his head. Isika's hands shook as she pulled the jug from the water, spilling it over herself. When she straightened, she saw everyone in the camp staring at her, wide-eyed.

"Well," she said. "This is going to be an interesting trip, isn't it?"

Chapter 17

*A*s they got closer to the Desert City, a pressure built in Aria's chest, hurting her. She was glad for Gavi beside her, and she leaned on him when the pain was bad. She was glad for the driver who helped her down from the cart in the evenings, offering her food and drink. She was glad for the lizards that Gavi shot, for their familiar roasted taste, reminding her of past journeys.

She felt feverish as the arrow hurt her more. She wondered, for the first time, whether she should go to her father. Then she shook herself. Of course. That was the plan.

As they traveled, the occasional smattering of towns grew closer together, until there were no longer spaces between them and Aria could see a tall smudge in the distance. *Dhahara.* It looked impossibly large. Her head felt too heavy for her neck. She leaned on Gavi's shoulder, her eyes only half open.

The driver looked back at them. "Let us stop for a rest," he said. "I feel that we need it."

He pulled the dromed up next to a shop, tying it to a rail. He nodded at them once, then disappeared inside. As people caught sight of Aria, they knelt to press their faces to the ground. Gavi jerked in his seat, then let his breath out in a long sigh.

"Are you sure about this, little bird?" he asked her. "It's not too late to turn back."

Her eyes widened at his nickname for her. She shook her head. "Of course I'm sure," she said. "How could we come this far, only to turn back?" But she shifted in her seat, trying to find comfort in her bones. The first time someone had bowed to her she had felt only pleasure, but as it happened more often, she felt shivers of pain at the people's lack of dignity. They pressed their faces into the ground when they saw the king's dromed, even the children and old women.

"What's wrong?" Gavi asked, watching her face.

"I don't know why I'm feeling worse as I'm getting closer to the city. I felt so strong when we were out in the desert."

He watched her face, his ser tied carefully around his head to keep the sun from burning through his white blond hair to his scalp. She saw that his face had browned over the weeks of travel, white showing in his smile lines. "You know, Aria," he said. "You may be feeling worse, but you're acting better."

She snorted. "Acting better how?"

"I can understand what you're saying, for one thing. Before, you would talk and talk and I swear that I couldn't understand a thing you were saying."

She stared at him. She knew she had been better in the desert. She had been fine.

"I think the poison was able to deceive you, tell you that

you felt good, even when you were actually getting worse. What is changing it now, though?"

But then the cart driver was back, holding three spiced yogurt drinks. He had a funny look on his face. Aria eyed him as she took the drink he handed her.

The driver took a deep breath. "You're not such a bad guy for a Worker," he said, speaking to Gavi.

"A Maweel, but thanks," Gavi mumbled. He buried his face in his drink.

"I feel honor-bound to tell you that the king will kill you if you come into the city."

Gavi choked on his yogurt, spraying it over the ground. Aria turned to look at him, feeling a rush of worry at the driver's words. Gavi tried to speak, but couldn't stop coughing, so Aria asked her own question.

"What do you think Gavi should do?"

"He can't come with us." The driver held up a hand as Gavi tried to interrupt. "I know, but you can't. He'll just execute you, immediately. He doesn't want anyone from Maween with her. Trust me, I've been in his service since I was a child. He is a fierce king. Follow at a distance if you must. Lose yourself in the city. But we should part here."

Aria looked back and forth between the two men.

"You are pretty easy to recognize, Gavi," she said finally. "Doesn't everyone know about the Maweel elders' two sons? One is dark as a night without a moon, one like the rising sun, with hair like light?"

The cart driver frowned, then laughed without mirth. "Not here," he said. "I don't even know what you are talking about. We don't know anything about Maween. Your country could fit in the smallest lake in Gariah. No, Worker, just lose yourself and no one will know who you are. But leave now. I'll give you a few minutes to say goodbye."

"What?" Gavi spluttered as the cart driver walked away. "He's crazy if he thinks I'm going to . . ."

"He's right," Aria said, feeling her stomach plummet. After all of this, after running off by herself, she didn't want to be alone in a strange land. "You need to go. Not least because I don't want him to be angry with me if I come in toting a pale-skinned Maweel boy." She smiled, her heart feeling sore and very, very tired. Her chest hurt again, a nudge of pressure from the arrow. "I'll be fine."

"Well, I'm not leaving. I'll go, yes, but I'll be very near. If anything happens to you, I'll know immediately."

"Okay."

"Aria, are you sure? We can run, even now. We can go back."

Aria raised her eyes to his. She searched them. He still felt hope, while she had none.

"The thing is, Gavi, I don't think we can."

He looked around and she saw him taking it all in—all the people watching them, the cart driver, the people who still knelt, forming a very effective barricade. It was too late. He nodded, squeezed her hands, and whispered, "Immediately, I'll know immediately." She smiled weakly as he disappeared into the crowd. The crowd absorbed him easily, interested only in her, and the cart driver came back, visibly relieved.

She draped her ser over her head as they went on, toward the city, so the people who were bowing to her couldn't see her cry.

She watched as more and more people came out to bow. The pain near her heart grew worse, and she had clarity as she went on. Was Gavi right? Was there something protecting her from the deception of the arrow? In the Desert City? She couldn't imagine what it would be.

The buildings grew taller and the great walled city was ahead. It was built on a craggy desert mountain, with tall imposing walls around the bottom, and winding roads leading to an imposing palace on the top. Soon they were too close for her to see the whole thing, and she was stuck craning her neck to try to get a better look.

She wanted to show it to Gavi. But he wasn't there, and she was alone, on her way to see her father, alone in a city of people who did not know her. She held back tears, holding her head high as they went on. Now there were waves of people bowing on each side of her, and she began to pay attention to how they looked, to catch glimpses of who and what they were.

A group of children, tugged from their game of ball, rings in their ears and on their fingers. An old woman, stooped half over, tugged into a bowing position by a guard who lined the street. Aria lifted a hand to protest, but they were already past the woman. The people were not all the same. Some had very dark skin, darker than Aria's or Isika's, and some had light brown skin, with long noses and intense brows, like Abbas. They were tall people with long necks and dark ringed eyes, decorated with gold and silver, and even those who were obviously poor, in their ragged clothing, wore metal of some kind clinking around their necks and wrists. Some people had long, straight hair that swung around their waists. Some had hair that looked like hers, thick and roped in braids or locks, or cut close to their heads. She caught sight of some Workers with their long gowns, covered against the intense sun. She stared at a man who was at least a couple of heads taller than Abbas. Even Jabari would seem short in this city.

The buildings got taller and the crowds more thick. The houses were made of some kind of sandstone, a tumble of rooms stacked on one another, red brown and tawny, with crumbling edges and brightly painted window frames and doors. Aria could barely take it all in. Every time she saw something, they were past it before she could take a closer look. Soon they were at the city gates, and there were a dozen white-robed servants to meet her, helping her get down from the cart and holding out robes for her. They put the clean robes on over her smelly ones, and Aria wished for a bath, but they held out water for her to wash her hands and face, and she did so, wrinkling her nose at the dark water running from her hands. She sighed.

They led her to a tall horse, and she widened her eyes.

"I don't ride," she said to the head servant, but he shook his head and leaned down to lift her into the saddle. She looked around. The cart driver was gone. She was alone in this huge group of people, and she knew no one.

She allowed the man to put her in the saddle, and thankfully the horse was docile, because the pain was growing worse in Aria's heart, and it was all she could do to stay upright. She barely noticed as they led her in through the gate, but she tried to keep her eyes open, to see, to be present in her own procession as nearby people cheered and threw flowers. Near the gate, the houses were flimsy and old and dirty children ran in the streets, jeering and dancing out of the way of the soldier's boots. Aria stared down at old people who sat hunched on the side of the road. This was her father's city? It was nothing like Azariyah.

She turned for a look behind her. Had Gavi made it through the gates? There was some sort of scuffle happening, people pouring through, the guards swinging clubs, unsuccessfully trying to press the doors closed against the rush of people. She caught a glimpse of a shock of blond hair and turned back to face forward, smiling.

They continued up the winding road, moving from the lower part of the city to cleaner, wider streets. People knelt on each side of the road, a sea of black hair and sparkling jewels, of color and tunics. Here the sandstone of the buildings was cleaner, they were stacked straighter, and the paint was intact on ornate doors and window frames. Small birds sang in cages that hung from the eaves, and a chant started up.

"Aria, princess, Aria, princess."

Aria's heart hurt as though she was being stabbed, and she wondered how they knew who she was. She breathed shallowly from the pain. Was she going to die right as she arrived at her father's palace? It would be a silly way to die, she thought, as they passed through yet another gate and into a new, gleaming section of the city. The streets here were incredibly wide, and paved, and the people on either side did not press their faces to the ground, but inclined their heads. Aria turned to look behind her again and saw that there were still scuffles behind them, a press of people from the lower parts of the city. She didn't see any blond head, but she felt reassured. There were towering headpieces on some of the women, and she frowned, trying to understand how the tall sculptures stayed on the heads of the women. She held a hand to her aching ribs and chest.

But then they turned a corner and the palace was before

them. All she could see was her father, flanked by red-robed men, a tall man in a black robe that seemed to pull all the light into it, until he alone glowed. He had long hair that swung free, nearly to his knees. He stepped toward her and held out a hand to help her down from her horse.

Aria looked at the red-robed men, and then back at her father, and as she caught the eyes of one of the men in a red robe, her heart spiked with a fierce pain, and she cried out. Her father put a hand around one foot, pulling her out of the saddle and into his arms.

And as soon as he touched her, she felt relief. All the pain left her, and the power she had been missing since they drew near to the city came flooding back into her. She stood before him, looking up into his face, and took the first deep breath she had taken in months.

"Welcome, daughter," the king said. And he turned with her hand in his, facing the people. "Your princess," he cried, "Aria, daughter of Ikajo." The people knelt as one. Aria's heart gave a sudden bound and she felt as though she had been reborn.

Chapter 18

The Karee camp was not quite as shocking as the Hadem village had been, perhaps because Isika had known Abbas for a while now, and it seemed like exactly the kind of place that would have made someone like him.

They came upon it suddenly, rounding past a formation of red stone to find a mile of white decorated tents unlike any Isika had ever seen. They were graceful and airy, with wings like birds and wide doors. A cluster of larger tents in the center of the camp trailed gold ribbons.

Abbas inclined his head toward the largest tent. "My father's," he said. "That's where we're going. But first we have to make it through the camp entrance."

Matters were complicated by the fact that the cats refused to stay outside the camp.

At the doors they were met by four guards who were even taller and wider than Abbas.

"I didn't know other Karee warriors were bigger than *our* Karee warrior," Brigid whispered to Isika, who giggled.

She was so tense she thought she might shatter. She was growing used to the cats as they ran alongside the little crew, but they were still terrifying. They rippled like water when they ran—as graceful as clouds—but the effect was spoiled because she could hear them arguing about who got to be closest to her. The mother cat always flanked her right side, while the three grown cubs argued over the left.

The men stared hard at the travelers until their eyes landed on Abbas and they bounded forward, each taking a turn to hug him, lifting him off the ground. The others stood there awkwardly, waiting.

"I feel small," Ben whispered, and Olumi shot him a hard look.

"How do you think I feel?" he asked.

Isika got the giggles and couldn't stop laughing. What was wrong with her? A combination of nerves, the cats, a long journey, and the fact that she thought she had heard Jabari call her "lovely one" last night. Just thinking about it brought heat to her face.

"You have . . . interesting company, big brother," one of the guards said.

"Did he just call Abbas *big* brother?" Brigid asked, and Isika got the giggles again, while Ben put his face in his elbow, his shoulders shaking. *Oh dear. This isn't the most dignified way to start a visit,* Isika thought.

The man was half a head taller than Abbas, with long tangled black hair that was braided away from his face at the sides but otherwise hung free. He wore more gold than Abbas, with bangles nearly to his elbows and rings in his ears. There were gold bands around his ankles, too, and he wore a skirt and vest, both edged in bands of red and yellow.

"You're staring at his arms," Brigid said.

"I am not," Isika retorted. "You are."

"I am," Ben said. "How many pushups do you think I would have to do to look like that?"

"There is not enough time left in our age," Olumi said mournfully.

Isika looked at Ben's arms and giggled again.

The cats pushed forward and came to stand around her, despite Keethior's best attempts at keeping them back. They seemed to want to be close enough to touch her. She had a cat head thrust under each palm, a cat sitting on one foot, and one leaning against the backs of her legs. The Karee warriors looked alarmed.

"You have . . . even more interesting companions, Abbas," said the man again.

"Yes, you have received my messages, have you not, little brother?"

"Yes we have . . . so this is her? The World Whisperer? And her . . . friends?"

"Yes."

You need to stay outside while I go into the camp, Isika told the cats, using her most commanding animal speech. *You are making them nervous.*

No, said the mother cat.

Yes, she said. *I order it.*

We like you, said another cat. *We will come with you.*

Their tails slowly twitched back and forth and Isika was horrified to hear herself gulp.

"I can't make them stay outside," she told Abbas in a loud whisper. "Either I have to stay outside with them or they have to come with me."

In the end it took several huddled consultations and a visit from the Karee king himself to figure out what to do. As they waited, Isika shifted her weight from foot to foot, feeling embarrassed and tired.

"Can't you do something?" she asked Keethior.

"I tried. They are stubborn."

"I noticed."

Finally the king came, looking like a mirror image of Abbas except for the lines in his face and gray streaks in his hair. They all bowed, but when Isika tried to bow as well, Olumi jabbed her in the ribs and shook his head. She stood, unsure of where to put her eyes, and the king never looked away from her standing there. Then he frowned, waved a hand, and said they could all enter the camp. Isika walked in behind Abbas and Olumi, trying to look unimposing as four huge cats flanked her. They kept so close to her that she couldn't be near Ben or Brigid, so she had to take in the sights without talking with anyone. It gave the people of the camp an excellent view of her as they came out of their tents to stare for what could have been many reasons: Prince Abbas coming home. Olumi, who was quite honestly odd looking, shorter than even most of the Karee children, with his locks dragging behind him. Isika, walking with her escort of cats. She felt worried. She had noticed that unlike the men at the gate, the king had not approached his son for a hug.

They reached the king's tent and a handful of servants helped them unlace and remove their soft traveling boots before they entered. Inside the tent, cool bowls of water with lemon awaited them, and servants helped again, holding out cloths for the travelers to wash their faces. Isika was used to the bare minimum of help from servants in the Maweel palace, and she was a little startled to realize that wherever she turned, a servant was there to guide her, or pull out a short stool, or offer a drink. They settled on the floor, on cushions or short stools. The Palipa stayed close, reclining around Isika in a pool of silver fur.

The king sat as well, and Abbas's younger brother sat beside him, and an older man on his other side.

"So," the king said, after a long moment, watching Isika closely as he spoke. "You're the one who has kept four of my best warriors."

Heat surged into Isika's face, and her eyes widened. Keethior spread his wings and uttered a short cry, and in the same moment, the silver cats around Isika hummed in their chests.

Shhh, she told them. *He's not going to hurt me.* At least I don't think so, she added to herself.

"She keeps them for all of us, Father," Abbas said.

In that moment, something became suddenly and irrevocably clear to Isika. The Karee king was nowhere near as humble in ambition as his son, and this imposing man in front of her had not approved of the prince's absence from his tribe.

Isika swallowed, looking at Abbas. He looked back at her, steady as he always was, though there was a muscle jumping near his eye. There were those, she thought, who looked out for their tribes and lands, and those who hoped to help all tribes and lands. Abbas was one of the second, though his father was the first. Isika supposed she was also one of the second, though she thought Andar would like to make her into the first.

"I have been thankful to have the wisdom of a people like the Karee near me, in Abbas," she said to the king. It didn't feel so bad, just then, to have some very large cats and a huge bird beside her. Otherwise she would have felt very small in front of the Karee king, who was as tall as Abbas, but bigger in the shoulders. He had a long beard with jewels braided into it, and intricate, woven robes in deep blue colors. He was truly a king.

"Father, men have come to tell us that people are disappearing," Abbas said, changing the subject. "Is it true?"

The king bowed his head, looking older suddenly. "Yes, son. It is true. They disappear from their tents or from their beds. They disappear when they travel to get water. A horse at the end of a procession is suddenly without a rider. We fight, but it is as though we are fighting the air, and we no longer know what to do. To add to that, our well has been poisoned and we have to travel long distances to get water. Soon we will have to move the camp if this does not change."

They were quiet, digesting this, and then a woman ran into the tent. Tears were streaming down her cheeks.

"Mama!" Abbas cried, and bounded over to her in one leap. She hugged him and sobbed, then stood back and looked at him, pummeling him on his arms and chest. She had long, graying hair, braided away from her face, and wore the long tunic and skirts that Isika had seen the other Karee wearing in Maween. She was breathtakingly lovely and very angry.

"How could you not come back immediately?" she cried, still hitting Abbas on the chest, though she was losing power. A look of pain flashed across his face, and Isika understood something else. It had cost him to bring her back here.

Leaving was not going to be easy for him. Unless . . . she drew in a breath. Unless he didn't plan to return to Maween. Jerutha's heart would break. But looking around, she saw all that he had lost by choosing to remain in Maween as a trainer to the seekers. He was a prince who had left his kingdom, nomadic or not, and had lost everything in it. For Isika. *Why for me?* she wondered and one cat turned to give her a reproachful look.

"This is my mother," Abbas said then, turning so they could bow to the Karee queen. This time Isika simply inclined her head. Isika saw that Abbas's face was gray with pain, and he didn't quite meet her eyes.

Ben grabbed one of Isika's hands, over a cat's back, and Isika knew her music must be wild with fear because her heart was beating rapidly. She couldn't face the thought of Jerutha going through any more sorrow. It was as though she had forgotten just how vulnerable people could be, how heartache seemed to follow some people no matter where they went.

Ben squeezed her hand hard and she shook herself. They were there for a reason, there was a reason that Abbas had agreed to come back here, a purpose. The prophecy, of course —she needed to ask about the prophecy—but pain and fear at the thought of more betrayal had stolen her voice. She looked at Olumi mutely, and he stirred himself, clearing his throat.

"Your highnesses, we have come to see if we can speak to your healer and hear the details of one of your Karee prophecies. I have forgotten the exact wording, you see. And I have heard that your healer is a kind of truth keeper himself, and that he will possibly be able to see whether the shadow of this prophecy lies on Isika and her sister."

The king looked back and forth between Olumi and Isika.

"You want to see Asafar?" he asked, his voice a rumble.

Keethior suddenly rose up and flew to sit on Isika's knee. She was having trouble breathing, and the coming of Keethior soothed her enough that she could pull air through her throat and into her lungs.

"Yes, Brightness," she said, bowing her head.

He turned then, to Abbas's brother and something wordless passed between them.

"Asafar is not well," the king said. "He cannot come to us. We will go to him."

They rose. Isika's knees creaked as though she had been sitting for a year. She knew it was because she was away from Maween, where her strength came to her in great bursts.

Why did you make me strong only in Maween, she asked Nenyi silently, *if you knew that you wanted me to look out for all people?* But then, why did Isika think Nenyi wanted her to look out for all people? Because others suggested it? It seemed that Isika needed to figure this out for herself. She sighed as they left the tent.

She followed close behind Abbas and his mother, close enough to hear them speak.

"Uncle Asafar is not well?" Abbas asked in a low voice. The queen clutched his arm and didn't let go, looking back at Isika, her eyes darting to the large cats that walked on either side of her. The queen clutched something in her free hand. After a moment, Isika realized that it was a knife. She eyed the cats.

Behave yourselves, she said.

We always behave ourselves, the mother said.

Somehow I doubt that, Isika replied.

The healer's tent was small, and this time, when Isika asked them to stay outside, the cats didn't deign to reply, but settled themselves on the ground outside the tent. She breathed a sigh of relief and gave Abbas's mother a look of apology, which the queen responded to with a glare that would fry ziti greens. Isika sighed again, feeling small and completely out of her depth.

What had she thought? That hers was the only kingdom worth anything? The only kingdom with righteousness and pride? She was flooded with shame as she realized that was exactly what she had thought.

She ducked into the coolness of the tent, determined to keep it together until she could be alone, find a tree somewhere in this desert and recover herself, or at least a body of water to hide the tears she wanted to cry.

But as soon as she entered, Asafar spoke from his bed, his voice vibrating with magic.

"Oh," he said, "it's you. It's happening then."

Isika began to shiver. Asafar lay on a pile of cushions at the back of the tent. His face was gaunt but startling in its calm. An almost beatific look came over him as he spoke and Isika shivered harder, her teeth rattling. Keethior let out a long wailing cry.

"Two sisters, a boat, and a road
Heart broken, lies taken
Grip of evil grip of pain
One will die for the other's gain
The world cracked open
The old voices return
One lies dead, the other in shame

Out of the night comes the way
The land cries out, the Shaper turns
One will die for the other's gain."

"Well," Isika said, when her shivering had stopped. "That doesn't sound good." They sat in silence for a while, and then she smiled. "And it's certainly different from the song you sang, Olumi."

Chapter 19

Herrith walked behind the king, darting glances at Aria, using every bit of self control within him to keep his face blank and still. He cursed the king for insisting that they walk with hoods off during the procession. He needed the safety of his hood now, to think, to allow ideas and thoughts to pass through his mind without having to focus on keeping them off his face. But years of careful work in the king's presence had trained him, and he was able to walk carefully behind them, keeping his eyes trained on the back of the king's head, only occasionally darting glances at sweet, sweet Aria.

She did not look well. She was thin and obviously exhausted, though the king's false energy was keeping her head up now. She needed food, a bath, and sleep and Herrith hoped desperately that the king wouldn't make her do too much before he allowed those things for her. He didn't believe for one second that Ikajo had any real love for her. Mercy would not come naturally. He would allow his poison arrow to make her feel as though she was doing well, even though she was near death.

Were they going to her private quarters? Or to the king's audience chambers? He had his answer when they turned down a corridor. The audience chambers. Herrith clenched a fist. He would need to intervene.

She looked so much like her dear mother. Amani would weep to see her daughter back in this palace when she had fought so valiantly to get her children away. And Aria had simply walked back into her father's trap.

Herrith had tried, as he sensed Aria getting nearer, to turn her away. He had lifted the deception of the arrow so she could feel its true pain, cleared her mind as the king tried to fog it. It was dangerous work. Surely the king noticed the lack of deception as he first touched her. But one touch from Ikajo had clouded the girl's mind immediately. Tears pressed behind Herrith's eyes.

Oh, Amani, what would you have me do? he thought. *She has walked right up and put her head in the lion's mouth. There is almost nothing left of her. How can we help her?*

First, he thought, to keep the child from dying of lack of sleep or nutrition. *What was Ikajo thinking?* he wondered angrily, as the king steered her toward the dais at the front of his audience chamber. He wasn't thinking, that was it. His own magic was so powerful that he hardly needed rest or sustenance. Herrith thought quickly.

"Brilliance," he said, a sneer in his voice. "May I have a word?"

The king turned to look at him, blinking as though he had forgotten that anyone else was there. His eyes were fever bright. Herrith would need to tread carefully here.

"You may."

"Alone?"

"No," the king said. "You may say it here."

Herrith took a deep breath. He didn't want to hurt the girl, but he pushed the thought away. There was much more at stake than her feelings or her opinion of him.

"The girl smells, Brilliance. She reeks of the Maweel, of the desert. Surely we can persuade her to bathe and rest before we hold any court events."

The king's nostrils flared. Herrith held his breath. He needed to tread the right line between dislike of the girl, for the king disliked her, and deference to her. It was an impossible task, but his whole life had been an impossible task.

Herrith looked at the beloved child, and she blinked at him, clearly stung, then turned to lift adoring eyes to her father.

"Yes, fine," Ikajo said, his lips curling as he took in the sight of her. "Take her, assign her rooms and servants."

He looked around, obviously frustrated. "Everyone be back here tomorrow so I can truly welcome my daughter," he said. And then he kicked at the slave who approached to offer him a drink, tripping her and sending her flying.

Herrith wasted no time. He gestured for some of the slaves to usher the girl along behind him. Who could he assign as her servants? He had given it some thought, but that was before he had seen how frail she was, how the arrow had taken nearly everything from her already.

He had few allies in the palace. That was purposeful, because people talked, people always talked, and they couldn't risk it. The Circle, the resistance would be useless without him. So there were only four of the Circle in the palace. Did he dare assign Lena to her? He glanced back at her and saw her sway.

Yes, he did dare. He had decided against it, but no one else would keep her alive. He cursed the king under his breath.

"Send Lena, Ola, and Keer to me," he told a nearby slave. "The princess will stay in the east wing."

"Wouldn't it be better to keep her in the west wing? Closer to the king?" one of the upper servants interjected.

"He doesn't want to be disturbed by a bratty child," Herrith spit out, alarmed. He wouldn't have thought the man had argument in him. "She is a princess, but she is a child, she needs to know the proper order of things."

She turned then, to him. "My father is happy that I am here," she enunciated clearly. It obviously took all her strength, and it was the first time he had heard her speak.

Oh, Amani, my darling. She is so brave.

"He will be happy if he has some space from you," Herrith said. "And you will like these rooms, princess."

She looked at him for a long minute, then nodded. Herrith let out a breath and continued along the corridor, touching the dark torches to light them as he went. The magicians didn't make it as far as this corridor often. It wasn't used as much as the king's quarters, which is why he wanted Aria here. Oh, he needed to keep her safe, he shook with the need to keep her safe. What a strange day this was. One of Amani's children was back in the palace, and it was more than his heart could bear. So much hope and grief combined in him that he stumbled. He kept his face perfectly still, and thankfully, at that moment, they rounded the corner and came to the doors to the suite of rooms he had chosen for the girl.

The king would never come here, which meant that he could take the time he needed to make it as comfortable as possible for her. He didn't want the king to know his heart, so he needed to be careful, but he knew the king would never come to the child's rooms. He didn't really care about Aria. She was bait, to him.

Lena, Ola, and Keer were already there, bowing low before the princess, and Herrith spoke to them.

"She is your charge, now. Lena, you will be her handmaid. Ola and Keer, you will serve and clean for her." The three women straightened and though Ola and Keer looked toward the girl they would be serving, Lena looked at Herrith for a brief moment, a question in her eyes. He made a tiny motion with his hand. Later. They would have to meet later.

And now he had much to do, because he must get to the hearth of the old woman by nightfall, and he must fight for Aria's life before then.

"Come, princess," he said, not stopping to see whether she followed. How he wanted to tell her who she was, that she was safe and loved, but he couldn't risk it while she was still poisoned. All her allegiance was to her father. He hoped Lena would see his example and follow it, and she did, catching his eyes and giving him a swift nod to show she understood.

"Ola, she needs food quickly. The kind for an uneasy stomach. It has been a long journey. And Keer, fix a bath."

Keer was already moving toward the bathroom. Herrith glanced at Aria and saw her turning in a slow circle, taking in the grandeur of the rooms. She looked ready to faint from exhaustion, but there was awe and pleasure in her face.

There were four rooms: a large bedroom with a huge bed, low to the ground and covered with cushions; an even larger room for eating and sitting; a bathroom with a deep pool of a bath; and a room that the servants would begin to fill with tunics and dresses, shoes and lotions to make a wardrobe for a princess.

"Lena," he said, still keeping his face very still. "She needs food, a bath, and sleep, in that order. She may need help to sleep."

Some of the intent of the demon's arrow was to keep the girl awake and fretful, with racing heart and eyes. He knew this poison. The king had used it many times. On him even. But Lena had skills. She could make a tea that would help Aria sleep. In the morning, when she was stronger, Herrith would see if he could help with the arrow. But not yet. He needed to meet with the Circle as quickly as possible.

"The evening will be long," he said to Lena. "Take care to finish your duties quickly."

This meant that she needed to meet him at Mara's hearth. Her eyes widened before she turned to Aria.

"Brightness, here comes the food. Can you eat a little porridge? It will settle your stomach after a long travel. Then let's get you out of those filthy clothes and into the bath."

Aria's eyes softened and she nodded, her shoulders slumping in relief. Herrith left the room silently, nodding to the guard who remained outside the room, then continued the difficult job of pretending everything was normal for the rest of the day.

It was only when he was alone in his own quarters that

he finally cracked, holding his face in his hands and shaking with sorrow and worry. Tears came, but he couldn't let them fall for long. He needed to attend the king.

The evening felt as though it stretched on forever. He received a message from Lena that said Aria was sleeping well. He told the king she was resting and would doubtless sleep through till morning. (Lena's teas were very good.) He listened to the king rant about Isika's refusal to come and how she would soon come running.

And then it was finally time, and he was slipping through the streets, hood down, his long braid out with the gold cord gleaming in the light that came from nearby homes. He tapped on the door and was let in. Lena was already there, as was the warrior princess and the two bricklayers, with their wives and children. He gave Mara the rose he had taken from the king's garden, and she took it from him, scolding and laughing, but the tension in the room was high.

He looked at Lena.

"I was waiting for you," she said softly.

"She's here," Herrith said, and there was a hiss as everyone let out the breath they had been holding. Questions rang out, and Herrith, exhausted, held up a hand.

"Let us sit and think this through. This is what we have been waiting for, because the king's plan is our plan too. We need the World Whisperer here, to fight with us and take this city back. But Aria is in the balance and we cannot let her be harmed. Oh, I wish there was another way. I tried to turn her back, not even sure that it was right to do, but she would not be turned."

He lifted his eyes to Mara, the old grandmother. "You should see her. She looks so much like her mother."

The old woman shuddered like a tree in a strong wind.

"Shaper, this is too hard," she whispered.

"It is not," the warrior princess said, her voice strong. "I know she is dear to you, but we have been losing people dear to us for years now, more people than you can imagine. You know it is time for this, you know this is the way. You need to be strong now for the sake of all the lands. How long do you think the Maweel can hold out against him without some strong show of might?"

The grandmother sucked in a breath.

"You are not wrong, princess," she said. "But have a little pity on an old woman."

The princess stabbed at her food with her knife.

"The shipment will go out within the next moon. We must stop it this time. It cannot go on like this."

The bricklayers nodded and began talking over one another. In one corner of the room, the old scholar sat with his head in his hands. He had wild gray hair from perpetually running his hands through it.

He muttered to himself, then said, "It is hard, but I cannot see another way."

Herrith held up his hands. "Yes, yes. We need a plan. But what?"

Lena moved in her seat then.

"Something, brother, that may be of use. Aria said something strange just as she drifted off to sleep."

"Yes?"

"She said, 'But where is Gavi? Did he make it all right? Is he safe?'"

Herrith sat back in his chair. He knew that name—they all did.

"You heard her clearly? You're sure? But the cart driver swore she was alone, that he picked her up alone."

"Maybe he was always hidden," said one of the bricklayers.

"Or maybe they made an ally," said Lena.

Could she be right? Could the second son of Andar have snuck into the Desert City? If so, everything was different now, and the balances were tipping in their favor. Finally. It had been a long day, but Herrith felt a slow smile creeping across his face, mirrored on the faces in the room. They stirred themselves and began to come up with a plan.

Chapter 20

*G*avi woke up to the sharp crack of a boot in the ribs.

"Ouch!" he said, sitting up in the doorway of the bakery he had chosen, only to get a cuff on the head. A man peered at him suspiciously.

"Worker slave, hey? Running away from your master? Get out of my way, I need to open up."

The sky was barely tinged with pink, and Gavi cursed himself for choosing a bakery. Of course it would open early. His body felt as though the cart had run him over rather than simply dropping him off. He hadn't slept properly for longer than he could remember. Aria had walked slowly but she had barely stopped to sleep, propelled by the wild energy of the arrow. He rolled the kinks out of his shoulders, longing for more sleep, then stood up.

The man was still staring at him, suspicion strong on his face.

"My master used to live in the city," Gavi said, hoping to placate him, "but now he lives in a village a day's journey away. He always loved your pastry and requested that I bring him some before I return."

The baker's face changed immediately, softening into a smug expression.

"Oh, well, people do love my pastry," he said. "What is your master's name?"

Gavi searched his memory for a Worker name.

"Nirloth," he said, wincing. What if the baker had heard of the priest? It didn't seem to bring any memories, though. The baker tipped his head to one side, thinking, then opened the door to the bakery, bustling through to get to the baking within.

"I don't remember a Nirloth. I do have so many customers though. So, so many."

The bakery smelled like heaven, and Gavi's stomach growled. He glanced down at his hands and frowned. They were black with desert silt. He needed to look for a job at the palace today, and he couldn't look like this when he did.

"Do you have work I can do in exchange for a bath? I want to clean up before I go back to my master." The lies sent twinges of discomfort into his chest. He had never been a liar. But this was a new life. A different person had followed Aria away from Maween.

The baker stopped in his tracks, his eyes widening as he turned to look at Gavi. "As a matter of fact, my delivery boy called in sick today." He looked Gavi up and down. "Bath's in the back. Soap on the upper shelf. We don't have fancy hot water here. Come back when you're clean and I'll give you work—till sundown, you hear? I'm not giving out water for free."

Gavi took a fast bath in the cold water, using a scrub

brush and soap from his pack. After, he felt better, invigorated from the scrubbing and certainly cleaner. He used his last set of clothes and felt more like a human being. But soon he would need to wash his clothing and find a place to hang it to dry, which meant he needed a place to stay.

Feeling better must have made him walk taller, because the baker looked at him funny when he came into the room.

"Where did you say you were from?" he asked.

Gavi slouched a bit. He couldn't walk around like a prince if he was supposed to be a slave. His father had drilled good posture into him from the time he was small.

"I don't know," he evaded. "I left when I was just a baby." It was partially true. The Maweel had rescued him from the boat when he was around two years old.

He took the basket the baker gave him and spent the day walking the city with the basket on his head, delivering flat bread and crusty bread, desserts, and even some vegetables. It was better than he had hoped. He was able to see the inner parts of the city without suspicion, for the baker gave him a baker's coat that allowed him to pass through without inspection from the city guards.

He saw many people stopped by the guards, questioned as to where they were going or what their business was. Gavi slipped right by them, pulling his ser over his face in case they had a description of him. But no one seemed to be looking for him, and he realized the cart driver must have kept quiet. He silently thanked the driver, an unexpected friend.

He saw that the city was built in tiers. He only had one order in the top tier—a tray of crusty, cream-filled pastries that sent their fragrance into his nostrils and tempted him until he could barely think straight. Then there was the middle tier, where the bakery was, a tangled web of well-trodden streets, packed full of bustling merchants and well-to-do housewives. Gavi delivered most of his baked goods there, observing the customs of the city. Shoes off at the door of most homes or shops. Women wore long tunics over loose skirts, decorated with tiny bits of embroidery or jewels. Their sers were also decorated with bits of mirror, and they called them sars, or at least their Gariah accent made it sound so. Women ducked their heads to avoid his eyes, but men stared straight at him, which was different from the Workers, who met no one's eyes.

As he loitered and observed in the second tier of the city, he heard whispers about a princess, which peaked his interest until he realized, with a sinking feeling in his stomach, that they were talking about Aria.

"She's come back," he heard people murmuring to one another. "At long last."

He felt slapped. It was as though a door had cracked when they trekked across the desert together, but now there was no denying that Aria's life could take another path, that there was another side to her lineage, people who had been waiting for her here, in the city of Maween's greatest enemy.

He took a break in the early afternoon. The baker had a slab of cheese and a crusty loaf of bread waiting for him.

"You're certainly the healthiest Worker I've ever seen," the baker said, "and you work twice as fast as any helper I've ever had in this bakery. Do you think your master might be willing to sell you?"

Gavi gaped at him. "No," he said, settling for the simplest

answer. How could people own and sell one another so easily?

"Pity," the baker said. He handed Gavi another basket, full of flatbreads and the dense grain-rich bread balls. "These are for the third tier. And then you're done, son. You've more than worked off that shower. I'll set you up with some food for the journey as well."

Gavi walked slowly down to the lower reaches of the city, noting again that things got worse the farther down he went. Beggars crawled along in the gutter, and filth covered the lower halves of many of the walls. He had to work to avoid water and other liquids thrown out of the tallest floors of the buildings. It smelled. It hurt him to be there. Dozens of people that he passed seemed in need of healing, and he wondered where the healers were to allow this to happen to their people.

He found the building the baker had directed him to and stood in front of it, looking at a short blue door, well below his head level, with a round symbol painted on it, like a circle with one piece missing. A line of people waited near the door, and he caught snatches of their conversation as he moved past them to get to the door.

Suddenly he froze at something he had heard. He looked hard at the speaker.

"What did you say?" he asked.

"I said," the man replied, his voice loud and coarse, "I heard that this isn't even the worthwhile princess, but some bit of trash the king has decided to take pity on."

Gavi took the baker's basket off his head and took a step toward the man, who was third in line and very near the door.

The door began to swing open just as he drew level with the man, his hands in fists at his sides.

"You watch your mouth," Gavi growled, and the man made to step closer to him, but stopped suddenly as a voice came from the open doorway.

"You, Ko, you know you get no food if you fight in the line." The speaker was a small elderly woman with deep black skin creased over with wrinkles, jingling with jewelry; rings in her nose and on her fingers, and bangles on her wrists. Ko looked abashed and stepped back into line.

"You, boy, are you delivering bread today?" the woman asked, glancing at the basket Gavi had retrieved from the ground. "Must be that the baker didn't warn you about the rules here. Come in then."

"How come he's delivering today?" Gavi heard the man ask as the old woman put a surprisingly strong hand on his shoulder and yanked him into a small, dimly lit room.

"What are you doing?" she hissed at him as soon as the door was shut. "Do you want everyone to know who you are?"

After a moment, Gavi realized his mouth had fallen open as he stared at the old woman, a thought that was confirmed by the snicker from the corner. He glanced up to see a woman who looked exactly like Abbas, so much so that he stepped toward her before realizing she wasn't Abbas. He frowned.

"No, no," the old woman said, leaning over a countertop and scribbling wildly on a piece of paper. "No time for questions now. You've been seen. Just dump the bread on the table and read this somewhere private."

"Are you sure he can read?" asked the woman in the corner. "He doesn't look very smart."

"Oh, I'm sure, as are you," the old woman said. "You're just trying to get him to crack. Get out of here, boy, unless you want to be suspected by every person in the lower reaches."

Gavi stumbled out the door and past the line of people, walking quickly in case the angry man decided to abandon his meal in favor of revenge. Not that he was worried about getting hurt. The man looked like he had seen a rough life but Gavi had been trained as a fighter. He didn't want more attention, though. The woman was right, he needed to be able to slip around the city. But what was that place? Did she know him somehow?

In a quiet corner, he opened the piece of paper he had crumpled in his hand. The paper was different here, he thought absently, rubbing it between his fingers. More slippery. And the writing was different. But those thoughts left him completely as he read the words on the page.

"Evening watch. North gate of the palace. Tell the guard you've stopped a fight near the mountain gate."

Well, that was cryptic. But Gavi felt a rush of excitement to think he had happened upon something that could help him get to Aria. If it was help. What if it was a trap? What was that place, and the symbol on its door? He walked back to the bakery and returned the basket, accepting his bread with thanks and turning down the baker's offer of more work the next day.

He walked toward the palace, wondering whether he could trust the old woman. But the woman seemed to know Gavi. A delivery boy wouldn't be able to read. How did she know him? He had to go to the North Gate if he wanted answers.

The guard at the North Gate was tall and broad. For a moment Gavi thought he might turn back. But then he thought of Aria, sick and alone in the palace, and he squared his shoulders and approached the guard.

"Yes?" the man asked in a gentle voice.

"I stopped a fight near the mountain gate," Gavi said. The man flinched, just a tiny bit, then stood back.

"By yourself?" he asked.

Desert spines, the woman hadn't said anything about any questions.

"Yes," Gavi said, hoping it was the right answer.

"Come with me," the man said, and he left his post to lead Gavi to a tiny walled garden, where he left him.

"Wait here," he said.

Gavi barely noticed him leave because the garden was filled with spiky gilgal bushes that flowered in every sunset color. He turned in circles, breathing in the scent of the gilgal flowers. After a while, he heard someone clearing his throat. He looked up from the flower he was examining, startled. He had nearly forgotten where he was—not his own garden at home, but the Desert King's palace garden, a dangerous place.

A man stood at the entrance to the garden. He was very tall, though not as wide as the guard. He wore a long red robe that reached the ground, but the hood wasn't pulled over his face so Gavi could see it clearly. The man was about as old as his father, and stern looking.

"Are you ready for this?" the man asked. "This is not going to be easy."

"What?" Gavi asked.

"Joining the Circle. Working with us. Are you playing, like a child who has lost his friend, or are you ready?"

Gavi nodded, shook his head, and nodded, startled. He had expected an introduction or something, not these cryptic questions.

"Is someone coming?" the man asked. "Will someone else help? Or is it only you?"

"Who are you?"

"We are Nenyi's Circle," the man said. "We have been here longer than Maween has been a country. Now tell me, is it only you?"

"For now, I suppose. But the Othra may come to bring and take messages. And," he shook his head, laughing. "I'm sure Jabari is on his way. He probably wants to take me back to Maween," he said. Then he frowned. "But I'll never go, I'll never leave her."

"So you shouldn't," the man said, crossing his arms and smiling faintly. "You are in the story, too."

Chapter 21

"There are too many cats in this tent," Ben said.

Isika looked up. One of the young male Palipa was chewing on a cushion, making a large hole in one corner. Isika jumped up and pulled it away from him.

No! she told him. *Go somewhere! Can you control your children?* she asked the mother cat, sending her a look. The mother cat heaved herself up and padded over to the younger cat, knocking him down and growling with her teeth at his throat.

"I agree," Brigid said. "I have to curl up in a ball to sleep."

"I don't know what you expect me to do about it," Isika said irritably, her arms crossed. She found her pack and rifled through it until she found her sewing kit. She threw herself down and began stitching the gorgeous cushion back together. It was one of many that were scattered around the tent the king had given them for the night.

She worried about growing soft on their journey. This tent was a far cry from a bedroll around a fire, thick with cushions in the sleeping area, cool in the day, warm at night. She worried about the prophecy, which didn't seem positive no matter which way you interpreted it.

"I don't know," Ben said. "Exert your mighty powers. Talk to them with your Isika ways."

Isika glared at him, but she did try.

Do you hear this? she asked the cats. *It makes people nervous to have you so close.* She tried her best to explain it as clearly as she could, showing them pictures of their claws and teeth.

Why? the young ones kept asking, and the mother simply fixed Isika with a level stare.

Because you are so big and there are so many of you.

Would it be better if some of us waited outside? The mother cat asked.

Yes, Isika said. *Absolutely.*

Okay, the mother cat said, but then nothing happened. She waited for a while and still nothing happened. The cats went to sleep.

"I tried," Isika told the others. "They didn't listen."

Olumi laughed quietly in a corner.

"Thanks for trying," Brigid said, eying the cats. "I think I'll find some space outside."

That night when the travelers came back from their meal, the three younger cats were gone, and only the mother was left.

What happened? Isika asked. *Where did they go?*

The cat blinked slowly at her and yawned. *You asked them to go. They went.*

Isika stared at her, then sighed and went off to prepare her bed. She hadn't known that any creature could be more irritating than Othra, but here they were. Othra, at least, had good qualities, like singing and calming people. They were helpful occasionally.

"I often help," a voice said, and Isika jumped.

"Keethior," she said, turning to look at the giant bird. His feathers gleamed in the lantern light in the tent. "We've talked about you reading my mind. Don't listen unless I'm talking to you!"

"It's hard not to when you're thinking so loudly. But you'll find that the cats are good friends when they are loyal to you. It just takes a dire situation to find that out."

Isika stared at him. "Well, we're not hoping for a dire situation."

Keethior hummed in his throat. "The cats showing up means you just might have one. They're made for killing."

It took Isika a long time to fall asleep.

THE NEXT MORNING was bright and hot, the sky almost metallic, and when Isika walked to the king's tent she found Abbas outside already, staring into the distance.

"It's going to storm," he said.

"Really?" Isika asked. She looked around. There wasn't a cloud in the sky.

"Yes, can't you feel it?"

She hesitated, shifting from foot to foot.

"I taste or smell something, almost like an old belt buckle."

Abbas grinned at her. "That is it. An approaching storm is like an old belt buckle. Very good, little sister."

She smiled back at him. "What are we doing today?"

"My father wants to talk more, tell you more of the Karee ways. Then you are free to explore our camp if you want."

"I would love that. I want to see everything."

Abbas gestured for her to go first, and she ducked through the opening in the king's tent, blinking when she realized that Brigid, Olumi, and Ben were already there. The mother cat stayed outside, settling onto her stomach, staring at the other people who passed into the tent in a disconcerting way. Isika shook her head at the cat.

Be less scary, she said. The cat looked at her with unblinking eyes.

When they were all there, the king offered spiced tea. Isika took a tiny glass, of the hot, sweet tea and sat forward quickly as she burned her tongue. She was brushing tea off her lap where she had spilled it and was taken by surprise when the king jumped right in.

"We need to discuss this prophecy," he said. "And what it means for all of us."

"We don't yet know that the prophecy is about Isika," Brigid said.

"True. Yet you said your sister has gone to Dhahara?" the king asked, directing the question at Isika.

She nodded. She felt the familiar ache that came whenever she thought of Aria marching into the city by herself.

The king leaned forward. "What I say next must not leave this tent, do you understand? Of course you may speak of it together, but it is guarded, dangerous information. Please do not breathe a word."

Isika nodded, as did the others. She felt a prickle of anticipation. What was he about to say?

"What do you know of the Circle?"

Isika blinked. She looked at the others. Ben had a blank face, along with Brigid. Only Olumi looked like he knew anything. He sat with his mouth open, mopping at his wet trouser knee. He had spilled his own tea at the question.

"Is it real?" he breathed in a whisper. "I believed it to be a wish or a myth. A wild rumor."

"Oh no," Abbas said. "The Circle is very real."

"Are you going to explain what the Circle is?" Isika asked, feeling irritated. "Or do we have to guess?"

The king shot her a quelling look and she sat back a little.

"The Circle has been around since before Maween was a country. It is Nenyi's resistance effort, built into the inner reaches of the Desert City."

"Nenyi's what?" Ben asked. His face had a slightly distant look, as it did when he was listening hard.

"Deep inside Dharhara there is a resistance effort against the Desert King and Mugunta, the goddesses and the Great Waste. But Ikajo will execute anyone who even breathes the name Nenyi, so it must be hidden. You knew already that many of the Karee fight for independence. Many are a part of the Circle, part of the resistance. And there are many more who only want to fight the Gariah.

"And the people who disappear?" Abbas asked.

"All part of the resistance in some way or another."

Abbas sat back, his face stricken, as Isika tried to take in what the king had just said.

"You mean they know?"

"They can't know. It is some magic from the Great Waste, a strong poison trying to wipe out the last of those who are willing to try to fight the king."

There was silence as everyone tried to digest this.

Isika spoke. "Long ago, in Batta, a Worker priest told me people weren't allowed to know the Desert King's name. But last year you said it, Abbas, and now here..."

"The Desert King does not allow Workers to speak his name," Abbas answered. "He feels that their low caste will taint it. But Gariah, including Karee, all refer to him as King Ikajo."

More silence. Then Isika sat forward.

"Is there anyone from the Circle in the palace?"

The king nodded. "Yes, though we hear there are only a handful, and they are so secretive that we don't even know who they are. But a few months ago, Abbas's sister Enfa went to the Desert City to learn what she could about the missing people. She has sent messages that she is in communication with members of the Circle from the palace, the inner Circle, if you will, but that is all she has said. She must be very careful. She already looks different. She is there on pretense of being a merchant selling our embroidered robes and blankets."

Isika looked at Abbas.

"You have a sister? I didn't know."

"I have three sisters and four brothers," Abbas said. "I have many siblings. But Enfa is close to me. She is my step down sister, just a year younger than me."

His face was clear of any struggle or anger, but again Isika thought about what it meant that he stayed with the World Whisperer. He had left his family—not a small thing. She couldn't imagine what would ever cause her to live far from Benayeem. The pain wouldn't be worth it.

"So the prophecy is important, you see. If you are the sisters, what does it mean?"

"It doesn't exactly give instructions," Brigid said.

"Wouldn't it be nice if it did?" Olumi said, smiling. "But it does seem to imply that Isika needs to be close to Aria."

"Yes!" Isika exclaimed, sitting forward. "That's what I've been saying!"

"But first you need to learn to hide yourself from her," Olumi said. He turned to the king.

"Aria can sense where Isika is."

"That's not safe," the king said immediately, gesturing to the servants for more tea. "You can learn how to block that. Asafar is the one who should teach you."

"But I thought he wasn't well," Isika said.

"The day that Asafar is not well enough to teach a lesson is the day he is no longer with us," the king said, and though his words were light, his face grew sad.

LATER THAT DAY, Isika went to Asafar's tent with the mother cat trailing her and Keethior flying overhead.

What is your name? Isika asked the cat as they walked, realizing she should probably stop calling her "the mother cat" in her head.

Heeeeeerrrra, the cat replied.

Isika stopped and stared at her.

"Hera?" she asked aloud.

If that is all your human mouth can say, it will do.

It's more like Heerrrrrra, Keethior added helpfully from above, rolling the *r*'s until they sounded like the ripple of waves on a shore.

"Hera," Isika said again, this time rolling the *r*. She scowled as the pair of them laughed at her.

Hera walked with Isika into the tent this time, and Isika turned and narrowed her eyes at the cat, but Asafar gestured with a weak hand.

"I don't mind her," he said. "I'm rather tickled that I get to see a mystical being I only ever thought was a myth."

Isika smiled at him. She regarded him as he lay back on his cushions. He didn't look well enough to teach. But the king had said he would do it. She hated to ask him but gritted her teeth and thought of Aria.

"Uncle, can you teach me to guard my mind?"

"Of course. Come closer."

She settled herself on the cushions. Hera stretched to her full length against Isika's side and began purring. The vibrations were so strong that Isika felt them in her teeth, but she did her best to ignore the cat, and Keethior also, who was standing to one side, lifting his wings idly every so often.

"Hiding from someone who can sense you is like finding a secret place inside yourself. You put your presence there, so people can't simply reach out and grab pieces of you. Let's try this. Imagine a room, a beautiful one. We'll call this your soul. And you merely have to go inside this space and shut the door."

Isika looked back at him. The old man had gentle eyes and a soothing presence, almost like an Othra.

"It sounds a lot like what Ben does in his mind to block the music, only he shuts the music in a room."

"Ah, but he would find it easier to put himself in the room."

"Will I still be able to focus on the world around me?" Isika asked.

"Try it and see," the old healer said.

Isika envisioned a room that looked very much like her bedroom at home, with white walls and a wooden ceiling, a simple bed and a mat on the floor. Then she went into the room and shut the door, sitting on the bed. As she did so, she opened her eyes. Everything around her looked the same, but she felt protected. It wasn't that she couldn't see, it was more that she wasn't flailing in the wind, ready for anything to pick her up and carry her off.

She blinked and suddenly she was back outside the room.

Asafar smiled and lifted a hand, but it was so weak that it fell back against his chest.

"Very good, young one," he said. "It will get easier in time, so that you won't be forced out of the room. You'll learn to live there, to practice everything there rather than living out in the open. You can invite Nenyi there, but no one else gets to come . . . into the room."

He was growing breathless, and his wife came forward. Isika nodded and stood to go, but something had been bothering her, itching just under her skin. It was a little like the feeling she had just before she found a wall to pull down. What was it? She had learned to listen to this sense, but it often took its sweet time to show her what it needed.

Hera raised her giant head and looked directly at Isika, and Keethior gave a long, low cry.

Isika knew then.

"Can I touch you?" she asked Asafar.

He looked at her from weary dark eyes and shrugged. "All the best healers have failed," he said. "Many more skilled than you. No one knows what this thing is."

But the feeling was very strong now, and Isika moved toward the healer as though she was in a trance. She fell to her knees beside him and tucked her feet under her, placing her hands on either side of his head, cupping his forehead gently.

His eyes flew open and then she couldn't see anymore, because she was following the sickness, deep inside, to the very center, where she found a deep poison that attacked him so he would be too weak to stop the kidnapping of his people. This was malevolent magic, from the bowels of the Great Waste, targeting the powerful healer to take his strength and eventually kill him. And it was strong because of betrayal magic. She pulled it, all of it, sending it deep inside her and smothering it with her pure water. It couldn't live within her. She drew it out slowly, without mercy, refusing to feel its panic, pulling and pulling until she opened her eyes to discover that she was on her feet, holding onto the healer's forehead, while he stood strong and impossibly tall in front of her, fire in his eyes, and now he had his hands on her elbows and he was holding her up.

She opened her mouth. "There is a spy in the camp," was all she could say before she fainted.

Chapter 22

From a long way off, Ben heard Isika's music suddenly change, so he broke into a run, searching for her. It grew poisonous, then soft and like her again, and he realized she had performed a healing. A big one. Her music was wispy and pale, as though she was barely alive. He ran faster.

He found her with the healer Asafar in his tent. Asafar look completely well, while Isika lay curled on the floor of the tent.

"Wow," Ben breathed, taking in the size and scope of what his sister had just done.

Asafar looked at him and nodded.

"What do we do?" Ben asked. "She's normally okay after some sleep, but this time her music is weak, too weak."

"The magic grows angrier," Asafar murmured. "It fights her in a different way, targeting her as though it has instructions to hurt her if it finds her."

"I think Mugunta is becoming wise to the fact that she will heal what she finds."

"I am trying to help, but I do not know what to do," Asafar said.

Ben thought, feeling frantic.

"Is there a tree in this desert?"

"A tree?" the healer looked at him with astonishment. "Yes, there are a few. There is a small grove of orange trees with precious fruit."

Abbas ran into the tent, Keethior directly behind him.

"The stream," he said. "We need to lay her in the stream."

"The stream is no more, young Abbas," the healer said. "At the same time that the well was poisoned, the stream dried up. Things are bad here."

"We'll go to the trees," Ben said.

Asafar turned to Abbas. "I'll carry her. I feel stronger than I have in years. But, Abbas, she said there is a spy here. We must find him."

He picked Isika up as though she weighed nothing. He was tall, like Abbas, with long silvery hair and a dark beard. He had rings in his ears and his nose, and his skin was almost as dark as Isika's but his hair was long, straight, and swinging free. He stooped to get through the tent opening, and then Ben had to stop staring and hurry to catch up as Abbas went after him. They moved swiftly through the camp, people staring and calling out as they passed by.

"Asafar!" the people called out. "Healer! You have come back to us!"

"Yes," the healer responded to their calls. "But my own healer is sick and I must help her." And then the people noticed Isika in his arms, and they cried out in fear. Ben was listening intently from behind, his heart beating quickly.

"Uncle, I can barely hear her!" he called, and Asafar began to run.

They ran into the desert, and the heat beat down on them until Ben was parched and exhausted, but as they ran he saw a low-lying mass on the horizon that grew larger as they drew closer. The mass became a stand of trees, then finally they were in a grove of stocky orange trees, fruit heavy on their branches. Ben could hear only the quietest strains of Isika's music and his heart was tight with fear.

Asafar turned to ask where he should put Isika, and Ben gestured to the ground at the foot of one of the trees. The healer laid her gently down and Ben placed her hands on the tree, while Abbas swung her knees so she was curled all the way around the tree, in its shade. Her music lifted and Ben heaved a sigh.

"We are in time," he said. "She will be okay, but I think she will sleep for a long while."

The three of them settled in a circle to wait, and Abbas retrieved a piece of fruit from one of the trees and pulled a knife from his belt. He removed a cloth and a few packages from the pack he always wore on his back. Inside was a chunk of goat cheese from the camp, a skin of water, and a few pieces of flat bread. He cut chunks of fruit, layered them with thin slices of goat cheese, and offered them to Asafar and Ben. Ben relaxed in the company of these men, reassured now about Isika and ready to lay down his fear for a time. The fruit was spicy and sweet and the cheese mellow and creamy, with that slight taste of goat that reminded him of traveling the desert with his mother, asking for milk from wandering goatherds.

He sat and listened for a while. He could hear the earth responding to Isika, and the sound of the tree finding her and lending her strength. He had never heard that before, and when Asafar asked him, he told the healer about what he heard.

"How far have you tried to send your hearing?" the healer asked.

"Across the city," Ben told him, "back in Azariyah."

Asafar took a bite of flatbread, then a bite of fruit and cheese, and watched Ben as he chewed. When he was finished, he sat forward and offered Ben one of his hands.

"Can I listen with you for a moment?" he asked.

"Listen with me?"

"One of my gifts allows me to experience the gifts of others with them. And I am a listener also, although I hear things other than music. I am fascinated by your own gift."

Ben felt stunned. He had never heard of a person who could hear the gifts of others, and suddenly he longed to share what he heard, to have someone else hear it. He put his hand between the two hands of the healer, and Asafar drew in a sharp breath.

"You hear this all the time?" he asked. Ben listened, becoming aware of what he heard. He heard Abbas and Asafar. He heard Isika's song and the way it mingled now with the song of the desert and the grove of orange trees. He heard the wild song of the Palipa, and turned to see that the mother cat had followed them and was lying not far away.

"Yes," he said, "though I have learned ways not to hear

everything all the time, only when I want to pay attention."
He grimaced. "Mostly."

"Yes," Asafar said. "I can see why you would have to. Try
to send your hearing farther."

"Farther."

"Yes, you are looking for your sister, yes? And her music
will be familiar to you? Try to find her."

Ben closed his eyes and listened. As he opened his
hearing up rather than blocking it, he could hear a cacophony
of sounds. Throughout the desert there were people rejoicing
at the healer's return. He heard the desperate sounds of the
sick. He listened harder, farther, skimming over the deep
waves of music and all the threads of song until he found a
spark that sounded familiar. It was Aria. He gasped and
almost lost her, but quickly found her again and listened. Her
music was deeply familiar to him. He had known it since she
was born, but he heard unfamiliar and sorrowful music
within hers now. The poison of the arrow. And the Desert
King's music, woven into hers now, nearly drowning her out.
And even in her own music, something new: an anthem,
almost, so different from the shy, quiet Aria that he knew.

He was listening so hard for Aria that he almost missed
other, familiar music coming closer and closer until Asafar
shook him. His eyes flew open. His hands were still held
between the hands of the healer.

"What is that?" the healer whispered, and Ben smiled
with relief.

"That is Eemia, the Othra," he said, and soon she swept
into the grove of trees, purple lights flickering within the deep
black of her feathers, bringing her distinctive, sweet,
wild song.

"Eemia," Abbas said, bowing his head slightly, and Ben followed suit. The bird drew close and looked at Asafar, her bright eyes flashing as she cocked her head to look at him.

"Well," she said, "that is an ancient one. Honor be on your head, ancient one."

"And yours," Asafar said, dropping Ben's hands and sitting straighter.

Ben looked at the bird, sure she had something important to tell them about Gavi and Aria, but not wanting to interrupt her conversation with Asafar. He caught movement out of the corner of his eye and turned to see the mother cat moving closer, stretching out close to Isika and giving Eemia her full attention.

"Is the cat safe for you?" Abbas asked, his voice wry but nervous.

Eemia gave the squawk that was an Othra laugh. "Ancient ones don't eat each other, don't worry," she said. "But I have news for you, Abbas and Benayeem."

"What is your news, Eemia?" Ben asked.

"Aria will be crowned heir within the week," Eemia said. "The king is naming her as next in line. She will be queen of Gariah one day."

"What?" Ben said. "What does that mean?"

"It means she will be tied to the magic of the city and the king, woven into it in a way that will be very hard to fix later. If we are going to help her, we must do it now."

THE SHOCK of Eemia's news took time to sink in. Ben asked himself over and over what it meant and what they could do. He finally agreed with Isika. They needed to go to Aria quickly. Isika needed to learn to hide herself, and soon. He looked at her, sleeping peacefully under the tree. He heard her coming back, her wild earth gift strong and powerful. He heard her song of worship, her link to Nenyi, the song so beautiful it made him want to get up and sing it out.

Ben, Abbas, and Asafar talked into the night, and when Isika didn't wake, they finally lay down and slept there in the orange grove, covering themselves with the thin blankets that Abbas had carried with him. A messenger came from the king at one point, asking if all was well, and when Asafar told him yes, and that they would be back in the morning, the messenger bowed low before Asafar and stood up with tears in his eyes. He laid a flower at Isika's side and went.

The healer smiled softly as he settled himself down to sleep.

"She will find it interesting to deal with my people's gratitude," he said. "Without their healer they felt lost. She has returned me to them and they will be loyal to her forever."

Ben laughed, and drifted off to sleep, his heart tangled between fear and grief for Aria and love and happiness for Isika.

AT FIRST HE didn't know what had woken him. The sky was dark, the moon had set, and the stars were like brilliant sparks. The air was chilly. Why was he awake? Then he sat up. Music. Harsh, discordant, wailing music that hurt his inner ears and made him want to run far away. Isika, under the tree, sat up suddenly, the mother cat at her side. Their eyes met.

"Hera says there is danger in the camp," Isika said.

"I hear it," Ben answered. They woke Abbas and Asafar, and Isika assured them she was well. They ran back toward the camp together, spotting the flames while they were still far away. Abbas cried out, his steps growing faster as he pulled ahead. Out of the distance, the three other cats joined them and ran on either side of Ben and Isika, flanking them.

The music was horrible, and Ben tried to protect himself from it so it wouldn't overwhelm him. He knew what he was hearing. It was betrayal.

THERE WERE FOUR OF THEM. Three young men and one woman. They had set fire to the tent where Isika, Olumi, Brigid, and Ben slept. Olumi and Brigid stood outside, shaking but unharmed, as fighting broke out between the Karee and the betrayers. Spies.

One of the men had a bow and arrow, and as Ben and Isika ran into the camp, he turned and sighted the arrow on Isika, a mad gleam in his eye, his lips curled back over bared teeth. He pulled back his arm to let an arrow fly and Ben was helpless, useless, but then four shapes tore toward the man, leaping like silver lightning to knock the arrow out of the air and leap on the man. He was dead before anyone else reached him, Hera standing on his chest, blood on her muzzle. There was smoke and confusion and when things cleared up, they discovered that the other three spies were gone.

ISIKA WAS SITTING with the mother cat, stroking her between the shoulders, when Ben finally reached her.

"Well," she said. "Olumi was right about the cats, although they may have terrified the Karee beyond repair. But no wonder they couldn't heal Asafar, with so many spies right here, sending waves of betrayal magic."

Ben nodded. He was exhausted and ready for sleep, wondering when someone would offer them a new tent.

Abbas came to them. Isika had her head on her knees, and the first streaks of light were showing over the desert horizon.

"Bring me to the well," she said, after a moment. "We will need clean water to help with healing."

She called the clean water back to the well, drawing the poison out of it and sending it far away. And then she lay near the dry stream bed and called the waters of Lake Ayo back to the surface. Soon the stream bed was running with water again and Isika sat pouring it over her head with her hands.

"That's better," she said. "But I still need to sleep for a week."

Ben laughed at her and let her lean on him while they walked to the new tent. He wasn't looking forward to telling Isika that their father was getting ready to install Aria as heir. He decided to tell her in the morning. Seas and skies, she could insist on leaving today if she knew.

Chapter 23

*J*abari squeezed through an opening between two walls and nearly tripped over a nest of snakes. He shouted, leaping back and smacking into Deto, who was right on his heels. Deto fell backward toward Ivy, and the three of them landed in a pile in the muck that lined the dark streets of the small city.

Oof.

"Jabari!" Ivy shrieked. "Look at this mess! Why can't you ever be careful?"

Jabari was too busy trying to untangle himself from the pile of arms and legs to answer. Several white snakes began slithering through the opening, looking for the people who had stumbled on their nest. Jabari couldn't move fast enough. Everything was slippery. He tried to warn the others but his voice stuttered.

"What?" Ivy snapped, thoroughly angry, but then she caught sight of the snakes whipping their long heads back and forth. She screamed.

"Go, go, go!" Jabari said, finally locating his voice, and they scrambled to their feet, tearing back down the narrow alleyway.

When it looked like the snakes weren't following, Jabari slowed to catch his breath, exchanging glances with Deto and Ivy, who shook their heads wordlessly. Jabari wound his way back out onto the main street. He was winded from the heat of the midday sun and the quick escape, sweating because of the stuffy air in the stacks of buildings on the edge of the Desert City. They hadn't even reached Dhahara and Jabari was already tired of the smell.

"Gavi, you are going to be in so much trouble," Jabari muttered fiercely as he tried in vain to wipe the slime from his hands and clothes. Ivy wrinkled her nose at him.

"You tackle Gavi. I'll take the first swipe," she said.

Deto looked back and forth between them, eyebrows raised. He peeled his ser off his head and used it to wipe at a line of mud that stretched from his shoulder to his wrist.

"You are both going to fall on him crying when you find him. You can't fool me."

Jabari wasn't so sure. They had been sleeping rolled up in their cloaks in ditches and behind barns. They had been eating flatbread and the occasional lizard, and now they were trying to find secret ways through alleys and cracks in walls so they could get into the Desert City without being discovered.

He looked up and realized they were attracting attention even now. The three of them stood out. Jabari the tallest, clearly from Maween, not really looking or walking like a slave or even a simple Gariah. Then Ivy, like a queen, not even a little bit subservient. Jabari had reminded her a hundred times that Gariah women didn't parade around looking like they ruled the world, but she didn't know how to make herself look miserable. It wasn't her way.

And Deto was a rarity in the desert. There were only a handful of people who looked like his mountain tribe, with his sand-colored skin, long eyes and wind-reddened cheeks, his flat, high cheekbones. People kept whispering and pointing at him, and Jabari had to agree that he looked like something out of a storybook, one of the old fighters whose birds fought just as fiercely as they.

"Now what are you going to put over your head?" he asked Deto testily. "You can't walk around like that. Look at the people staring at you."

"I have a spare," Deto said mildly. "A clean one. Don't worry, I'll hide my strange face. You should also hide your princeliness, but if you want to pretend I'm the odd one of the bunch, you can. What's with you, anyway?"

"He's been like this ever since we had to leave Isika," Ivy said.

Jabari scowled, refusing to acknowledge that comment. "So," he said, ignoring their smirks, "obviously that snake road isn't open. Let's find another way." He grinned suddenly. "And you're ones to talk. Don't think I haven't seen you holding hands when you think I'm not looking."

This city was little more than a grouping of tottery buildings that leaned against the walls of Dhahara, and Jabari felt there must be a passage through the walls. They needed to find it. He didn't want to announce himself at the front gate of the city. Jabari would love to avoid getting pulled into the Desert King's prison right from the start.

"Where is Eemia when we need her?" Ivy asked.

"She told me she was going to search ahead a bit," Jabari said. "Hopefully she'll come back. But you know Eemia. She's sweeter than Keethior but more imperious, if that's possible." He scanned the buildings around them, then settled on one that looked promising. "I'm going to climb up to the top of that roof and see if I can find us a way into the city."

"You're not going to blend in that way," Deto commented.

"It's the lesser of two evils," Jabari said.

"Says you," Ivy said, but she made herself comfortable, leaning against a stone wall.

Jabari sprang to the top of a short wall, then found footholds to launch himself up the sides of the building he had chosen, a short, two-storied sandstone thing that had a sign proclaiming it was a tailor's house. It was easy to climb. He used the edge of an open window on the second story as a handhold and had a shock when he found himself face to face with a cross-legged tailor. The old man regarded him for a few moments, then spoke.

"Do you mean me harm?" he asked.

"Not at all," Jabari responded. "I'm just trying to get a better view from the top of your roof."

The old man gestured with one hand. "As you wish. And on your way back down, come and tell me what you are seeking. I may be able to help." He adjusted the glasses perched on the end of his beaky nose and went back to his stitching.

Jabari watched him for a moment, then said, "Thank you, Uncle." He kept climbing. At the top of the house, he peered down at the back alleys and thought about what he had seen on this journey so far.

The Gariah were not what he had expected. The people were not evil. They were much like the Maweel, but bent and broken by their harsh ruler, Isika's father. He thought also about what Ivy had said to him, about being grumpy because he was away from Isika. She was right, but it was only part of his situation. Jabari had a sharp pain in his chest. It stayed with him from morning until night and he knew what caused it. Gavi's absence. His brother was his closest friend and companion. No one knew him better and he hadn't known how much he counted on that understanding. Until that seeking journey last year, the brothers hadn't been separated since Gavi's rescue day. Their mother said there was no way Jabari could remember that, but Jabari knew she was wrong.

That day had changed his life. His parents had come home and told two-year-old Jabari that he had a new brother, and there was Gavi, the tiny pale boy with huge eyes. His hair was so white and stuck straight up from his head. And after that there was Gavi, there was always Gavi, and Jabari was never alone again.

Until now.

Jabari saw nothing but dead ends. Alley after alley seemed to be blocked by buildings, or wood, or simply the solid wall. He gritted his teeth, vibrating with impatience. The sooner Jabari could get to Gavi, the sooner he could gather him up and bring him back, find Isika again, and all would be well. As for Aria, he only hoped they could convince her to come too. The things going on with her seemed deeper than any of them could fix.

He was going to have to trust the tailor.

He clambered back down to the window and rested his

elbows on the opening. The tailor seemed much the same as when Jabari had left, unperturbed by the young man at his window.

"We need to get into the Desert City unseen," Jabari said. "There is no alley that appears to lead inside."

The tailor took a pin out of his mouth and regarded Jabari from beneath bushy eyebrows. "Oh, is that all? Well you wouldn't find that on your own." He looked at him for a few moments. "Do you mean harm to our people?" he asked.

Jabari gave a start. The man knew he was not Gariah.

"Is it that obvious that I'm not from here?" he asked.

The tailor laughed a wheezy laugh. "You can't imagine that you, or your companions are passing as Gariah," he gestured down to Ivy and Deto leaning against the wall. Holding hands again. Jabari scowled. "You are as obvious as that ancient bird that has been flying past every day."

Jabari swallowed. "No," he said. "We mean harm to no one. I am seeking my brother and my friend. They have come this way."

"Do they wish to be found?" the man asked.

"Yes," Jabari said. "At least I think so."

"Well then, head to the Hardy Cactus and find a woman named Eva. She will show you the way."

"Thank you," Jabari said.

"Tell that friend of yours to keep his head covered. His people are only in the city as slaves. He could get picked up by sellers or the palace guard." Jabari nodded, feeling a kind of sad justification at his accurate predictions about Deto. What kind of horror was this city?

When Jabari was back on the ground, relaying these instructions, both Ivy and Deto burst out laughing at him.

"Are you serious, cousin-brother?" Ivy asked. "You really think we should follow a tailor you met in the sky, searching for a pub with what—a secret door?"

Jabari shrugged. "It's the best we've got. And you need to get that first punch at Gavi's face, don't you?"

Ivy and Deto were still laughing when they finally found the Hardy Cactus, which was located at the wall that opened into Dhahara itself. But they stopped laughing when the woman named Eva showed them through crowds of sleepy and drunk people to a small closet. She opened the door to reveal dusty bottles . . . and a door.

"It's a long walk," the woman said. "And I don't show so many people the way anymore, since the soldiers have been growing smarter about the secret ways. But you will find a corridor that eventually comes to the filth of the lowest part of the city. Get ready to be dirty."

Jabari glanced at Ivy and grinned. "Too late."

Ivy grimaced. "He's in so much trouble," she muttered.

They thanked the woman and pushed through what felt like miles of cobwebs in a narrow corridor that was barely wider than their shoulders. The corridor smelled damp, like old earth, and the coolness was a welcome respite from the bright heat of the desert above.

"This is disgusting," Ivy said, wiping slime and cobwebs off of her arms.

"What are you talking about?" Jabari asked, turning to untangle himself from a beam that was broken at the top of the corridor. "It's delightful."

"I'm glad you're having fun," Deto grumbled. He was picking cobwebs out of his long braid.

"I see light ahead," Ivy said. "So we don't have to talk any more about whether this is delightful or disgusting. In fact, we should be quiet, because we have no idea where we're going to turn up."

They drew near the opening of the corridor in silence, peering outside, blinking in the bright sunlight. When they wiggled out of the opening, they were at the the end of an alleyway, sheltered from sight by stacks of old sacks of rotting onions. The stench was horrible. Jabari covered his face and gestured for the others to follow him. He made his way as quickly as he could up the alley toward a busier street ahead, only to bump into a tall woman at the beginning of the alley.

She was taller than him. He stared at her in shock. She looked so familiar. Then he remembered they weren't supposed to be noticed, and looked down, but not before she got a good look at him.

"What are you three doing down that way?" she demanded, leaning back on her heels and crossing her arms. "There's nothing to see over there."

Abbas, that's who it was. The woman looked like Abbas. She was dressed in the simple earth-colored clothes of the Gariah people, though, not like a Karee woman.

"We're lost," Jabari said. "Have you by any chance seen . . ." he grasped for something, "a blacksmith around here?"

"A blacksmith." The woman didn't move, keeping her arms crossed. "You were looking for a blacksmith in the trash alley."

Ivy and Deto were giving Jabari looks.

"Oh," Jabari said. "Is that the trash alley? We're totally turned around," he said to Ivy and Deto. "Why did you think it was down there?" He held in a gasp as the sharp point of

Ivy's elbow jammed into his ribs. "Well, we'll just be on our way, then."

They scurried off and it wasn't until they had turned down a few streets that Jabari lost the feeling of the woman's eyes on his back. In his panic to get away, he almost didn't see what was around him, but eventually he noticed that they were in some kind of horrible slum. Filth coated the sidewalks, people lay on the side of the road, beggars reached out their hands to them.

They stopped for a moment.

"Where are we going?" Ivy asked.

"And who was the woman who looked like Abbas?" Deto whispered loudly.

"His sister," a voice said, and the three of them turned to find the woman standing beside them again, her arms still crossed.

"Argh!" Jabari exclaimed, jumping away from her.

"Are you done pretending to look for a blacksmith now? We've been expecting you. Come."

"Is this wise?" Deto whispered, as they followed the woman.

"She said she was Abbas's sister?"

"Anyone could say they were anyone's sister after someone else says they look like that person," Deto muttered.

"Now you're just saying words that make no sense," Ivy said. "Do you have a better idea? How about you, blacksmith?"

Jabari narrowed his eyes at her, but he didn't have a better idea, so they continued to follow the tall woman who was clearly a warrior, judging by her stance and bearing. After a few turns of her head, Jabari grew increasingly convinced that it was actually Abbas's sister. She looked enough like him to be his twin.

After a while, they stood before a small doorway with a symbol of an unfinished circle etched into it. The woman gave a complicated knock, and the door swung open. Gavi stood before them, surprise on his face, blond hair sticking up into ten different directions.

Emotion welled up in Jabari and he tackled his brother, gripping him in a hug that tumbled them into the doorway and had Gavi gasping and laughing. Ivy and Deto joined in the hug, and the warrior woman shoved them farther into the room, closing the door behind them.

Finally they released one another and Jabari dashed tears out of his eyes. His brother clasped his shoulder.

"You are in so much trouble," Jabari said in a cracking voice.

"Mmm, I thought you would say that," Gavi answered. "But why is your hair coated in cobwebs?" He pulled some out of Jabari's hair, wiping them off his hands.

"They came through the eastern tunnel," the tall woman said. She was now sitting at a table, eating sections of an orange. "I was watching that entrance."

It took a moment, but then Jabari understood that she had known who they were from the first. He felt embarrassed and aware that Ivy would probably call him "blacksmith" for a year. He looked around at the other people in the room. There was an old woman, a couple of Gariah men, a few children, some women who came back and forth from another room with food, and a man who wore a long, red robe.

"You," Jabari said, his mouth open. "You were with him.

At the fire. You are in my dreams. Who are you? What is this place?"

The man gazed back at Jabari. "You will learn all you wish about the Circle in time, son of Andar. But what about your future queen? Where is she? For our plan to work, she must be here."

Chapter 24

*A*fter the healing of the well and stream, Isika recovered slowly. Along with resting to get strong again, she was trying to learn to shield herself. Asafar spent hours teaching her. Olumi sat in on the lessons, listening in perfect stillness, his hair coiled around him on the ground. He and Asafar became good friends, and Isika loved the sight of them striding around the camp together, Asafar nearly twice the height of the short librarian, the librarian's long locks swinging in the dust. He sometimes carried them over his arm to keep them out of the sand, like he was a servant carrying a towel.

At times, waves of poison ache nearly overcame her, and she would stumble and fall while walking, losing all strength. For some time she thought it was exhaustion from such a big healing, but Asafar shook his head at her theory. He pulled her up after she had fallen on a walk with him and Olumi.

"No," he said. "You are recovered from the healing. This is poison from Aria's betrayal."

Isika stared at him. "But she hasn't betrayed us yet."

"Even walking in the direction of your father was a form of betrayal. It only gets stronger as she plans to become heir. She will get stronger as the time grows close, and you will grow weaker. Betrayal is truly the most evil sort of magic."

"The arrow," Isika said. "It's the arrow that is making her do this. You must come and heal her."

"No," Asafar said, taking a step back. His face was shocked. "I will never leave my people and put myself in danger by going to the Desert City. They are lost without me."

"But I healed you. They wouldn't even have you if I hadn't come!"

As soon as she spoke, Isika knew what she said was childish and not of the ways of Nenyi, but the serious, disappointed looks on Olumi and Asafar's faces made it even more clear.

"Dear Isika, you are upset," Olumi started, but Asafar held up a hand.

"Young one, there are no transactions or borrowing and lending between Nenyi's servants. But if you can bring Aria to me here, I promise I will try to heal her of the demon's arrow."

"Demon's arrow?"

"You didn't know? This arrow was crafted by a mud demon. It will suck life and strength out of Aria as well as deceiving her, telling her that she is better and more fulfilled. It is a most deceptive kind of poison."

Isika felt like her heart was being torn open. *Aria*.

"And you still won't come!"

Asafar sighed and began walking again, holding an arm out for Isika. Olumi hurried to catch up.

"If I left my people for every person who needed my healing, I couldn't be what Nenyi wants, young one. I know where the Shaper has placed me, and I live only to please her. I am sorry I cannot help you in this way, but bring the girl to me and I will do my utmost to heal her."

"How can I bring her to you if she is still poisoned by this arrow?"

"You must find that out for yourself. You are far more gifted than I am."

"Then why could I not pull the arrow out of her?"

"I suspect because it was put there by your own father. This makes both you and Aria weaker to its magic. It is a powerful betrayal, layer upon layer."

Isika looked at the sky. Dusk drew a curtain across the length of it. She saw the first stars appearing in the deep blue expanse.

"We leave tomorrow," she said. "We will collect Aria and bring her back to Asafar."

"And find something of the stolen ones, if you can, daughter," Asafar said.

Asafar, true to his word, did not come with them. But two other Karee warriors came, wearing dull Gariah clothes. And the cats came, of course, easily traveling alongside them and sleeping beside Isika whenever they stopped for rest. They moved quickly over the landscape, walking at night, stopping to raise shelter during the day. Traveling with the Karee made it easier. The king had given them tents as gifts, and the shade was welcome as trees were nonexistent. The silver of the cats' fur flowed like a river in the moonlight as they walked easily over the uneven ground.

As they drew out of the deep desert that the Karee inhabited, more buildings appeared, and they had to work harder to avoid them. One of the warriors approached Isika.

"We will attract attention with the cats following us," he said. "And as we come near the city, we need less attention."

Will you go? Isika asked Hera. *The man is saying that it is not safe for you to come with us.*

Do you want us to be less visible? Hera asked, blinking at her.

Isika stared at her. Hera sat at attention before her, gazing into Isika's eyes with her own silver ones. The other Palipa lolled at her feet. One cleaned his paws, another turned on his back, batting at the edge of a tent with one paw. The youngest, the female, cleaned her fur.

What do you mean? You can become invisible? Isika asked.

She sensed them laughing at her in their deep humming purrs.

Well, we don't disappear, if that's what you're thinking, like some common magician's trick. But we have ways of directing attention away from ourselves, of thinning our presence, so people don't notice us. Your friends the Keerza can do it too. And the Othra, but they rarely want to, because they like to be seen and admired. You also could learn it. You are the World Whisperer.

"What are they saying?" Ben demanded. "You have a very strange look on your face."

Olumi stroked at his beard after Isika relayed what the cat had told her.

"I suppose that makes sense. It is a little like what you have been practicing with hiding yourself from Aria."

"Except that I'm hiding what she senses of my presence, and they are hiding their presence from everybody."

"That would be an incredibly useful trick if you really could use it, Isika," Brigid said. "Teach me! I want to be invisible."

The tension broke as they all laughed, and the cats had their way, traveling even into the towns on the outskirts of the city with the others. As Isika watched, people's eyes clouded over briefly when they looked past the huge cats who padded along city streets, careful not to touch anyone.

One night when they were traveling in near darkness, the moon only a sliver in the sky, the Keerza turned up out of nowhere. Isika felt a jolt of gladness in seeing her old friends, but the Karee warriors sighed and shook their heads.

"This is getting ridiculous," one of them said when he thought Isika wasn't listening. Ben met Isika's eyes and grinned.

Are you sure this is the mission for you? Isika asked the Keerza. *I know about your ability to be unseen, but we are going into a city, and you are so wild, made for wide spaces.*

We come to help, said the head Keerza, and Isika couldn't turn him away. Later that night, Keethior came back from wherever he had been, and behind him, Isika heard hoofbeats.

Friend? Friend? she heard, and gasped. Ben turned to ask what she was hearing, but then he smiled as he recognized the music, and Wind and Night, their horses, galloped up to them. For a while, there was a mess of talking and laughing and exclaiming over how far they had come and how secretive Keethior was to summon them without saying anything.

"But Keethior, why?" Isika asked, leaning her head on her horse's side.

"Isika," he said, cocking his head to look at her out of one bright eye. "You don't know what you are walking into. This is not Batta, this is not a fire in your own city. You are walking into Mugunta's heart, and you need every strong friend, every bit of ancient magic you can get. You will need everything you have to get through this city and not succumb to its malice toward you."

"It's time to actually do it," Abbas said. "Maybe we should discuss how we will get into the city."

Isika, is there a stable where we can wait for you? We will be able to feel if you are in trouble.

"The Keerza are wondering if they can come inside, too," Isika said. "They want to know if there is a stable."

Olumi frowned. "How can we hide twenty gazelles in a city with walls?" he asked.

Abbas shook his head. "It's not possible, Isika. They take up space, even if they can be unseen. The cats can come, but the Keerza . . . I can't see how it will work!"

Isika looked at the head Keerza. *He says it won't work. Can you stay outside the walls?*

We must send one or two with you, he told her. *The others will wait outside the bounds of the city, but they will be ready to enter if they must.*

And where will you stay?

We are nearly as good at hiding as the cats, the ancient animal replied. *Don't worry about us.*

Isika filled the others in on what the Keerza had said, and though Abbas sighed again and shook his head, he shrugged and got the warrior to permit two of the Keerza to come, and the two horses, and all four of the cats. And the Othra.

"Have you ever tried to do anything secretly before?" Abbas asked Isika. "You're not so great at it."

"It's not my fault," she said, laughing.

"How do we get in?" Brigid asked.

"You forget that the Karee have been here for a very long time," Abbas said. "We have ways."

THE WAY TURNED out to be an underground road, a tunnel that was wide enough for the two horses to walk shoulder to shoulder. Isika was focused on calming their spirits as they went, because the presence of so much poison had them skittish and dancing from side to side.

Abbas glanced at her as she walked. He held a lantern in one hand and seemed at ease, though there was so much earth that could potentially fall on them and they were walking straight toward his people's most dreaded enemy, the one who had imprisoned him as a slave.

"This is why we don't have horses in the city or in our camps," he said. "Mules and camels are less vulnerable to magic. The magicians of the city lay some kind of spell on their horses, but it makes them sluggish. Horses would be useful to us, but they are sensitive."

"Yes, I can see that," Isika said, bringing Wind back down to all four feet and laying her face against his cheek. He settled with a shaky sigh. She glanced at Olumi.

"Do you know of anything I can do to help them?" she asked.

He shook his head. Unlike Abbas, he seemed quite nervous to be in the tunnel, jumping at sounds and cringing away from the ceiling, which was a long way above his head.

"I think you should ask your cat friends," he said. "They must have secrets and tricks."

Ask us what? The Palipa were different from the Keerza or the horses. They seemed to be able to understand everything Isika and the others said, even when Isika wasn't using animal speech. But they tuned out for long sections of time, catching bits and then demanding to know what everyone was talking about.

Do you have any advice for the horses? Ways that they can feel more calm?

They don't like us.

Well, you are predators and they are prey. But they can control their dislike if you can help them.

We would have to lay our magic on them. Are they willing?

Isika asked the horses, who shuddered and snorted and finally said yes. So the cats laid protective magic on them, and though the smell of it bothered the horses, Isika could feel the moment when they settled, when their muscles weren't hard as iron and their minds quieted.

"Wow," Ben said. "That worked."

Isika looked back at him.

"Their songs are more like their pasture songs now, and not their imminent danger songs," he told her. She smiled.

It was a lot easier to walk along the underground road with calm horses, and Isika let herself relax. She thought of

Aria being installed as heir and shuddered. She felt a spike of resolve in her heart. She would simply not allow the king to lay more of his magic on her sister. She wouldn't allow it. They would stop this, she and Abbas and Jabari, the cats and Olumi, the Keerza and Brigid and Ben and Keethior. Surely there were enough of them. And Nenyi would help them, as she always did. She walked faster.

"Let's not be in the tunnel any longer than we have to be," she said. "We have to get to Aria."

Chapter 25

The holes in Aria's memory seemed to be getting larger.

There were whole days when she would arrive back at her rooms and it was time for sleep, but she had no memory of the day that had passed.

Or sometimes on the small throne that her father had had set up next to his, she would blink and realize she didn't know how she had come to be there.

One thing was certain, though. She loved her father. She loved everything about him, and she couldn't wait to be named heir. He had told her of the festivities that would happen, starting with a procession early in the morning before they did the actual ceremony. They would travel through the whole city. And then would come the ceremony that would tie her to the throne and her ultimate destiny to be the queen of Gariah, and maybe, her father said, the whole world. She blinked. That was odd. Why the whole world? She must have heard him wrong.

"Why not do the ceremony first?" she heard herself asking one day, and even as she asked, she wondered why she was asking. Her father knew what was best, why would she question him?

She thought she saw his eyes tighten at the edges before he laughed.

"It will be so much better if they know you before the ceremony, Aria. The power of the ceremony will be stronger, bigger, grander, and they will love you more fully."

Well, that sounded good. So she avoided Herrith's eyes and the uncomfortable feeling in her stomach at the sound of her father's laugh.

There were so many things that her father taught her. She had been deceived for so long by people she had considered friends and family members. For instance, Nenyi was part of Mugunta, imagine that! The two were intertwined and could not be separated. And Isika was weak, because she had only chosen one half of the whole.

This and many things she learned from her father while they sat in their chairs, eating giant plates of food—Aria nibbled at hers—and being waited on by the slaves. Sometimes Aria got a funny feeling in her stomach when her father hit a slave, but he never hit Aria. Only once, when she was walking back to her room, her cheek throbbed with pain, and Herrith seemed very angry. When Lena saw her, she burst into tears.

She also spent a lot of time with Herrith. It was different from being with her father, mostly because her stomach hurt more when she was with Herrith, and she didn't have those gaps in time. She could see more clearly, but sometimes she didn't want to see more clearly. Lena had this effect on her too, so that she was mostly awake when she was in her own rooms, but often sleepy in the king's chambers.

She mentioned this to Herrith one day as they were walking in the gardens. He looked down at her with what she had begun to think of as his soft face.

"Why do you think that is?" he asked.

She thought about it. She loved her father so desperately. She loved his face and his strength, his way of being commanding and the way he made her feel like she would be the most powerful queen he had ever seen. She loved how he was strong with the slaves, hitting them when they were disobedient. No—wait. She looked up at Herrith. She didn't like it when her father hit the slaves. She and Herrith had talked about that before. What had Herrith asked? She couldn't remember. She asked him, and he sighed and shook his head gently.

"It's okay Aria. Let's talk about Nenyi."

"Nenyi is the same as Mugunta."

"No. Remember? We're talking about how maybe that's not true. But that you shouldn't tell your father that. Because he gets mad and he might hit you, right?"

It came back then, and with it, her stomachache, which she thought had more to do with understanding what was really going on than an actual problem with her stomach. She had told her father the things she and Herrith had been speaking about, that Nenyi was actually quite different from Mugunta, and her father had whipped his hand back and slapped her. She had fallen off her stool and laid on the floor crying while her father strode around the room shouting, the wild colors in the floor going mad. He had left the room, still shouting, and after a moment, one of the slaves had run over to Aria and picked her up, murmuring to her and stroking her hair. After a while, Herrith came, his face like a storm, and when she was ready, they walked back to her rooms, where she curled on the couch while Lena and Herrith had one of their angry whispered conversations. Lena had made her hot tea and given her a soothing balm for her face, and Herrith paced, then abruptly left.

She looked at him, her eyes wide.

"You remember?" he asked.

She nodded, her eyes very wide.

They sat in a corner of the garden, under the shade of a large palm.

"Aria," Herrith said. "Do you feel more clear right now?"

She nodded again. Her stomach hurt so bad it was moving into her chest, so her heart hurt as well, feeling as though it was going to come out of her. She stared at him, the white in his beard and at his temples.

"Are you very old?" she asked him.

"Quite old," he said, "But maybe not as old as you think."

"Do you remember my mother?"

"She was my dearest friend," he said. "But Aria, even when you are with the king, when your mind feels less clear and you are forgetting things, you can never ever tell him about my friendship with your mother. You can't tell him what we talk about here in the garden. You can't tell him I told you these things. You can't. You have to ask Nenyi to help you be quiet, and not tell about what we say here."

"Because the king will grow angry and hit me?"

"Worse," Herrith said, his eyes very, very serious. "He assumed what you said today was only what you had learned in Maween. But if he knows it is coming from me, he will take me from you. And then you won't have anyone to help you clear your mind."

Aria considered that. In a way, it would be easier if she never cleared her mind. It was such a painful thing to do. When she was foggy, things seemed nice, her stomach and heart didn't hurt, and she didn't have to think about all the things that hurt her. In a way, it seemed like the healing she had been seeking for so, so long.

"What will happen to you?" she asked. "Where will he take you?"

"He will kill me," Herrith told her.

And that was different. Because even if it hurt when her mind was clear, she didn't want Herrith to die. Herrith and Lena had been very kind to her, kinder than anyone else in the palace. She wouldn't tell her father anything. She would keep the secret.

"How can I remember?" she asked.

"I think you need to remind yourself over and over again. Tell yourself not to talk about what we have learned here."

She looked back at him.

"Why would you risk telling me?" she asked. "If you know my mind is cloudy and I will tell him if I forget? And then you might . . . you know?"

"Ah," he said. He looked off into the distance. When he looked at her again, he blinked as though he was surprised to see her there.

"Because of your mother. And because I have stayed here all this time, within reach of the king, because of you. Waiting for you."

"Not for Isika?" she asked him.

"For both of you."

She frowned, but then there was a rustling of leaves and one of the palace guards stood before them.

"Robed one," he said.

"Yes?"

The man started to say something, then stopped himself, looking at Aria. He paced back and forth quickly.

"Things are happening," he said finally. "There are new guests in the south wing."

Oh, Aria thought. That was all. Then why did Herrith turn pale and press a hand to his heart? She turned to him, seeing a significant look pass between him and the guard.

"What is it, Uncle?" she asked.

"I haven't prepared enough sheets for the new guests," he murmured. "Come child, let us go back to Lena. We'll find her and ask for your cooking lesson."

As they walked back into the palace, Aria forgot all about the palace guard. She smiled at Lena vaguely, excited because they were going to learn about making the sweet pastries that Aria loved most for breakfast.

Later, in the throne room, she blinked at her father as he praised her for something good she had done.

"Did you do anything interesting today?" he asked. "Learn anything?"

Aria thought about her mother and Herrith, and she leaned forward to tell her father that Herrith and her mother had been dearest of friends, but then Herrith moved and she saw his face under his hood, and a picture of Herrith dead on the floor suddenly presented itself to her. She sat back.

"I made pastries with Lena," she said.

Out of the corner of her eye, she saw Herrith settle back on his heels.

Chapter 26

*J*abari watched Gavi across the low table as his brother addressed the room. Gavi had come to give the resistance members of the Circle an update on the palace. Days had gone by since they had arrived, days filled with ideas and plans for how to extricate Aria. Nothing had come up that made any sense, and Jabari grew frustrated. He had tried to talk to Isika in his mind, but she wasn't within his reach somehow, and he didn't know where she was anymore. He tapped his fingers on the table until a look from Ivy made him stop.

Nearly everyone was there—Enfa the Karee warrior, Mara, the handful of laborers who were part of the resistance in some way Jabari didn't understand, Jabari, Ivy, and Deto, of course. Herrith was late, so Gavi had started without him. Herrith was having more trouble getting around undetected, Gavi told them, and at a time when it was most important that he not be discovered. Children whispered and tumbled on cushions in the corner, their little legs flashing out of their tunics as they turned somersaults. Once in a while, one of the adults would turn and shush them, and they grew more quiet, only to increase volume gradually until they were shushed again.

Jabari could tell that his brother wasn't sleeping well. Gavi kept running his hands through his hair, which stood straight up from his head in blond stalks. His face was weary. He kept glancing at the door, as though he couldn't bear to be away from the palace.

"Aria comes back to herself sometimes, when she is with Herrith," Gavi told them. "But the demon poison runs through her, gripping her, especially when she is with the king. She barely knows where she is, half the time. And he hit her, when she accidentally told him something that Herrith had told her." Gavi clenched his fists.

Jabari frowned, staring at his hands. How could they help her if she was under the king's sway? He ran through ideas in his mind, but none were any good.

"The most important thing is that we don't get Herrith killed," Gavi said. "He's the only hope for Aria right now. She's only clear-headed when she's with him, and he's the only protection she has in that court."

"And he is precious to us," the old woman, Mara, added gently. Gavi flushed and nodded, his eyes darting to Jabari's and then away.

They continued to discuss ideas and Mara brought out some flatbread and spicy peas. Jabari had his mouth full when the rush of well-being swept over all of them and everyone relaxed visibly. Jabari swallowed his food and grinned. It was a sense of well being that he knew well. An

Othra was somewhere nearby. Eemia must be back with news.

But then there was a knock at the door.

The old woman got up slowly just as Jabari heard a grumpy Othra voice in his head.

Get up, lazy! She's here!

He leapt to his feet and past Mara, lunging for the door. Vaguely he heard the old woman cautioning him not to open the door until he knew who it was, but he ignored her and threw it open.

Isika stood in the doorway. There was silence in the room. Jabari stared at her, holding his breath, unable to speak. She looked different, taller somehow, and she was flanked by two giant silver cats. Her eyes widened at the sight of him, and a brilliant smile split her face. He could feel by the ache in his cheeks that he was smiling too, though he could barely tell if his head was still attached to his body. Behind him was a flurry of words and bodies he barely heard or felt.

"Let them in, Jabari!" Ivy said. "They're going to attract attention, standing there at the doorway with those creatures."

He stood back to let them in. He reached out to touch Isika briefly on the arm as she passed by, and she smiled at him with her eyes as the familiar magical sparks leapt between them. As she went into the room, two more cats walked in behind her, making four. And there was Ben and Brigid, Olumi and Abbas.

There were introductions all around. In the corner Abbas and Enfa embraced and she was wiping tears out of her eyes. Gavi, Ben, and Isika hugged and laughed.

Jabari went to them and hugged Ben, bowed to Olumi,

clapped Abbas on the back, and then turned to see Isika looking at him.

"I wouldn't have thought it possible," she said, a glint in her eye. "But I actually missed you, Yab."

He grinned at her and gave her a hug, reluctantly letting her go.

Mara fussed around them, urging everyone to sit. They all found stools, cushions, or places on the floor, and sat looking foolishly at one another, smiling and wiping away tears.

"I thought you were dead," Enfa told Abbas in a low voice.

"You didn't get my messages?" he asked.

"I didn't believe them. I couldn't until I saw you."

Quiet descended in the little room, very full now. Jabari wondered where to start. There were those cats, but it seemed rude to start with them.

"So . . . Isika, I take it you learned to hide yourself from your sister," he said.

Isika nodded. "Yes. The Karee healer taught me well." She pointed her chin at the cats. "And they also could teach us things about how to hide ourselves. They can go unseen among people. Imagine how helpful that would be."

The silence was heavy with questions.

"Would you . . . introduce us?" Ivy asked.

"Oh, yes. I'm sorry. I'm used to them now. These are the Palipa. They are, um, well, quite attached to me."

"Of course they are," Jabari said, breaking the tension, and everyone smiled. It wasn't the first time that creatures had come out of nowhere to profess allegiance to Isika.

"Yes, but they don't listen to me," Isika said, shooting a

look at one of the cats, who turned her huge head and began licking one of her paws. "For example, I asked them not to come inside with me, since they can be . . . intimidating, but they wouldn't listen. I tried to explain that they needed to request permission of the house owner, but they don't understand ownership."

Isika looked at Jabari with a question in her eyes, and he nodded at Mara. Isika bowed her head in apology to the old woman, and Mara smiled gently, shaking her head and waving the apology away. Her eyes sparkled with tears.

Then Herrith's knock sounded at the door and he burst in as soon as one of the laborers opened it for him, heading straight for Isika and Ben. He knelt down before them, surprising everyone.

"I have known you since you were born," he said. "And long have I waited for this day."

Everyone was too keyed up to make more plans, so Gavi went back to the palace, and Ivy, Deto, Olumi, and Abbas went off to the home of one of the families to spend the night.

Jabari, Isika, and Ben stayed with Mara and prepared to sleep. The cats finally stretched out along the wall when Isika told them to get out of the way. She had to tell them three times.

"You have an interesting relationship," Jabari said under his breath, watching the heavy lidded stare the biggest cat gave her before rising slowly to move out of the way.

"You don't know the half of it," Isika muttered. Then she shook her head. "But they are valuable allies, and Olumi says I will need all I can get in this city."

This reminded Jabari that Isika was within reach of the Desert King, and he felt sick to his stomach. He had hoped so much to prevent this. Herrith lingered while Isika and Ben ate. Jabari noticed that neither Mara or Herrith could take their eyes off of Isika or Ben for very long.

Also, Ben kept looking up with a puzzled look on his face, but he never said anything, so Jabari finally asked him about it.

"Are you hearing something strange?"

Ben took his time answering.

"Yes, something like a mass of people, but I can't figure it out. Maybe it's just that I've never been in a city this size before."

As Herrith and Mara watched Isika and Ben, Jabari also stole glances at Isika. He had never seen anyone so beautiful in his life. The line of her neck. Her hands on the flatbread, scooping curry. She already looked like a queen, even sitting in this shack eating on the floor.

She looked up and he looked away quickly.

"You said you have known us since we were born?" Isika asked Herrith and Mara. "I'm sorry, but I don't remember you. Can you tell me how you knew us?"

The old woman smiled, then wiped at her eyes. "I was in the palace with Herrith's father when your grandmother was first captured. I remember your mother as a little girl, then I remember her growing up to be Amani, a strong woman who was wedded to the king's son against her will. When her husband became the king, she became more wary with you, trying to protect you, and she would often leave you with me when she went to visit the king. I took care of you often when you were a tiny thing."

Jabari would have given anything to wipe the sorrow away from Isika's face.

"But the king insisted on keeping Ben with the boy slaves. We still don't know why," Herrith said. "I tried to watch over Ben as Mara did over Isika, but I couldn't watch all the time."

Ben nodded, his eyes on his hands. It struck Jabari then, just how hard it must be for Ben to come back to this city. He carried the memories of being a slave boy here, of being hit and afraid and unloved in this place. Jabari knew from past conversations that Isika's memory of this city was very vague. Right now she was staring at Mara as though trying to remember her.

She shook her head, looking disappointed, but Ben nodded suddenly.

"Yes," he said. "I remember both of your songs. They are as familiar to me as Isika's, though it has been a long time since I heard them. Let your heart be comforted, Uncle. You did help me as a boy. I remember how soothing your song was, how I would try to sit as near to you as possible, especially in the king's chambers."

Herrith's face contorted, then he dashed tears away with the back of one hand.

"I loved your mother more than life," he said. "I'm sorry that I couldn't do more to help her."

Isika sat back, watching the two of them. "I'm so surprised to find a resistance here," she said. "I would never have expected it."

"That was the same way your grandmother felt when she came," the old woman said. "Herrith's father spent a long time trying to convince her of the resistance, of the people in this land who are loyal to Nenyi."

"I feel like everything is being turned upside down," Isika said.

"Yes, I do as well," Jabari said.

"You are very like your father in appearance," the old woman told Isika suddenly. "But even more like your grandmother."

Isika turned her head to smile at Jabari, and he remembered the portrait of the stolen queen that had revealed Isika's identity, back when none of them had known who she was. She did look very much like the queen.

"Aria is more like your mother," Herrith said. "And she is soft like Amani too, not as strong as you are."

"How is she?" Isika asked, leaning forward eagerly. "Do you see her every day?"

As Herrith began to tell them of Aria's condition, Jabari sat back against the wall and stared at the silver cats, sleeping now with light snores that drifted through the dark room.

Something was bothering him and he tried to identify it. The other four talked for a long time, exchanging memories of Amani, and Jabari slowly understood what it was. Isika was part of Gariah as well as Maween. How could it be that the future queen of the Maweel had a history and tie to their enemies? The Maweel had always stayed pure and dedicated to Nenyi by keeping themselves away from the goddess worshipers and living the life they knew Nenyi wanted them to live. How could it be that Isika was the long-awaited child of the resistance? How could she be this part of the plan that the Circle had been forming all these years? It didn't make sense. Jabari felt, as he often had since meeting Isika, that unwieldy assumptions were rearranging themselves in his head, and it was physically painful.

Ben lifted his head again, looking off into the distance, cocking his head to one side and closing his eyes. He shook his head and returned to the conversation, then after a few moments, he did it again.

"What is it, little brother?" Jabari asked him.

He looked at Jabari, his face puzzled. "This sound. It's unlike any other sound I have heard . . . a clamoring of music, different strands packed close together. I mean, this is a big city, bigger than Batta or Azariyah, but the songs are so strange, it might not only be the city."

"What do you think it is?" Isika asked. They were all paying close attention to Ben now.

He shook his head, looking distressed, then reached out to grab Isika's hand.

"I will try to find out," he told her. "Stay close to me. I will have to open up to the music and it might overwhelm me."

He closed his eyes and immediately gasped and shuddered. His eyes were closed, but emotions rippled over his face, and Jabari nearly reached out and shook him to make him come back as he saw extreme pain in Ben's tightly gripped hands and strained forehead. Isika put her hands on either side of his forehead and his face eased a bit. After a few moments, he opened his eyes. They looked haunted.

"It is not the city," he said. "It is the missing Karee people. And many others, I think, from other lands. They are imprisoned here in Dhahara. Afraid—in pain. And I think I know where they are."

Chapter 27

*J*sika wanted to go to the prisoners right away. Herrith thought they should wait.

"Benayeem knows where they are now," she told the older man, feeling panicked. "What if they are gone tomorrow? We can't wait."

"It's late, daughter, and the city isn't safe at night."

Hera sat up and switched her tail back and forth, just enough for the five of them to notice her. Then Keethior pulled his head out from under his wing and and opened and closed his wings. Neither one of the ancients said anything, but the message was clear. They were perfectly capable of protecting Isika.

Herrith sat wide-eyed for a few moments, then a smile spread across his elegant, wise face, transforming him. He shook his head.

"You are not what I expected, daughter. Yes, then, let us go carefully. Mara, will you come?"

"Of course I'm coming," said the old woman, bustling

around the room, extinguishing candles and gathering a wrap for herself. "After all these years, if you think I'm going to miss the first adventure with Amani's daughter, you are not the sharpest twig on the branch."

Next to Isika, Jabari laughed. She smiled at him. He grinned back at her, then turned to Ben.

"And you, little brother? Are you ready to lead us to these captives?"

Isika felt a twinge. She had been thinking of her own desire to find the captives, not about Ben's well-being. His face was weary with pain, but he nodded.

"Yes," he said. "It's better that we go now. I want to close the connection as soon as I can. They are too much for me."

They left the little house and silently crept into the night. Ben led the way, with Herrith beside him to make sure Ben's intuition didn't carry them down any lethal paths.

"Down here in the lowest tier killers come out at night," Herrith said. "They are desperate, addicted to the illegal juice of the night-blooming cactus, hungry, sometimes mad. Do you hear me, cats? Watch out for them."

Hera regarded Herrith through half-lidded eyes as though she didn't appreciate orders, but she walked so close to Isika that Isika felt like she might fall over.

I can't walk if you are leaning on me like that.

You heard the man. He is forceful and arrogant, but right.

Just a tiny bit of space. You're pushing me into the wall.

The cat relented and Isika could walk upright again.

Mara walked behind Ben and Herrith, which left Jabari and Isika to walk together. The other three cats walked behind them. Keethior flew overhead. And Isika could hear her horses and the Keerza in a far-off barn.

As if he read her thoughts, Jabari said, "Is that Keerza that I hear? And your horses?"

Isika nodded. "They joined us yesterday. There are many more Keerza waiting outside the walls of the city."

"How are the horses able to stand the poison around us? Even I have a difficult time with it. I feel as though I haven't breathed properly in weeks."

Now that Isika thought about it, she felt it also. The air was hazy with poison. She felt a sharp longing for Maween and the clear air. For the market tree and the waterfall where she met with Nenyi.

"The cats gave them some protection," she said. "So the poison doesn't reach them."

Jabari looked impressed. "Those are some helpful friends," he said.

"Yes," Isika said. It all felt a bit dreamlike. The cats, the horses who wouldn't leave her, and this place. She was in the last place she had ever expected to be, especially after the events of last year—the fire and her father's words to her.

You are warrior and whisperer, you are the perfect instrument of Mugunta, formed to wield a great blow.

Ben stopped and they halted and waited for him. Herrith stood beside him, looking down at Isika's brother, worry clear in his eyes and his rigid shoulders. It was also strange to find people who knew her, people she didn't remember, who had dreamed of her all these years. If she had known these people were here when she was back in the Worker village, toiling away . . . well, she couldn't have known it. But what did they want from her and could she give it to them? For a moment her throat tightened and she gasped for air, but Hera bumped her leg with her head and Isika's breathing eased.

Thank you, she told the cat.

You think too much, Hera said.

Some of the alleys were very narrow, and Isika and Jabari had to squeeze into single file, he in front, she following. A few times they had to climb a set of slippery steps or through a hole in the wall and Jabari turned to offer Isika a hand. There were no sparks when she grasped it.

You're getting good at that, she told him in her mind.

I've been practicing masking my own magic a bit.

Without the sparks, Isika could concentrate on the feeling of Jabari's hand gripping her own carefully. Her face felt hot. She let go quickly, though part of her wanted to hold on. *It's comforting in a strange place, that's all,* she told herself. *Calm down.*

There were lights in the houses around them. Isika saw faces peering out a few times, but no one stopped them. Ben halted and listened hard.

"I can't tell anymore," he said, panting. "They are somewhere near here, but it's overwhelming and it feels like a storm coming. Like the pressure of air and water in a huge cloud."

From the sky above, Keethior let out a long, haunting cry. Isika looked up.

I see a large space, he told her. *Something that looks like an old stadium. Come with me.*

Instantly, she was seeing through his eyes. She saw herself and the others beneath the bird, small bits of color in the dark. Then they flew low and she saw a large, ancient structure, a stadium out of old stories, where games or races would be held, a big oval with a covered area and a large open space in the middle. It looked abandoned. They flew lower, under the covered roof, and Isika saw a set of stairs that led underground. From there she could hear noises, crying children and moans. Keethior landed on the stairs.

Go farther? he asked.

She didn't want to. She wanted to fly far away, back to Maween, back to Auntie and spiced tea in the mornings. But she couldn't leave.

Yes, she told the Othra.

They flew down the stairwell, and at the bottom, through his eyes she saw long narrow corridors lit by a few magical red lamps, with bars on either side. Through the bars were . . . but no, she couldn't believe it, and guards ran toward them now, and she gasped and found herself thrown out of Keethior's head.

She opened her eyes to find herself lying on the ground with her head on Jabari's knee. He was stroking her hair and looking down at her with an extremely worried face. When she tried to sit up, she found she couldn't, so she stayed where she was and closed her eyes. Jabari's hands on her hair felt nice.

"Can you warn us when you're going to do that?" Jabari asked. His voice was light but Isika could tell he was worried. "You fall hard when you go off with Keethior. This time, thankfully, I caught you, but what if I had been walking up ahead, too far to catch you? And you go into some kind of trance, and it's a little alarming."

"Sorry," she murmured. She lay there breathing through the disgust and fear in her heart. When she felt ready, she sat up slowly.

"What was it?" Jabari asked, his voice soft. Ben was there

too, and Herrith and Mara, but Isika couldn't focus on their faces. Her bird senses were pinging.

Are you out? She asked Keethior.

Nearly, he answered, out of breath. *I'm just trying to see how far this thing goes.*

She faced her friends.

"It's under the stadium," she told Herrith, and he gave a start and then nodded. "There are rooms, so many I couldn't see them all. Room after room, closed in with bars, and when I looked in, I saw more people than I could count huddled on the ground, sleeping so close to one another that they could barely move. There were guards, and they chased us . . ." She swallowed. "Some of the people looked like they had been hurt, and some of them were crying."

Keethior came then and flew to Isika, opening his wings to send comforting air over her. Tears began to roll down her cheeks.

"There were corridors like the one we saw in every part of the stadium," he said. "There are thousands of people."

They looked at each other, stunned. Isika became suddenly aware that they were in a dark alley, sitting on the ground, windows cracked around them and listening ears, and also that she was still leaning on Jabari.

Herrith stood. "We can do no more tonight," he said. "Tomorrow morning we will find a way to speak with the prisoners. Perhaps Isika, through the eyes of the bird. But you two need rest before you collapse."

He nodded at Isika and Ben, and Isika wanted to protest but she found that she had no words and what was more, tears still streamed down her cheeks. Jabari handed her his ser, and she used it to wipe her face. It smelled like him, and that made her cry harder.

She hardly remembered getting back to Mara's house. She dreamed of the circle on the door, and the captives, and in her dream she wept. When she woke up, her face was wet. At breakfast they talked about what to do.

"It's Keethior," Jabari said. "It has to be. We can't get in, not with so many guards, and you can follow Keethior from here, right Isika? So we don't have to be out in the open, making people curious."

"I don't know," Isika said. In the daytime, the old woman's house was gentle and full of light. Isika took a sip of her coffee. Mara had given it to her in a thick clay mug that made Isika long for the pottery workshop. She cupped the mug in her hands and held her face over the steam. The coffee was hot and strong, and light from the house's window streamed across the clean earthen floor. Daylight made Isika feel better.

"I've never tried. But let's see. Keethior, do you think you can find someone who looks like they know what they are talking about and ask them questions?"

Keethior ruffled his feathers, making himself twice as fat as he normally was, displeased.

Friend, I don't know how to ask these questions. Isika told him. *Don't be offended by my puny human mind.*

He laid his feathers down and told them he would try. "I noticed that the guards walk in circles," he said. "If they do the same today, I can wait for one of them to pass before asking questions. I will find the right person before I bring you in, Isika, so that you don't have to fly with me very long. I know you humans are too weak for much of this."

Isika exchanged a glance with Ben, trying to hide a smile. Jabari opened the door and Keethior flew out, giving a low cry as he went.

"You had better get comfortable," Mara said to Isika. "Yesterday you fell like a tree, and it was just a good thing that this boy was there to catch you."

Isika smiled up at "this boy," who towered over the diminutive old woman. Mara bustled around, arranging pillows, and Isika obligingly went to lie on them. Two of the cats came and stretched out on either side of her while she waited.

We will help, the mother cat said. *We will lend you power so you can see from afar. I believe this is out of your range.*

Isika didn't have time to ask how they knew before she was pulled away from herself and into Keethior's eyes. He had found someone quickly. It took her a moment to understand what she was seeing.

A woman crouched by the bars, looking eagerly into Keethior's face. With a shock, Isika realized the woman knew what Keethior was, because she was Maweel! She had large eyes and her beautiful dark face was too thin. She held a sleeping baby. Had people from Maween disappeared and Isika didn't even know it?

"What are they planning to do with you?" Keethior was asking.

"We only hear whispers," the woman said quietly. Behind her, several people were watching the exchange with wide eyes, but they were silent. Isika recognized the Karee, as well as people with the faces and long hair of Deto. She saw a few Workers, their faces pale in the gloom. The woman went on. "But we hear that we are waiting for ships, and that we will be sent across the sea to be the emperor's slaves."

Isika felt the shock of the woman's words as though they were echoing through her entire body.

She had no idea that this was so big, that the Desert King was involved in such horrible evil from the Great Waste. All these people, slaves? Sent across the sea to the shadowy fear of the emperor? She couldn't bear it. Keethior thanked the woman and assured her that there were people who would try to help. A small flame of hope shone in her eyes, and Isika felt sick. How could they do anything against poison as deep as this? This evil was too big.

Keethior flew through the corridors so that Isika could see the thousands of people pressed into the stone rooms, damp and sick-smelling. It was too much, and she threw herself away from it, landing back in her own body in Mara's house. There were tears on her cheeks. The others watched her with concern. Jabari and Ben came to sit near her, and as she sat up, Mara handed her a cup of spice tea. She held her face over the steam and cried.

This was so much bigger than she had ever known. All she wanted was to get her sister and go, but she couldn't. She couldn't leave those people as they were.

She told them all she had seen and what the woman had told her.

Jabari looked thoughtful rather than overwhelmed.

"There has to be a way to do both at once," he said. "How can we get Aria out of here and help the captives get out of the stadium?"

In the sweet-smelling room they began to make plans. There was love and beauty in the little room. The rightness of what they were doing poured strength back into Isika, and the sad hopelessness left her bones. She remembered the strength and hope in the Maweel woman, and she set her mind to this plan, determined to help every one of the prisoners reach freedom.

Chapter 28

a plan was forming. Ben sat in the meetings with the others but he was barely there. It was hard to focus in this city full of sad and terrifying music. More and more he felt that he was in a different world than his friends and companions. While they could laugh and joke, get some respite after a difficult day, he always lived in the sorrow, bombarded by the emotions of people he passed on the street. An old man with a lonely song. A woman full of fear. He shrunk from it but could not stop listening.

When he could get away from the little house, he walked to the stadium where the prisoners were and slowly circled it, listening to the haunting music of the people inside. Sometimes he heard a strain of music that was full of despair, and he asked Keethior to fly in and soothe that person, to help their distress. Surprisingly, Keethior listened to him. It was a rare good thing to hear the change the Othra brought to people.

Isika told him she was worried about him.

"Why don't you block it out?"

"I don't want to," he said.

"Why under Nenyi's skies not?"

"Because it keeps me here."

Isika couldn't understand, because she had no memories of Dhahara. Ben was two steps from bolting with every heartbeat that passed. He heard his father's music in everything, insidious and terrible. To make himself stay, he needed to remind himself of Aria, and he needed to remind himself of these captives and the plan to set them free. Nothing else was enough to counteract the terror. So he didn't block out the music. But it meant he lived in the world of others, and at times he wondered if there was anything to him at all, or if he was only made of the shapes of other people. They lived in him with their fears and pain, and true, the little bits of joy.

One day, after a night of little sleep, he went out to listen for the captives. He walked around the stadium slowly, listening. Keethior flew alongside him.

"There," he told Keethior, "just beyond this wall, is a young mother with her small child. Please help them."

Keethior made a soft clicking noise and flew off. Ben was still surprised that Keethior helped with this. It occurred to him that Isika might have given Keethior instructions. He nodded. That made sense, in her worry. Ben didn't care. He only wanted to help.

He kept walking, listening hard for the music of the young mother and her terrified child. He smiled as he heard it soften and grow calm from the soothing effect of the Othra and the hopeful things he was telling the woman. He wandered, without thinking, down an alleyway. He was listening so hard that he didn't see them. He first knew they were there by the heavy hand on his shoulder.

"Got you, boy," the guard said, and Ben's heart plummeted into his stomach.

He struggled, but there were three of them and he had no chance. They led him up through winding streets and Benayeem's heart beat with terror as they approached the place of his nightmares. The palace.

HE WAS GOING to face his father. His wrists were bound behind him. He stood and watched the empty throne of the king's chambers. Vaguely, he saw that there were two thrones instead of one. His heart was pounding so hard he could feel it in his feet. The room spun and he took a deep breath, looking around.

The familiar sight of the shiny black floor, the dozens of slaves. He was back in his nightmare and he heard everything. The drum beats of doom and the discordant screeching of strings. He thought he would pass out as the music came flooding into him. He stood unseeing until he heard the soft murmur of his name, and then he looked up.

The Desert King had entered. He sat now in the throne, staring down at Ben. But the sound had not come from him. His younger sister sat in the chair beside the king, gazing at him with worry in her eyes. One of Ben's eyes was swollen shut from a blow from the guards, so he had to tilt his head to look at her properly. She was gaunt and dazed. Aria. Sister. He shook his head.

"Aria," he said, but the guard beside him raised a fist in a threat. He stopped talking.

"Father, why is Ben here? Why is he chained and hurt?" Aria asked slowly, as though through a great fog.

"Oh, dearest," the Desert King said, and Ben cringed and reached up to cover his ears at the horrible sound of his father's voice. "This one has ever been a disappointment. He has tricked and hurt us. Even now he wants to betray us."

Aria stared at Ben, her mouth open, her eyes confused. She started to say something again, but the king gestured for her to sit back. Ben could see his father's anger rippling in the lights of the floor beneath his feet. He could feel and hear the horrible, screeching music coming from his father. He didn't want to set the king off. He didn't want his terrible anger to turn toward Aria, so he stayed silent. But he tried to tell her with his eyes that he loved her. She stared back at him, distressed, lovely, waif-like.

"Disgusting Maweel brat," the king said, and Ben jolted with the ugly sounds behind the words, "you need to tell us where everyone else . . . is."

He stood up and walked down to Ben's level. Ben shook. He tried to breathe. His vision darkened and he saw flecks of color in the corners of his eyes. What had Asafar taught them? *Make a room.* Be in the room with only his own music. But it was hard to focus. When the king stepped, rays of light shot from his feet. His angry music shrieked. The anger hurt Ben's stomach and made it hard for him to breathe.

"I imagine you will resist. But you will talk. You will regret your disobedience. You always were a disobedient brat." He paced, then came very close to Ben and looked into his face. Ben's eyes darted everywhere, terrified of seeing Mugunta deep in his own father's eyes. His eyes lit on Herrith, standing against the wall. Ben gasped, thinking the resistance leader might help him, but Herrith gave a quick shake of the head and Ben realized he couldn't. He looked back into his father's face and met his eyes.

Music like nothing he had ever heard rolled over him. He fell to his knees and his father yanked him back up. Where the king's hands touched Ben, they burned him. He had no bones, he was straw, he would burn away. His father lifted a hand to strike him. Ben prepared for the blow, but then he heard a voice.

"Father." At the sound of Aria's voice, strength returned to Ben's limbs, and he stood on his own power, his father's hands still burning him. He looked toward the dais and saw that she had stood and walked to the edge. He shuddered to see how thin she was, how sickly. "Why are you hurting my brother?"

At the words, "my brother," Ben felt even more strength returning to him. He realized that though Aria had come to the Desert City, she had not quite betrayed them. There were strands of love-soaked music woven into the mat of demon's evil the Desert King had laid over her.

The king pulled his hand back. He stood motionless. Ben dared a glance at his face. It was a mask, but behind it, Ben could hear a tumult of conflicting music, and it confused him. He couldn't figure it out. He was sure the king felt no love for Aria. What was his game?

Whatever it was, it won out, and the king barked an order while he strode back to the dais.

"Herrith, take the boy to his quarters. Boy, I will give you time to consider. At the end of one day, we will bring the persuader."

Herrith came to Ben and roughly turned him toward the door.

"You heard the king," he said. "Walk. I'm not sure you're going to like these quarters. They're not quite as fancy as your . . . hovels in Maween."

Ben walked, listening hard to the contradictory music in Herrith. Herrith was trying to help him, despite the harsh tone of his words.

Once they were in the corridor, and gaining distance from the king's chambers, Herrith spoke in a barely audible voice.

"Your sister spoke of learning to hide her presence from Aria. Do you have the same skill?"

"I was there when she was taught. It is somewhat similar to what I do to hide myself from noises. Or I'm trying to learn it, anyway."

Herrith looked around and made sure no one was there, then pulled Ben into an alcove.

"He can see, though not far. He can see within the palace, so if you escape and hide here, and he cannot see you, he will assume that you are out of the palace. You can hide for a few days, until it is safe to leave."

"Now?"

"No, you need to practice this skill, and it needs to happen at another time, when I am not guarding you. It is more important than ever that he does not suspect me. Wait for the sign."

Herrith took him to a prison cell. Ben felt fierce longing for Auntie's house and the calm sweet music that filled it. He practiced using the room many times that night. Going in. Shutting the door. Cleaning and making the space bright. In the night, he dreamed. He dreamed he was in the room and Nenyi came to him there, as an old man. He looked a little like Ivram, but with more kindness, more wisdom.

You are not a disappointment, he said, and Ben felt a great weight lift, as though he had been under heavy blankets and something had suddenly pulled them off.

It happened the next day. A guard came in and shoved a bowl of some kind of disgusting mush at Ben, then left. When he left, he didn't quite fasten the door, and when Ben looked, he saw that no one guarded the corridor. He didn't hesitate, leaving as quickly as possible. He ran soundlessly down the corridor in his soft leather boots.

He climbed out of the prison cellar and ran in the opposite direction of the king's chambers. Using his memory of the palace, he found the secret ways through the inner walls, making sure as he went that he was inside the room, with the door closed, the curtains drawn. It also had the effect of dampening the evil music he heard, so that he felt better. He knew where to go. Near the women's chambers, where his mother had lived, there was a series of linen closets. In the very back, a small room held clothing only used for fancy banquets. The closet was generally ignored unless there was a high function. The king's wives wore fancy clothing every day, but this closet contained robes sewn over with gold pieces and jewels, things that were rarely used. He had spent time hiding here as a small boy.

He found the rooms without too much difficulty and squeezed himself inside the closet, pulling a mattress from another closet to the very back. As he curled up on the mattress, he spotted a dress wrapped in thin paper. The paper had torn, and he recognized the color and jewels of the dress underneath. His mother's banquet dress. He had seen her in it many times, attending banquets as a slave boy. He remembered his mother in the dress, greeting him and warning him with only her eyes, putting a soft hand on his head as he served her food, hugging him to her if the king's attention was directed elsewhere.

He pulled the dress close. It still smelled of her rose perfume. For a moment he thought that the smell would make him cry, but instead he found himself remembering his mother's fierce bravery. When Benayeem was in danger from the king, she had run from the palace, taking him and the girls across the desert to the Worker village. Which eventually had led him to Maween. Which had formed him into the young man he was today. Not the cowering child whose only iden-tity was disappointment, deserving of hatred. His mother had loved him. She left for his sake. He slept and dreamed of her. *You are not a disappointment,* she told him. He held her hands and kissed them.

At night he left the closet to look for food, no longer able to ignore the pain in his stomach. Distressed music flowed from the guards. The king knew he was gone, then. He hid behind statues and under stairwells, taking care to stick to the shadows in the dimly lit corridors. At one point he heard Herrith striding along, barking at the guards who scurried along behind him.

"How could this happen? I want the whole palace searched!"

Ben grinned to himself behind a giant vase, feeling his heart lift. It was a good thing the corridors in the king's palace were cluttered with unnecessary things. They made for good hiding spaces in the dark evenings. He had the sudden realization that he was in the nightmare that had followed him for his whole life, and yet he was alive, whole, and not terrified.

He made his way slowly to the kitchens, intending to find some scraps of food if they were empty, but when he got there he heard voices.

"Give her this. It will revive her and hopefully nourish her. She is wasting away."

"Thank you, young one. It is good that you are working here. You know what she likes. We can't tempt her with the palace food."

"Any sight of her brother?"

Ben peeked around the doorway to see Gavi standing with a diminutive older woman. Gavi had his back turned to Ben, but the woman's sharp eyes saw him and widened.

"I believe he has come now, for his supper," she said to Gavi, and a smile transformed her serious face.

Chapter 29

*I*sika was helping the old woman make dinner when Keethior called out to her.

Your brother . . .

She dropped the carrot she was peeling as her hands suddenly stopped working.

What? Keethior? What happened?

He's been taken. They took him. I'm so sorry.

What do you mean? Who took him? She was already walking toward the door, ready to throw it open and rush outside, but Hera stood up and walked in front of her, leaning against her legs so she couldn't take another step.

You can't go out there. They took him to find you, the mother cat said.

No, no, Isika told both of them. *You can't keep me here. You don't understand. Benayeem will crumble under this. This is his worst nightmare, his living demon.*

You have to trust him, Keethior told her. *He has been changing and growing, training for this day. We need a plan.*

You cannot just act without thought, or the Desert King will have you and we will all be trapped in this city, unable to retrieve you or leave without you.

Isika sat down very suddenly, all her arguments leaving her in a rush. There was a painful ache in her chest. The room swam in front of her. A cat came and sat on either side of her, leaning against her body, purring, so that the vibrations brought her back. When she opened her eyes, Mara knelt before her, concern and love in her eyes.

"What has happened, daughter?"

Isika stared at the woman, speechless. She couldn't imagine anything more horrible than her brother, so dear to her, trapped with the man who had made his life unlivable for so long. The Desert King had tried to pour the Great Waste and all its fear and poison into Benayeem. He had wanted to destroy him. First Aria, now Ben. Isika's hands trembled.

The front door swung open and the room was full of noise and light. Abbas and Jabari strode inside, laughing and talking until they spotted Isika on the floor. Jabari rushed to her and sank to his knees in front of her.

"What is it, Isika? What happened?"

Are you okay? Did he hurt you?

She looked at him. *Not me. Benayeem. The king has captured Benayeem.* Then she said it aloud, for everyone else, and also because it was still secret that they could speak to each other with animal speech.

The mother cat flicked a lazy look at her.

This one speaks the language of the animals?

I do, Jabari told her. *Do you want me to go look for him?*

No, she said. *Let's stop and think first.*

Jabari offered her a hand and she stood up. They moved over to the table and sat at the low seats around it.

"What happens now?" Isika asked.

Abbas looked thoughtful. He stood and began to pace in the small room.

"He knows that we are here. That means we need to be more careful. And we need to split up. My sister and I will work together. Gavi is in the palace."

"And Herrith," Jabari said. "Isika, this isn't like last time. There are allies at the palace. Hopefully they can help Ben."

"Should we send Keethior?" Isika asked.

"No," Abbas said, and Jabari shook his head at the same time. "We should not risk what we have. We need time, and we need a plan. Let's watch and wait. The king wants to draw you in, Isika. He has found your weakest place—your siblings—and he is multiplying the effect by taking many of them at once."

The old woman had made spice tea and brought it over, just as Ivy and Deto came through the door, Keethior flying in behind them.

The others told Ivy and Deto what had happened while Keethior landed on the table and spoke to Isika, his head taller than hers in the small space.

"Where is Brigid?" Ivy asked suddenly.

"I thought she was with you," Jabari said, startled.

"We thought she was with Ben," they said.

"She was with him early in the morning, before he was taken, but I didn't see her afterward," Keethior said. "I tried to locate her but couldn't."

They all stared at him.

"You didn't think that was important information?" Jabari asked the bird. The bird turned his back on Jabari.

"I don't answer to the son of Andar," he told Isika. "And I have just informed you of what I know." Jabari and Isika exchanged a glance.

"Deto and I will search for her," Ivy said. " And we will change to another inn, in case we have been followed."

Isika glanced at Jabari. "We will look for her too. And then we need a plan for Ben and Aria."

Jabari nodded and Isika could tell that he was thinking about Gavi.

"Not before you drink a cup of tea," the old woman said. "You still look like you're about to fall over."

ABBAS, Deto, and Ivy left to retrieve Abbas's sister and change inns. The plan for now was that Jabari and Isika would continue to stay with the old woman. Now that Ben was gone, Jabari wouldn't hear of Isika being alone anywhere.

"Sorry," he said. "You'll have to get used to me, because I'm not leaving your side."

Isika felt a rush of surprising happiness, and she turned away as her face grew hot.

They drank tea, and then they ate, and when the old woman was satisfied, they covered their faces with their sers and left with the cats to look for Brigid.

Which one is lost again? The youngest cat asked.

Do you really not know?

We only pay attention to you.

Isika frowned at the cat. *You shouldn't do that. Perhaps if you paid more attention, we wouldn't lose people.*

You are the only interesting one, the cat said.

Beside Isika, Jabari sniffed. "They're not so polite, are they?" he asked.

"No," Isika muttered, glaring at the cat again.

She's the pale skinned one, with long hair that reaches her knees. She walked with us for many miles.

Oh! The cat said. *The one who likes to sing to herself.*

Isika supposed Brigid did sing to herself. *Yes.*

We don't notice all these markings that you do, skin color and hair. But we do notice singing.

THEY WANDERED down corridors and into dark alleys, looking for something that would tell them where Brigid was. The streets were crowded and Isika made sure her face was covered so that only her eyes showed. People still looked at them, and watching Jabari, Isika could see why. There was no hiding that he was some kind of royalty, striding through the city with his shoulders back and his head high.

"Can't you slouch a bit?" she muttered. "Everyone is looking at us."

He looked at her. She could only see his eyes and thought for a moment that she had never noticed how they swept into up-tilting points at the corners.

"Do you really think they're looking at me?" he asked. "You're radiating power."

"I am not."

"You're walking around like a queen. You're supposed to be hiding. Turn it down."

"I didn't turn it up! How am I supposed to turn it down?"

They were still arguing when they walked down a road

and Isika felt awareness coursing over her like water. She stopped in her tracks and turned slowly, looking toward a narrow entrance that had an archway over it, with overgrown trees on each side.

An old man saw her looking at it.

"That's the queen's old garden," he said in a thick Gariah accent. "It's been long abandoned now. They've tried to build over it, but it turns the spades back."

"Turns the spades back?" Jabari asked.

"Yes, it protects itself somehow. Can't dig in the earth there."

Isika was drawn into the garden by a familiar strong pull. She thought it was friendly, though it was wild and powerful. The cats didn't seem to want to stop her. She thought she recognized this wild power, but surely . . . no, it couldn't be. She pushed through the overgrown trees and stepped inside the garden.

She had only taken a few steps before the singing caused her to fall to her knees on the grass. The garden was a wild place inside a dirty city, with huge trees and desert plants and she wondered briefly how they got the water to keep this place alive. But that wasn't what had her on her knees. The presence and the power in this place could only be Nenyi. But how? How was Nenyi here?

She lay face down on the grass and stretched both arms and legs out, her cheek pressed against the earth, and breathed it in. It was as though she had slowly adjusted to the thin air around her, the lack of power she felt in the city, the dust choking her. And now here it was: life. Buzzing through her, humming all around the garden. The cats stretched out and Jabari sat crosslegged nearby, watching her with a slight smile.

"It's amazing," she said.

"It is. But you are going to be pretty obvious to anyone who walks through that entryway. What do you say we go a little farther in?"

"Farther in?"

"Yes, I think the garden stretches a long way down the hill."

He held out a hand and she took it and rose to her feet. They walked farther in, down the long stretch of hill, and the cats ran alongside them, their silver flanks rippling and shining in the sun. One tackled another and they rolled around in the grass, biting at each other in glee.

Isika heard something then, in a far-off corner of the garden. It sounded like a person crying. She exchanged a concerned glance with Jabari. When she went toward the sound, she found a cactus garden with rows of flowering cacti, arms reaching to the sky, stones on the ground between them. Underneath a large cactus, a dark-skinned woman sat holding a baby, weeping. Her clothes were barely clothes anymore, they were so old and dirty. Tear tracks ran down her cheeks. And waves of power emanated from her. Isika and Jabari fell on their faces.

Nenyi. Nenyi was neither male nor female. Nenyi was not a person. But he had come to Isika in many forms. The form of a large cat, the form of a whale, the form of a man. And now this woman, in her rags, cradling a baby.

Then she stood and she didn't hold a baby but a white owl, wings outstretched on her arm, and she wasn't wearing rags anymore. Her skin seemed made of stars.

What are you doing to me? Isika cried out. *Why have you taken my brother?*

Love forms through pain, beloved, the woman said, bending over so her hair brushed Isika's face. The owl hooted and flew off, for suddenly it was night and Isika saw a vision of her grandmother crying in the garden, planting these cacti, walking with a man who looked like Herrith, reaching out to ragged children.

How else can love form you? If it only comforts, its worth is dead. If it only protects, it cuts off the world.

I don't want to lose Aria, Isika moaned.

You will lose her before you regain her.

Two sisters . . .

Isika sat up and it was day. Nenyi looked like the woman with the baby again. Her eyes were very gentle. She glanced at Jabari and he sat up as well. There were tear tracks on his face. But Isika didn't have time to wonder at that because the Shaper spoke to them.

Be true to each other. Hold fast to hope. It will look very dark, dear ones, but you will know what to do.

And then she was gone and Isika sobbed. Jabari came close to her and held her and she turned her face into his neck and cried. Nenyi had come again, and then she had left, and they were in the Desert City and Ben was gone and Aria hated her and her mother was still dead and she was filled with grief.

Slowly she calmed, and as she did she became aware of where she was, of the steady beat of Jabari's heart under her ear. She pulled back, her heart fluttering strangely, embarrassed. They sat like that in the grass, knees touching, Jabari's arm around Isika's shoulder, her head resting on his arm, until a plan came to her, fully formed. The cats sat up as one.

"Jabari," she said, turning and meeting his eyes. "I know what to do. I know how we get the prisoners and Aria back. And I know where we can find the power to do it."

He looked at her and smiled. Then he leaned forward and kissed her on the forehead, his soft lips briefly touching her skin and then pulling away.

No, she thought. *Don't go.*

"Well, then," he said, jumping to his feet and offering her a hand. "What are we waiting for? Get your lazy cats and let's go!"

Chapter 30

Gavi wiped a floury hand over his forehead and wrinkled his nose as the fine white powder dusted his face. The amount of cooking he had to do here tested even his love of cooking. He would be happier, he thought, if he could harvest the ingredients himself, like he did at home.

He had a pang of longing for his kitchen garden, but shook it off and went on preparing the mix for the next day's flatbread. The head cook was a good one. She had quickly seen Gavi's talents in the kitchen. She switched him from station to station throughout the week, and this week was his week for bread. He mixed the batter until it was even and smooth, then put the cloth over it so it could ferment overnight. It was late. He had worked slowly, so that all the other kitchen workers had left for the night, finally leaving only the head cook, who was preparing sauces for tomorrow's breakfast.

She finished her work and took off her apron, throwing it

into the large laundry barrel. The cleanliness in the king's kitchens was impressive, considering how big they were and how many people moved through them each day. Gavi had seen the mess and muck of the lower city, though, and he knew the comfort of the palace was a thin veneer over the misery in the rest of the city.

"Make sure the lamps are out before you go," the cook told him. "Tomorrow you'll start with the stew, okay?"

Gavi smiled at her. "Of course," he said.

She lingered and watched him for a moment, and in his mind he urged her to leave.

"You're an odd servant," she said. He slumped his shoulders and tried to look more like a servant, and after a shake of her head, she left the kitchen. He breathed a sigh of relief. After a few minutes, watchful Ben would come to eat, and Herrith and Lena would come too, so they could meet together. It had become their ritual. Poor Ben had been waiting a long time today.

Gavi wanted to see his friend, but he also wanted to know if Herrith had any news. Today Herrith had gone down to the lower tier of the city for the first time in a week. All that time, Isika and Jabari and the others had been working on their plan. Gavi wanted to know what it was.

Gavi knew he was meant to be in the palace—one of the team who had their eyes on Aria—but he missed his brother and friends more than he could express. He missed the fun that radiated from Jabari, bringing everyone around him into the joke. Herrith and Lena were great, but they were grave, and even Ben was serious for his age. Gavi missed the lightheartedness of his youth. He was just starting to realize that it didn't come to him naturally, as it did to Ivy and Jabari. He needed them to bring it out in him.

He started to make Aria's stew. Each night he made her favorite soup. Lena said she barely touched any food except his. He carefully stole into the kitchen gardens when he could to take the fresh herbs that he knew would nourish her. He used his own dried mushrooms and spices. And sometimes he carried it in to her. He was careful only to talk to her when she was especially lucid, so she would know not to betray him to a passing guard. Somehow she still hadn't told her father that he was in the palace. It was a dangerous game to play. She had whole days where she barely inhabited her own skin.

Shaper! He cried, as he often did when he thought about what Aria was going through. *What do we do? How do we help her?*

There was a quiet knock at the back door of the kitchen. When Gavi opened it, all three of them were there. Herrith was shaking his head as he walked in.

"It is foolish of us to arrive together," he said to Ben. "You were supposed to already be here, young one."

"It isn't his fault," Gavi said lightly. "The cook left late today. He's been waiting a while."

He retrieved Ben's plate of food and handed it to him. Ben sat on a short stool and began to eat, barely pausing for breath.

"Should we wait for him to be finished?" Lena asked.

"No," Gavi said, as Ben shook his head. "We don't know how much time we have. Our starving boy can listen and eat at the same time. Herrith, do you have news for us?"

"Much news," the older man said. He settled himself on a

stool in a corner of the kitchen while Gavi kept one eye on the soup simmering for Aria. "I told them that we have Benayeem." He looked up at Ben. "Isika burst into tears."

Ben nodded, chewed, and swallowed. "I knew she would be worried. I am thankful she knows now."

"Brigid was missing for some time, but she was found in a hospital in the deepest part of the lower city. She was trying to make sense of visions she had seen, and someone picked her up as a crazy person and committed her. Enfa managed to sneak her out."

Gavi and Ben stared at him with their mouths hanging open.

"Well," Gavi said, after a moment. "That is a lot of news."

"That's not all. Isika and Jabari have made a plan."

"Yes?" Gavi said, when Herrith paused.

"They will split up. Some will rescue Aria from the Desert King while the others spring the captives out of the stadium prison."

Gavi was shaking his head, holding up a hand.

"They are going to what? Rescue Aria? But she came here of her own accord. She isn't planning to leave. Are they going to forcibly remove her?"

"That seems to be the plan."

Gavi frowned. He felt a familiar old anger rise up in him at the presumption of the plan. He turned and spiced the soup, then stood and crossed his arms over his chest. He looked at Herrith.

"They can't do that."

Herrith watched him. "Who will stop them?"

"I will," Gavi said, extinguishing the fire under the pot of soup. He reached and took a large clay bowl from a high shelf, ladling the soup into the bowl, then handing it to Lena with a spoon. "She'll like this one," he said. He glanced at Herrith again. "When are they next meeting? When can I talk to all of them at once?"

A few days later, Gavi hurried down the narrow streets of the lower city, which baked and stank in the sun. He had told the head cook he needed to look for ingredients they did not have. The hottest part of the day was the easiest for moving around undetected, because most people slept and there were few people on the streets. He adjusted his ser. The sun was unrelenting. He slipped along the streets quietly and eventually stood in front of the blue door with the circle symbol. He knocked. The door opened to reveal Jabari, who quickly pulled Gavi into a hug, shutting the door behind him.

"Brother!" Jabari said, his white grin splitting his face. "It has been so long!"

Gavi soaked the warm welcome of the room into his skin. His brother, radiant Isika who shone with life even when she didn't know it, Ivy, his cousin sister, and Deto, an old friend were there. Brigid was in the corner on a mat, looking paler than usual.

"Are you okay, Brigid?" Gavi asked. "Herrith told us what happened and we couldn't believe it."

She smiled faintly. "Much better," she said.

"How is Ben?" Isika asked while Ivy and Deto were in line for their hugs. "Why has he not come back yet?"

"He's fine. Don't worry about him. He's strong and growing stronger. He spends his time in the palace listening for who might be sympathetic, who might eventually be convinced to join the Circle. He does good work. He also listens for times when it might be easier to speak with Aria." He paused. It felt wonderful to be in a safe place, to be on good terms with the people he loved, and if he knew Jabari and Isika at all, he knew that they wouldn't like what he had to say. He sighed.

"Aria's the reason I have come," he said, jumping straight in. "Don't go through with your plan. It won't work."

Jabari took a step back, crossing his arms over his chest. "What do you mean it won't work?"

"You can't take her by force. She will never be healed if you do."

"Are we supposed to leave her here?" Isika said, her voice rising.

"I will not leave her," Gavi said in a low voice.

"Wait, what?" Jabari's face was shocked. "You're planning to stay here? You know we're getting the prisoners out and then leaving, right?"

"I will stay with Aria as long as she needs me."

"You're going to leave us?" Ivy's voice was a whisper.

"No," Isika said, shaking her head. "No one is staying. We are taking Aria, whether or not she wants to come, and we are going home to Azariyah."

"Isika, no," Gavi said. "You don't know how it is to be a rescued one."

"You think I don't understand you, brother?" Jabari asked, pain in his voice.

"How could you understand, loved as you are? How could you know what it is like to live, knowing that you were thrown away?" Gavi asked him. He cleared his throat, upset that his voice was cracking.

"You were loved too! You were chosen!" Jabari took a step toward Gavi, but Gavi moved away, determined to make Jabari hear.

"Can being chosen make up for being rejected?" he asked. "Is one more powerful than the other?"

Deto and Brigid were looking at each other. Deto nodded.

"What he says is true," Deto told Jabari. "It is a heavy poison. It doesn't go away, but seeps through most of life."

"But what does it have to do with our plan?" Jabari said. "So she is under a heavy poison. All the more reason to get her out of here and back to Azariyah where she belongs."

"No, brother," Gavi said. "The song that rejection sings to her is that she doesn't belong, that she will never find a home. That's why she came to her father. Trust me. I understand her. I'm waiting for the right moment. For Aria to heal, peace needs to come from within her. We can't just steal her."

Jabari stared at Gavi like he didn't know him, then turned abruptly and began pacing. Isika sat on a stool with her head in her hands. Deto and Brigid sat as if frozen, immense sorrow on their faces.

Suddenly Jabari turned to Gavi, fists clenched. "No, brother!" he said, and his voice was loud enough to make Brigid flinch. "The moment is now! We cannot allow this! If she gains power she could try to destroy Maween. Don't you see how much poison could come from her betrayal if she is actually named heir!"

"So are you doing this for her good? Or for the good of Maween?"

"For both, brother! Listen to yourself! What are you saying?"

Gavi shook his head sadly, gazing at Jabari. "I don't want to fight you, Yab. But you are wrong. You need to reconsider your actions." He glanced at each of them, pain lancing through him at the sight of their faces. "Keep well, all of you. I must get back now."

He let himself out. No one tried to stop him or follow him. As he hurried back to the palace he felt that he had never been more alone.

Chapter 31

*J*abari was in the city stables, going through the
motions of taking care of the horses, but his
mind was far from the task. He couldn't believe
that Gavi had come and told them that breaking Aria out of
the Desert City was the wrong thing to do. Stay in Dhahara?
Stay?! Impossible. They had been brainwashed, both of them.

What about Ben? Would Ben be brainwashed also, now
that he was in the palace? What about Herrith? Jabari didn't
know who he could trust anymore.

Isika's horse, Wind, turned his head suddenly and nipped
at Jabari's arm. Jabari loosened his grip on the brush when he
realized how hard he was pulling it through the horse's mane.

Sorry, friend, he said.

You are angry, the horse replied.

He was angry. He was angry with Gavi, at Jabari's side as
long as he could remember. How could Gavi leave him? How
could he imagine that Nenyi wanted him to stay in this poisonous city? How could he have alliances away from Jabari and

his family, the people who had rescued him? And for that matter, how could the rescued ones band together like that and say they had never felt loved? Not as loved as Jabari? Jabari didn't have something they were lacking! They were all loved! What was the point of loving rescued ones if they turned on you and decided to stay in evil cities with evil kings?

Wind turned and kicked the stable door, hard, and Jabari realized he should put the brush down.

I'm sorry, friend, he said again.

I am glad I am not on two legs, Wind said. *You have tangled minds.*

Jabari felt like there was a stone sitting in his gut. He sighed. *We will come for you in two days. You need to look very good, so try not to get dirty before then.*

We are standing in a stable, and sometimes they let us walk in the yard. I don't think we will get dirty.

Good.

Jabari left the stables and started to walk across the city in the growing twilight, feeling the familiar heaviness that had settled on him since he came here. Somehow he was luckier than everyone who had been born in this city. But that thought made him think he was undeserving, and he shrugged it off, even as he stooped to help a thin little girl who was having trouble picking her brother up. Jabari picked up the toddler and held him while the girl tied him in the cloth on her back. She grinned at him, then raised her hand for a coin. He gave her one reluctantly, not even sure he knew where the reluctance came from. He had enough to spare.

Heavy, it was so heavy. The houses rose on either side of the road, corners jutting where no one had bothered to match them up, water dripping from ledges where people had thrown their dregs after cleaning laundry or dishes. He heard the crying of hot little babies who couldn't sleep, the shouting of cranky men after a long day of work.

As he rounded a corner he came upon a crowd of angry people who were clustered around a boy younger than Ben. A man advanced on the boy with a raised club.

"What are you doing?" Jabari cried, already pushing through the crowd, toward the boy.

The man with the club lowered it. He turned to look at Jabari with a scowl on his face.

"Who are you?" he growled. "And what are you doing on this street after nightfall?"

"I'm just a stranger coming from the stables, no concern of yours. What are you doing to that boy?"

"We're the guards, stupid," another man said, and spittle flicked from his mouth as he came closer to Jabari. Jabari flinched, noticing two other men who left the crowd to walk closer to him. Four. There were four of them. "Everything here is our concern. That boy is a thief." He turned to point at the boy, but he had taken his chance and run. Jabari grinned, but the malice of the guards made him refocus. He would need something special to get out of this mess.

Keethior? he called.

Out loud he said, "That's how you guard the city? With brute force?"

"A language all people understand," the man with the club said, his face contorted with anger, even while he grinned with broken teeth. "As I'm sure you do as well. And we have an empty spot where we had a thief. How nice of you to take his place."

Keethior!

I don't answer to you, son of Andar. How many times do I have to remind . . .

Isika! Can you send Keethior to help me?

There was a flurry of activity in the animal speech part of his mind, and Jabari got himself ready as the four men lunged at him.

He dodged the first, then kicked his legs out from under him, as the man with the club roared and came toward him, attacking with his club. Jabari tried to dodge it, but the club caught him over the eyebrow. Instantly, blood sheeted down his forehead and into his eyes, as pain erupted in his head and he stumbled. Another man used the opportunity to catch his arm and twist it behind his back. Jabari gasped, caught against the wall, unable to move without breaking his arm.

And then there was a roaring sound, like a mountain falling, and a cold chill of fear and strong wind blasted through the space. Jabari looked up as the man released his arm and through the blood in his eyes he saw a flurry of feathers and glimpse of two sharp beaks stabbing at the men. It was only a few moments before they fled, wailing as they went.

"Nenyi's skies!" Jabari said, his words slurring as he tried to stand. "I've never seen you do *that* before."

"Stupid boy," Keethior said. "What have you done? You may as well have walked into the king's chambers and told them where you were!"

"Now, now," murmured Eemia, and Jabari stood a little straighter.

"You wouldn't have been able to watch a young boy take a beating either," he said, limping down the street. The houses were dead silent as everyone stayed inside and prayed that the commotion would pass by. "Oh wait, you probably would have. I forgot who I was talking to. Not you, Eemia."

They were at the door. Jabari barely touched it before Isika flung it open and shrieked at the sight of him. She pulled him inside. He winced as the force jolted him, reminding him that he was close to passing out. She helped him over to some cushions that Mara pulled together.

He told them briefly what had happened and Mara's lips grew thin. She went to get some water from the kitchen and came back holding a towel.

"If Keethior had come the first time I asked, I may not have taken a club to the face," he said, looking at Isika, who had tears in her eyes as she stood with her hand on his shoulder.

She whirled and faced Keethior.

"No," Keethior said. "I am not his to beckon and send. If he wants to get into trouble, he can sort it out."

"He is like a part of my heart, Keethior. You may guard him like you guard me."

Jabari's heart jumped and sped up. The room was silent. Isika went on. "As Benayeem is a part of my heart, or Aria."

"I can't guard everyone, Isika," Keethior said, his voice sullen. "So you have to choose who is a part of your heart."

Isika wouldn't meet Jabari's eyes after that, though he wanted her to, but he was distracted anyway by the painful medical work that Mara was attempting. Finally she said, "He will be fine. He'll have quite a scar, though."

Brigid gasped from the corner and Ivy said, "Oh no, Yab. Your perfect face. Do you want me to get Gavi?"

Gavi would have been able to help Jabari instantly. But it

was Isika who came forward, finally meeting Jabari's eyes. He felt a sharp twinge near his heart.

"No need," she said. "I'm sorry. I don't know where my head has been."

"Isika, if this kind of magic will wipe you out, don't do it," Jabari said. "The naming ceremony is in three days and we need you."

"We need you too. I'll be fine."

She came very near, near enough that Jabari could feel her breath on his cheek, and leaned her forehead gently against the unhurt side of his head. He sucked in a breath. Magic. He could feel her wild, unfiltered magic, connected to the very deepest parts of the earth. It moved around him and enveloped him. He smelled fresh earth and sweet flowers, rain on the desert floor. When she sat back, a few minutes later, she smiled at him drowsily and he realized that he felt no pain. He touched his head and found the tiniest ridge, a thin scar.

Ivy leaned over and touched it as well.

"It's not too bad. No one wants to be friends with someone with a perfect face, so I'd have to say I like you better."

"I'm happy to have it. I've been healed by the World Whisperer, so I'll carry this with me as a sign. Lucky, lucky me." He smiled at Isika and she smiled back at him, then swayed where she sat.

Ivy pulled her up and helped her over to the cushions against the wall. She lay on them and closed her eyes.

The old woman muttered to herself and brought tea that burned Jabari's throat and brought strength back to him.

Then she brought bowls of thick stew and flatbread to scoop it with.

"We need to plan," Brigid said, stroking Isika's hair.

"We do," Ivy said, "though these two aren't good for much right now."

"I'm fine," Jabari said. "Isika healed me, remember?"

"I'm fine too," Isika said. "Just a little sleepy." She yawned. "Let's talk about it though. Jabari, did you speak with the horses?"

"Yes," Jabari said, frowning. He remembered how he could hardly get through brushing them, and why he had been so tense. The altercation with the brutish guards had nearly driven it from his mind. "They know we will come for them."

The plan was for Jabari and Isika to join the parade. Herrith would get two guard costumes for them and the decoration necessary for the shiny, brushed horses. While Aria was being named heir, everyone except Isika and Jabari would overpower the guards at the stadium prison, and open the doors to set the prisoners free. Herrith had told them that most of the guards would be occupied at the parade and ceremony, so it would be the easiest day to do it. Then, when the ceremony was finished, Jabari and Isika would take advantage of the chaos of the prison break, and spirit Aria away, escaping with her through the tunnels. Olumi had suggested that Isika should bring her staff and wear her circlet under the guard uniform. She couldn't imagine why she would need them, since their plan didn't involve any fighting, but she had agreed.

"There's something we're missing," Isika said, her voice soft and slow. She seemed barely awake. "I can feel it."

"We've gone over everything," Jabari said, trying to keep his impatience from showing. "We know exactly what we're getting into and why. We know where she will be. We know the closest safe spot with access to a tunnel. We might even be able to get her down the alley before anyone notices, if the skirmish at the stadium is big enough."

"It's just that something doesn't feel right," Isika said. "I can't explain it."

"I feel it too," Brigid said. "But there doesn't seem to be a better plan."

Jabari felt a squirm of worry for his brother and Benayeem in the palace. Would they all get out of the city alive and uninjured? It did feel like too many things could go wrong, and he wondered for a heartbeat whether Gavi was right. Maybe taking Aria by force wasn't the best thing. But the heartbeat passed and he shrugged it off.

There were only three more days. They couldn't let these captives be shipped across the sea as slaves. So they would go through with their plan. They had to take Aria with them! If she was named heir, the backlash of betrayal magic might cripple Isika and Maween beyond repair. No matter what Gavi said, the ceremony had to be stopped.

But it took Jabari a long time to get to sleep that night.

Chapter 32

*H*errith walked with his head down, wearing something he had never in his life dared to wear—a brown robe. A brown robe said he was a regular palace servant, with none of the privileges or powers of a red robe. He could be killed wearing a brown robe by the people, who didn't respect a brown robe, or by the king, if Herrith was ever discovered wearing a brown robe.

But he had gone back and forth from Mara's house, the home of the resistance, too many times recently. The king's spies knew the old woman had been Herrith's nurse when he was a boy, so they ignored his visits. But Herrith had begun to notice odd effects rippling out around him. Did King Ikajo have suspicions about his most loyal red robe, the cousin who had always been by his side? It seemed Herrith might finally be found out.

Wisdom would counsel that he lay low and stay in the palace, but he couldn't. This was the time to act. He needed to continue his work, but very, very carefully.

So he wore a brown cloak and stuffed the two guard uniforms that were for Jabari and Isika deep in its folds. Head down, moving quickly, he didn't see the woman until it was too late, slamming into her roughly and knocking her down. He caught himself before he landed on the scummy street with her, then held out a hand to pick her up. It was one of the moments when he was torn by who his role needed him to be, and who he truly was. He wanted to apologize, to claim fault, to say, "Sorry for making you fall in the scum that people throw out of their windows," but no one from the palace would do that, and acting out of character would start another ripple.

"Be more careful," he said gruffly, then turned and left the woman to shriek at him about how he had knocked her down and he was the one who needed to be more careful.

He was used to being hated. He was hated by everyone except a handful of people who knew who he truly was. He would have hated himself if he was who everyone thought he was, the loyal servant of an evil man.

It was why he loved Mara's house. The old woman had known his true identity since he was a small boy. She knew how he must behave so the king would keep him close. She had been with him when his father gave him lessons in duplicity, in keeping an evil face, in the delicate balance between weak and too strong that the king wanted him to hold. Not pathetic but not a threat. This was his life. He had been raised for it.

But with the coming of Aria, a window had cracked open and the fresh breeze outside whispered to Herrith. He dreamed of good, of how it would be to walk openly as a good man, in a place where it was safe to be good. It tormented him like a tray of flat bread cooling on a windowsill torments a starving man.

Meeting Isika had only strengthened the goodness he felt. For the second time in his life, he was tempted to leave the palace. How could he continue, surrounded by evil, filth, and hatred, now that he had felt the presence that Isika carried with her? Now that he had smelled that fragrance that didn't curl his toes or make him blink like his eyes were filled with dust?

His heart thudded with grief. If he left, it would mean the abandonment of his people. The Gariah would be without a gold cord, a prophet from the line of prophets that had begun with his ancestors. And he wouldn't be able to face the Shaper, not even in his dreams. So he determined to stay, even while Isika made plans to take Aria and leave. He mourned his birth, he questioned everything, but he would not leave. He would not leave.

He was nearly there. He worked at clearing his face of grief. He would present strength and clarity to the children who held the fate of his people in their hands.

The first time he was tempted was when Amani left, begging him to come with her. If she asked him now, he just might go. But back then he was so sure of the strength of his role the gold cord, so full of the idealism passed to him by his father, who had been friends with Queen Azariyah herself. It was barely even care for his people, back then, that made him stay. He stayed because of his principles, and felt righteous doing it.

He spit on the side of the road now. If he knew then that he would never see Amani again . . . if he knew that she would die believing that Aria had been sent to her death . . .

He wasn't doing a very good job of pulling himself together.

Amani was gone, and with her his heart. So he might as well stay here. She had died in the great tide of poison that came from the Great Waste. He was holding out against the tide with all his might, but if he had to be brave like Amani and die without seeing the true light . . . so be it.

He knocked his special pattern on the door.

LATER, sitting with the others, he submitted to questions about Aria, Gavi, and Ben.

"Have you seen Ben lately? How does he look?" Isika asked, leaning forward. "Does he have that pinched look that he gets when he's hearing too much insanity?"

"I saw him last night, and I don't know about a pinched look, but he seems to be doing okay. He was with Gavi."

He watched as Isika exchanged a long glance with Jabari —desert spines, the feelings between those two!—and waited for more questions. Jabari shook his head and stared at the ground, and Isika huffed a sigh, then leaned forward again.

"And Gavi? How does he seem?"

Ah, that was it. Something had happened between the brothers. He had wondered about the new grimness around Gavi.

"He seems fine. He's concentrating on cooking for Aria and speaking to her when he can."

"Has Ben seen Aria?"

"We don't feel it's safe for her to see him. She could so easily betray him."

"But she hasn't betrayed Gavi."

Herrith shifted where he sat.

"We believe that is because the poison of the arrow leaves him untouched in her mind. But it makes her angry with the two of you."

He watched as Isika's face folded up on itself, an endless well of grief just beneath the surface. He wished he could take back his words, but they were the truth. Aria must not learn that Isika and Ben were nearby until the very last moment, when they had her and could break free with her. Herrith believed she had forgotten that she had seen Ben in the king's chambers. She never spoke of him.

"Where will you go when you have her?" he asked. "She is still very sick."

"We will take her to the Karee," Jabari said, speaking for the first time. "We believe that their healer will be able to save her."

Herrith nodded. And them? Their plan? The Gariah? But he knew no further than this moment. His ability to understand the will of Nenyi extended to Aria returning and Isika coming after her. It was the moment he had been waiting for since the night Amani escaped. As he watched his beloved disappear into the night, he had been struck by a vision of Nenyi that left him weak and shaking—the perfect alibi. He had been sick in his bed for weeks, feverish and uncomprehending. The king had assumed that Herrith knew nothing of the escape.

He had never even kissed Amani. Never once done anything more than rest a hand on her shoulder. When they were young, they had held hands, but then she had been married to someone else against her will and he had been forced to retreat, except as a friend.

He bowed his head. What was this? Why would Nenyi prepare him for this moment for so many years, only to have Isika come and take Aria away, leaving him alone again? He didn't understand it, but he would serve these children, as he had promised the Shaper on the night Amani had gone from him forever.

HE SLIPPED BACK up the streets to the palace without incident, changing cloaks in a dark alley in the upper streets, then brushing past the guards and into the bright light of the evening palace.

That night, Aria seemed restless in her father's chambers, playing with her food when he insisted that she stay with him for dinner. She fiddled with her braids and refused to meet her father's eyes.

"What is it?" he finally barked. She looked up then, startled.

"Sorry, Father?"

"What is wrong with you? Your naming day is tomorrow, one of the most important days in the history of Gariah, and yet you sit and sulk."

"I'm sorry, Brilliance. I am not trying to sulk. I am nervous. There is something wrong . . . I feel something . . ."

Herrith cast an eye at one of the senior guards, who stumbled into a slave and knocked her to the ground, where the plate she was carrying shattered.

"Whip her!" the king roared.

"No, Brilliance, punish me," the guard said, falling to his knees. "I fell and shoved her."

The king stopped, his mouth hanging open. He was more

likely to order a guard to his death than whip him, as everyone in the room knew. Herrith held his breath, nodding three slaves forward to clean the mess, while the king considered the giant of a man, his largest guard, his boasting point, his favorite.

"Be less clumsy," the king said finally, and Herrith breathed again. The king turned back to the table, but Lena had already whisked Aria away. With a puzzled look, the king fell back to eating his enormous plate of food.

HERRITH FOUND Aria in the garden with Lena. The night was mild, a small breeze playing among the trees in the garden. The stars were out, and he sat on the bench beside the girl, but kept his eyes trained on the sky, searching for the Shaper.

What is it you would have me do? How can I be your prophet if I do not hear from you?

"Something is very strange, Uncle," Aria said then, and Lena got up and left them. "Something will happen tomorrow, and I think . . . I will be attacked, but I know that it will not hurt me."

He looked down at her, spooked by the sound in her voice.

"Nothing can hurt me anymore."

HE NEEDED to warn the others, but when he hurried down to the house, all of them were gone. The house was gone. He looked for them as though he was in a bad dream, running up and down streets, asking neighbors, barely able to speak, unable to hide his face as he knew he should. He went back to the palace. This was it, the king would find him and kill him. Only the king's magic could hide the Circle from him. But when he stepped into the king's chambers, the king was asleep. It wasn't him. Even he couldn't make a spell that big while he was sleeping.

He found Gavi in the kitchen, and began to tell him what had happened, but Gavi interrupted. His eyes were red.

"She won't eat," he said. "She's in some sort of trance. She keeps saying they are here."

It was Aria, Herrith realized with a sinking feeling, falling to his knees. She had blocked him from the Circle with her magic, far more powerful than any of them had realized.

He fell for a long time, and when he landed, he was suspended in a net in a dark cavern, lost in his own trance. Nenyi paced before him like a giant, like the father of the giant guard that the king was so proud of.

"She won't go," Nenyi said. "Her place is here for now. And it will get worse, but then it will get better, and all will be well. Believe me as I say these words to you."

Herrith tried to get something out through his cracked lips.

"It has been so long," he gasped.

Nenyi laughed, then turned and grasped Herrith's chin with a gentle hand.

"It has not been so long. You still haven't learned, dear one."

"I need to warn the others," he said.

"I cannot allow you. They have to go through many trials to break this great poison. You cannot save them from it. I have touched you in your sleep. You will wake up when you are needed."

Herrith's last thought before he sank into blackness was that he hoped he hadn't fallen in the kitchen fire.

Chapter 33

*B*en and Gavi half dragged, half carried Herrith to the little closet off the kitchen where Gavi slept. Gavi kept trying to talk to Ben, but Ben hushed him. He was listening and Gavi needed to be quiet. The music coming from Herrith was strange—wild and angry, but not menacing or tinged with evil, the way much of the palace music was.

"Are you quite finished?" Gavi asked.

Ben looked up, startled. "Yes, I think so."

"What is happening? First thing tomorrow morning Aria is going to be named heir. I was counting on Herrith to help keep her safe."

"Safe from . . ."

"From Jabari and Isika and their plan to steal her!" Gavi roared, and grabbed two fistfuls of his hair.

Ben had never seen Gavi like this. He was alarmed. "I'm confused. Do you mean that you are going to work against Isika and Jabari tomorrow?" Ben felt a flash of fear and bent to take Herrith's shoes off. He needed to hide his face. He straightened from his task and looked around, avoiding the older boy's eyes.

Gavi's closet room was tiny and neat. On the wall, near the corner of the bed, he had pinned a drawing of his family —Andar, Laylit, and there were Jabari and Gavi, their arms thrown around each other.

"Ben," Gavi said. "Look at me, Ben."

Ben dragged his eyes away from the drawing. He couldn't understand the unfamiliar music he was hearing from Gavi.

"I would never fight or lay a hand on my brother. I hope you know that. But I am convinced that he is wrong, that his plans are wrong. You know Yab, though. He has never listened to me in his life."

Bitterness. That's what the music was. Bitterness, from sweet Gavi who was the one to always find a good way to view the world. Ben felt shock. What had happened? They had to get out of the palace.

"Gavi, I can hear things in you that I never heard before. We need to leave. There is barely anything left of Aria, and the king's music spreads. I feel like I can't breathe. We can't stay here. Aria can't stay here. And you—you are changing."

Gavi stared back at Ben, arms crossed. Finally he sighed and relaxed his shoulders.

"Perhaps you are right, little brother. Maybe it is bad for me to be here, away from beautiful Maween and the bright air. But I know with complete certainty that Nenyi has asked me to be here, and that trying to steal Aria will only make things worse for her."

"How can Nenyi ask you to do something that is bad for you? It doesn't make sense! Look at Maween. The Shaper has given us a good way to live and we do well there. The Uncreated One wouldn't ask you to stay here! She wouldn't do that to you!"

Gavi shrugged and pointed at Herrith. "This man has spent his entire life here. It seems that Nenyi asks things that we couldn't have fathomed in our safe world. Look around you. This whole world belongs to Nenyi, not just our part of it. What is going on here? What is going on across the seas? It's time for us to wake up."

BEN WAS up at the break of dawn after a fitful sleep. He had wrestled with Gavi's words all night long. What was his part? Why was it that he could hear everything, the life song of every person, but didn't know what to do with what he heard?

He got dressed and went to the kitchens to see if Herrith had awoken. Gavi was preparing the morning bread and the head chef had not yet entered the kitchen, so Ben peeked into the closet room. Herrith was still in there, eyes closed, breathing softly. Ben heard Herrith's dimmed music and the wild music that was laid over it. He hurried away. It was time to escape the palace and find the others.

The palace was in an uproar as the king searched for Herrith and couldn't find him. Ben kept his head down and his ser over his head as he crept behind the hedge, through the garden toward the outer wall, overhearing snatches of conversation.

"They've dressed her. The king will continue, despite the red robe's disappearance."

"He believes something is trying to prevent the naming day."

"The horses are ready . . ."

The web of magic over Herrith must be hiding him from the king's sight. Ben slipped through the garden door while the guard had his back turned. If there was any less chaos he would never have been able to get away. In his head he cracked the door open to hear the music. He braced himself, nearly sinking to his knees, as the sounds rushed at him, and he listened for only a moment before he had to shut the door again. He leaned against a nearby wall, trying to catch his breath, and jumped when he heard a voice.

"Ben."

He turned and gasped. "Brigid, what are you doing here?"

"Looking for you. We need your help with the plan today. We're supposed to be over at the stadium prison."

"I . . . don't think I can come. I need to stay here. There's something wrong, Brigid. I can't explain how bad it sounds . . . but it is very bad."

She nodded, eyes wide in her pale face. "I have seen visions that are very confusing. But I have also seen the captives running out of their cages. I must go and help them. Please come with me."

He stared at her outstretched hand. He put his hand in hers and squeezed it, briefly. "Brigid, no, I'm sorry. I need to stay near Aria. Something is wrong."

She sighed, then nodded. "The Shaper be with you."

A call went out. "The procession is starting!"

Benayeem fled, looking for a safe place to watch. This was all wrong. Herrith was supposed to be here, helping. But Herrith had told them the king's plan, and Ben tried to remember it as best he could. He ran down the hill. The procession would start at the palace and then move down toward the king's lower gardens, where Aria would be named heir.

As he stepped into the garden, he heard the wild notes of Nenyi's song that permeated the place and felt shaken as he recognized it. What was the Shaper doing? Surely the Desert King would never allow Aria to be named heir in this garden, where Nenyi's magic was so strong. And why did Herrith's sleep sound like Nenyi's song?

There were many people already gathered, waiting for the procession, talking quietly among themselves. Ben slipped through the crowd, listening for signs, wishing he could understand what was happening. It was a colorful group. The people were dressed for celebration, wearing long embroidered tunics over shimmering pants, and great, glittering turbans or headdresses. In one corner, Ben found three little children standing on tiptoe, trying to see over the garden wall. Ben helped the littlest one up to sit on top, and as he did so, he laid his hand on part of the wall and a small section crumbled away to dust. He quickly took his hand away. The children stared at him with wide eyes.

"That's a very old wall," he told them, and left, making sure not to touch the wall anymore. Nenyi's magic was strong in this place. What was the king thinking? Murmurs of the procession's progress were being passed along by the people who lined the roads, so they knew that it was up near the market, and then it was by the ancient school, and moving closer. As Ben paced, he realized that he could see shapes in the edges of his vision, transparent and fiery, shimmers of fire flying around the garden. When he turned to look straight at them, they disappeared. "Firebirds," he breathed. He had heard of firebirds but he had never seen them. And there were tall beings, barely shaped like anything he knew, striding around the garden. What were they? Was he losing his mind?

There was a shout. The procession had been spotted. In the very front, Aria rode a horse led by a guard. Around her were more guards on horses, and Ben saw his own horse, Night, directly behind her. Isika's horse, Wind, was beside him. They pranced more than the other horses, unused to the strong poison of the Desert City. Ben felt despair as he watched them toss their heads. Of course they would be recognized, how had Isika and Jabari not seen it? The two horses were larger, stronger, and more spirited than the other horses of the procession, and though their riders were dressed in the colors of the other guards, they also stood out. Of course they couldn't go unseen. The cheers of the people grew louder and louder as the procession came close, until Ben could barely hear his music. He needed to listen. Something was wrong. What was it?

The Desert King. Herrith had said that the Desert King would be here in the garden. Ben looked around. There he was, right over there, in the pavilion where the ceremony would be held. But his music wasn't with him in the garden. It was with Aria as she rode. How was he doing that?

Ben stood waiting for them to enter the garden, but the procession stopped just before the gate, and then the Desert King's music was very, very strong, and Ben was slipping through the crowd, toward the gates, as fast as he could, running to Isika and Jabari to warn them. The Desert King wasn't where he was supposed to be. The king in the garden must be a fake.

There was another shout. Dirty, angry, ragged people poured into the garden over the walls. Abbas and Enfa were there, and so was Brigid with her teeth bared and a staff in one hand. The prisoners had been set free.

Chaos erupted. Ben shut the door very firmly in his mind. He needed to reach Isika but he couldn't break through the crowd.

He saw it as though dreaming. Isika, dressed in the guard uniform, moved toward Aria and snatched up the reins of her horse, pulling them away from the guard leading her. The horses turned and Isika began to ride away, Aria in tow. They made their way out, one step, two steps, and the plan was working because the other guards were lost in the chaos of the escaping captives!

But then Aria pulled a sword from her cloak and leaned across her horse, swinging at Isika's arm, leaving a long gash on her shoulder. Isika screamed, and the sound did something crazy to Ben's brain. Aria struck again, this time slicing along Isika's leg. Ben broke away from the crowd and sprinted toward the horses, his heart in his mouth.

The rider on Night roared. Jabari tore his helmet and ser off his face as Night reared up on his hind legs.

"Aria, stop!" he shouted. "You don't know what you're doing!"

Olumi was there very suddenly, tiny before the horses, his hair piled on his head, both hands stretched out. As Ben listened, he heard a low humming noise coming from the keeper of truth, and something happened to Aria's face. She blinked and did not strike again.

Ben ran as fast as he could toward them, strangely able to get through the crowd. But as he did, the guard near Aria rippled in the air. Something seemed to fall from him and his music blasted Ben, who stumbled and nearly fell. He became taller and his face changed. He became Ikajo, the Desert King.

"She knows exactly what she is doing," he told Jabari, his lip curled. Then, to Isika, he said, "I knew you would come."

Chapter 34

The world shrank and became very narrow, as though all of it was centered on one spot—the Desert King's face. Isika felt like her shoulder was on fire. Blood continued to spill from the wound, soaking her guard uniform. Her circlet flared with heat and she gripped Queen Azariyah's staff in her good hand. It glowed with light, sending waves of power up her arm and across, to her injured shoulder. But the pain was relentless.

The four cats had come running when the sword sliced her. Now they stood around her, muscles tensed. Their eyes were on Aria.

Do not attack, Isika warned them.

We will wait for your word, Hera said, even as the youngest cat hissed in disapproval.

Isika dragged her eyes away from her father's face and looked at her sister.

"I will not fight you, sister," she said. "You are in my heart forever."

Aria stood frozen, holding the bloody sword in front of her like a spear, like she didn't know what she was doing with it. Olumi stood nearby, holding his hands out toward Aria. Tiny shimmers of light came from his finger tips and flew to land gently on Aria's face. She blinked and Isika saw her in there, behind the mask of Ikajo on her face, looking out from inside a cage.

Isika turned back to the Desert King and screamed at him. "Let her go! This is you, all of it is you! Stop hurting her! Let her go back where she belongs!"

The king narrowed his eyes and took small steps toward her, hands out. Isika could barely see for pain in her shoulder and leg. It was going to make her faint and she felt paralyzed on her horse. She needed to dismount before she fell off.

She looked for Jabari. Oh, he was beside her with Ben, holding a hand to the wound in her leg. She met his frantic eyes. *Help me get down,* she said in her mind.

He went to the other side of the horse and put one hand on her good leg while she swung the hurt leg over the horse and slithered to the ground. She realized immediately that she couldn't put any weight on her hurt leg, so she leaned on Jabari heavily, her good arm around his shoulders, and the two of them turned to face the Desert King. She gripped her staff with the hand that was around Jabari's shoulders. Ben was behind them. Isika took a breath that was more like a moan, as behind the king, four giant ashy lizards poured out of the ground and wove toward them, hissing as one.

"Never," they said in their hissing, sing-song voices. "Aria has the poison of the mud demons, she is of the Baloto now."

The Desert King held up a hand, and the lizards stopped in their tracks, standing there waving back and forth. Isika pulled her eyes away from them, but she could see that Aria was transfixed.

"You still don't understand," the king said coldly, frowning at them. "She is mine. You are mine. He," he scowled at Ben and pointed at him, "is mine, though I don't want him. There is nothing you can do to persuade me to let you go. I will never let you go."

"You have never had me!" Isika shrieked at him with all the power she had left. Her head felt woozy, her face hot and cold. There were spots in her vision. Her circlet felt as though it was burning into her forehead. Vaguely, she noticed crowds of people running and fighting around them. She saw Abbas guiding half the captives up one alley and his sister guiding the rest up another. She saw other palace guards laid out on the ground and she realized that it was working. They had gotten the captives out and soon they would be away from here. Now all they needed was Aria and they would be able to leave this horrible place.

Palipa, be ready, Isika called. *Keerza, I need you now.*

The cats shimmered in front of Isika, becoming visible as they prepared for a jump, muscles tense, holding very still. They locked eyes on the king, who glared down at them and held his hands out as if he only waited to blast them.

"You don't understand, King Ikajo," Isika said, trying to stay awake. "You are not our father in anything but blood. You lost your right to be our father when you hurt our mother. I do not belong to you. I do not belong to any one person, but I belong to the earth and the sky and these cats and the Keerza and Othra. I belong to my people and I belong to water. I belong to the Naia and I belong to Aria and I belong to Ben and to Jabari. I am everyone's and no one's. I belong to Nenyi but I will never belong to you. Even if you kill me right now I will not belong to you."

The earth was shaking under her feet. Jabari tightened his arm on her shoulder and stood very tall. She let go of him and allowed him to hold onto her as the king continued to walk toward them, holding his hands out. The cats hissed and spit as he drew near. Isika held the staff out in front of her, pointing it at the tall, hateful man who was her father.

"I don't quite think you understand how powerful my magic is, child," he said, in a soft voice that hurt Isika's ears. Behind him, Aria tried to dismount, but she was too weak and couldn't get her leg over the saddle. Isika longed to go help her, but suddenly Gavi was there, offering her a hand. She looked at it for a long moment, then put her hand into his. As she did, her eyes changed again. She stared first at Isika, then the sword in her hand with horror on her face.

"Isika?" she asked. "Did I hurt you?" She slid down the side of the horse and held onto Gavi's shoulder, then took a step toward Isika.

"Aria!" Isika called. Her shoulder and leg throbbed and the pain filled her brain until she almost couldn't think. She panted, her breaths coming in short, painful gasps. "Aria, come, sister. Come with us."

Jabari looked at her with wild eyes. "We have to get you to a healer," he said, his voice urgent. "You're bleeding too much. We can't stay here."

Ikajo had paused when Aria spoke, but seeing that she wasn't going anywhere, he took another step toward Isika.

"Stop there," Jabari warned.

Ikajo smiled, then held his hands out and the ground shook beneath them, sending waves of pain through Isika.

She gasped and her horse neighed loudly and lifted his feet off the ground, stomping down.

Keerza, Isika called. *Now I need you. Can you come?*

We don't need them, Hera told her, and in one long ripple of muscle, she leapt at the king, claws out. He lifted a hand and deflected the attack, knocking the cat to the side as easily as if she was a kitten. She slammed into a wall and lay still.

Ikajo smiled again. Isika hated his smile, hated him being happy. He was only happy with evil things.

"What happened to you?" she whispered. "How did you get like this?"

"What's that, little girl? Are your whisperer powers deserting you in my city? Not so powerful here, are they? That's the problem with only drawing on your whisperer blood. You have no power away from nature. Weak." He glared at Jabari. "And you, boy, remind me of a man I have heard about. Isika's grandfather, a man who desperately wanted to protect the woman he loved, his wife. He died too."

He lifted a hand as he said it and Isika flinched, preparing herself for a blast toward Jabari, which would hit her as well, but as Ikajo lifted his hand, another long, lithe shape leapt at him. The youngest cat sprang at Ikajo's face, and this time he didn't see it in time. Her claws made contact and Ikajo screamed and fell. Jabari whirled, picking Isika up, shouting, "Gavi! The garden!"

Isika may have passed out as Jabari ran, because the next thing she knew, she was lying on her good side in the garden, her cheek pressed to the grass. The earth's life song was sending strength into her, and through her half-closed eyes she could see that the garden was filled with the fire of a thousand flaming birds.

She closed her eyes. She could still see the fire birds. She watched them behind her eyelids for a while, but Jabari wouldn't leave her alone.

"Wake up, Isika. He'll be back. You have to stay here to use your power. The garden will help you. I will fight him as long as I can, but he is much stronger than me. You are the only one stronger than him. You need to fight. Come on, my friend, you can do it."

She shook her head. *Sleep,* she told him.

"Come on Isika, my love. You can sleep later. We'll go to the tree at home. You can rest there. I'll go with you every day. Right now you need to fight. Open your eyes. Aria is here and she wants to talk to you."

Isika felt Jabari's soft lips on her forehead and she smiled, then her eyes flew open to find him very near. She reached for his hand, then sat up slowly. The garden had stopped her bleeding, but pain overwhelmed her until she wanted to scream. She looked at Aria, who sat on the grass, flanked by Olumi and Gavi.

"Sister," she said.

"Isika," Aria murmured, her voice heartbroken.

Isika stood shakily, walking close to her sister and sinking down beside her, gasping in pain. She put her good arm around Aria's shoulder and Aria turned her head into Isika's shirt and wept.

"What have I done?" she asked. "I'm so tired. I can't trust anything, not my heart, not my thoughts. I very nearly share his head."

"We'll get you out of here," Isika murmured, content to

have her sister in her arms. She listened for the sound of the Keerza. They were coming, she heard their distant hoofbeats. And the fire birds flew around them, filling the garden with song and fire that radiated warmth and light.

"You are wrong." The voice was loud, filling the air with a piercing, metal-tinged anger, and Isika winced. Beside her, Aria wilted and Jabari tensed.

Isika sighed. "What now?" she asked, turning her head to look at the king. He stood just outside the gate of the garden, she noted with interest. But then she saw the cats lying in heaps around him. "What did you do to them?" she demanded.

"What I will do to every one of you if you do not cease this futile resistance. You can't take Aria anywhere. She has already completed the inheritance ceremony, this morning in my chambers." He brushed at his robes and hair, which were messy and dusty. "Of course we wouldn't leave it to chance, how could you think it? If you try to take her out of the walls of this city, she will die immediately. If you try to keep her away from the palace, she will wither and die slowly. Her life is tied to mine as surely as if I held it in my hand." He held one hand out and then closed it quickly. As he did, Aria fainted.

Isika was on her feet, and in the back of her mind she noticed that her wounds were not bothering her like before. The garden was healing her. Her circlet blazed and she held out the staff. The fire birds swirled up in one long column above her, reaching so high she couldn't see where they stopped. She took a step toward her father and the birds came with her. The sound of Keerza hoofbeats was stronger and stronger in her mind.

We are coming, they told her. *We are coming.*

"That is a lie," Isika said to her father.

He laughed without kindness or mirth. "It is not a lie. And under it all, my dear firstborn daughter, are the strands of betrayal which will eventually be your downfall. You cannot heal this pain. You cannot undo the betrayal magic that took your grandmother, that followed you to the Worker village where you betrayed your sister by not going to the sea in her place. None of it can be undone. It is permanent and will cast you down eventually. Even if you manage to leave here, even if you manage to become queen." He sneered the word at her. "You will never escape this betrayal magic. And Aria can never leave this city alive again."

She stood there, enraged, and looked for Keethior above her.

Brother, let me see with your eyes, she asked him, and in a moment she was flying, free from the pain of her wounds, free from the heaviness of her father's words, in the mind of the Othra. Above all, seeing all. She saw the captives running with Abbas and Enfa and the others. They were leaving the city, going through the underground tunnels. She saw herself, lit by the staff's light.

She came back to her own eyes. She needed time to think, but there was no time.

The Keerza came closer and the garden made Isika stronger. The fire birds gave long, low calls, and Isika held the staff high with her good arm. All eyes were on her. She looked down to see that she was ablaze, cool flames flickering from her arms and legs.

"That is enough of that kind of talk," she said calmly, and she drove the staff down so that it stabbed into the earth of the garden. It flared with blazing light and suddenly, the city was on fire. King Ikajo fell to his knees and threw his arms over his head. Isika sensed the flames of the birds, purifying, seeking poison and destroying it. Walls toppled and disintegrated. People cried out in surprise and fear.

And then she was alone. She looked around, wondering where everyone had gone. The circlet was cool on her forehead. Then Isika sighed with relief to see Nenyi striding through the garden toward her, taller than any tree. But the look on his face was infinitely sorrowful and she shrank from him. She didn't want to hear what he would say.

"You have to leave Aria here," he said. He stood beside her with skin like the night sky, filled with stars.

"Never," she said. "I would rather die."

"She will be the one to die, if you take her from here."

"Isn't there a way around this poison? How can it be that I must leave my sister here to die?"

"Do you believe him? Do you believe that betrayal magic can never be undone?"

"No! If it is so, we are tied to the evil that has betrayed each one of us, back through the long line of our ancestors. My grandmother, yes, but what about every small betrayal before that? I will not be tied to the evil that was done to those who came before me!"

"He is right, though, little one."

"How can you say that?" Isika fell and lay with her face against the earth. Nenyi stooped and picked her up as though she was a small child, holding her against his heart.

"If there is a way, you will be the one to find it," he told her. "But you won't find it today, and that is the truth. I'm sorry, daughter. It will take more time than we have right now. And you are badly wounded by a betraying sword. You must get back to Azariyah. You will feel the pain of your wounds as soon as you leave this garden. Entrust Aria to me. Leave her here."

Tears streamed down Isika's face. "How can I know he won't hurt her?"

Nenyi looked down at her. His face was fierce.

"Isn't she my daughter too? Do you think you can take care of her, with all your fumbling ways?"

It feels as though you haven't cared for her well, she told him.

"Oh, but my daughter, you don't know anything of this fierce fire, or how it will change Aria into the brightest morning. Go soon. Go now. Leave her here and don't imagine that you are her protector. You have your own work to do. No one got the prophecy quite right. It's like this:

TWO SISTERS, *a boat and a road*
    Hearts broken, lies and shame
    Grip of evil grip of pain
    Whisperer and warrior
    One will die for the other's gain
    The world opens
    Whisperer and warrior
    One lies dead, the other in pain
    Out of the night comes the way
    The land cries out, the Shaper turns
    One will die for the other's gain."

"WHAT DOES IT MEAN? Can you tell me what it means?"

Nenyi shook his head sadly. "You need to figure it out. This is your question: What does it mean that you are whisperer and warrior, and how will you sever the strands of betrayal poison?"

NENYI DISAPPEARED. Isika found herself sitting with Jabari, Benayeem, Gavi, Olumi, and Aria in the garden. The land was quiet, a herd of Keerza grazed, the horses and guards were gone, and her father was nowhere to be seen.

Chapter 35

*W*hen Isika opened her eyes, Jabari could see the slight shimmery look that meant she had visited with Nenyi. He felt the strong longing he always had when this happened. The longing to protect her and the longing to be like her. Jabari had served Nenyi all his life and he wanted to meet the Shaper. He wondered if Isika knew how lucky she was. And then he saw the fear in her eyes and he moved to sit closer to her, tentatively putting an arm around her. She leaned her head on his shoulder for a moment, then sat up and reached her hands out to Aria.

"You have to stay here," she said, her voice breaking.

"That's what our father said. Or I could go . . . and let what happens happen," Aria responded, her eyes on the ground.

"No, Aria, you would die."

"Would that be worse than living as his puppet?"

Jabari shifted, angry because he couldn't do anything

about this. He had never felt so powerless. *What are my powers, Shaper?*

"Aria, you can't say that," he said, leaning forward. "If he kills you, he cuts off all the possible futures where you beat this and come back to be with us. We will find a way to set you free from his power. You need to trust us and trust Herrith."

"I don't want to be alone here," she said, and she looked like the small girl she was when they had rescued her.

"I will never let you be alone here," Gavi said.

"You can't—" Jabari started, feeling a rush of hot anger and fear mixed with love.

"Yes, I must," Gavi said, turning to give Jabari a look. Jabari sat back, swallowing the rest of his words. "The Shaper's instructions to me have been clear. I will stay here with Aria."

Aria gazed at Gavi with a small bit of hope alight on her face. Jabari crossed his arms on his knees and put his face down on them.

"What if he makes me declare war on you?" Aria whispered.

Jabari jerked his head up. "What makes you think he will do that?"

"Feelings I have about his plans. He will be very angry, Isika. He wants your power so badly. I am only bait. But I am bait that he has poisoned, and I can't see clearly most of the time." Her words ended on a sob.

"You can't stay here!" Isika exclaimed again, and Jabari couldn't bear the look on her face. She winced in pain and Jabari remembered with a start that she was wounded.

"Isika," he said. "We need to get you to the Karee healer."

"Yes, and then to Azariyah," she said. "The Shaper told me I wouldn't be healed until I could be back in our lands."

"What else did he tell you?" Ben asked, leaning forward eagerly.

"He said that he loves Aria more than we do, that he is taking care of her."

Aria had a look on her face, a raw, untamed hope that made Jabari's stomach turn over.

"We'll see," was all she said.

"We must go," Isika said to her sister. "But sister, hold onto these moments of clarity. You need to fight to be free of him. Gavi will help you, and Herrith. And this garden."

She shook her head. "I do not know where the king is or what has happened to him. If he has been hurt he will be very angry. He will tighten his power around me."

"We will find a way to heal this," Ben said. "There is a way."

"I don't understand why Nenyi hasn't shown us yet," Gavi said.

"Nenyi said that this goes back farther than any of us knows," Isika said gently. "That we need to find a way to sever ourselves from the betrayal magic of the past."

THEY CAREFULLY MADE their way to Mara's house. As soon as they left the garden, Isika's face turned gray and she slumped against Jabari until he was half carrying her. The cats walked on either side of them, pressing against Isika's sides. It helped to keep her upright, but Jabari nearly tripped over them several times, cursing the cats under his breath while Isika smiled a wan smile.

The city was empty of people, the streets dusty and still smelling faintly of smoke. Jabari was surprised to find the city still standing after seeing the fire Isika had called down, but Mara told them it had not been a physical fire, but a fire that destroyed poison from the Great Waste.

"I imagine that many people feel themselves quite empty right now," she told them as they came in, bustling to find bandages for Isika, "after a cleansing like that."

Jabari laid Isika gently on the cushions in the corner and the old woman brought warm water and bandages, needle, and thread. Jabari felt his stomach drop at the sight of the crude tools. Gavi's healing skills weren't up to the job, especially so far from Azariyah. The cats moved against the walls to make space. Jabari bent his face close to Isika's while the old woman sewed her up, whispering and humming to her as she breathed deeply. Isika bit her lips hard at the pain, and after Mara made a dozen stitches, she fainted. Jabari kissed her forehead gently.

"I don't know how we're going to get her home," he said.

No one responded. He looked up. Gavi, Ben, and Aria were staring at him.

"What?" he said.

"When did that start?" Gavi asked.

"When did what start? Nothing 'started.'" I'm just taking care of my sister."

To his surprise, Aria burst out laughing. "That's my sister," she said. "Mine and Benayeem's. She's definitely not yours."

Jabari turned away to hide his smile.

"Have you heard anything about the king?" he asked the old woman, who had a faint smile on her face as well. She shook her head, but just then, there was a knock at the door. Herrith's knock.

"Oh, thank the Shaper," Mara said, hurrying toward the door. She opened it and Herrith stumbled in, looking spent.

He leaned against a wall, breathing heavily, his face gray. "What have you children done?" he said, when he had recovered his breath. "The king is in bed, the palace is in an uproar, and somehow, every one of our captives has escaped. Not to mention our heir." He turned to Aria and held out his hands. She stood and went to him, wrapping her arms around his waist. He tucked her under his chin and held her close.

THERE WERE many assurances as they parted. Herrith would look after Gavi and Aria, and so would Mara and the other members of the Circle. Jabari and Ben would make sure Isika got home safely. Assurances didn't stop the tears, but they all felt a bit better.

Once Isika revived from her stitches, Jabari knew they had no time to lose. She didn't want to leave Aria, but he acted quickly anyway.

He reached out to the horses. *Where are you?*

Stables, they told him.

You need to come here, Jabari said. *Bring some of the Keerza. There is no time to be secretive and perhaps they can help her.*

"Keethior," he said aloud. "Do you know where the freed captives are? Is Eemia with them? We need their help to get Isika home."

Jabari could almost see the struggle within the bird. Keethior most likely wanted to remind Jabari that he didn't answer to him, but the Othra looked at Isika for a long moment and then spoke. Maybe he saw what Jabari saw. It would be impossible to get Isika home without help.

"Eemia is outside the city walls," Keethior said. "I will tell her, and I will go and hurry the horses." Herrith opened the door and the giant bird flew off.

"We need to go," Jabari said. He felt prickling in his hands and feet. The king was asleep but couldn't stay that way for long. They needed to be far from the city when he woke.

Jabari's heart wrenched. He grabbed Gavi and pulled him into a long hug, then stepped back to look his brother in the face. Gavi's blue eyes were calm, though sad.

"You are not from here," Jabari told his brother. "No matter that you are rescued, no matter that I can't ever really understand what that is like. You are Maweel, our own, through and through. Don't let this place make you forget it."

Gavi smiled and looked back at him very seriously.

"Thank you, brother," he said softly. "That is true. But that is only half the truth. I am of another people as well, the unloved, the thrown away. The Shaper loves us in a different way, because of our need. I want to learn how to be with people like me. And I will always be half there and half with you."

Jabari had so many things he wanted to say. How could Gavi separate himself this way, make himself *other*? He knew the questions weren't for now. He looked back at Gavi.

"I share a heart with you," he said, "so maybe I can try to be half there with you."

Gavi grinned, and in that moment, all the past months

and years fell away and they were just two boys running down the road together.

"Oh, Yab, I should have known you'd elbow your way into anything," he told Jabari, then gave him another swift hug. "You need to go now. Isika is not doing well."

Jabari jerked his head to where Isika was lying. Her eyes were closed but moving quickly. He felt a swooping panic in his gut.

When he opened the door, he found the horses and fourteen Keerza. The cats poured out with them and stood in all their brilliance, not bothering to mask themselves. Seas and skies!" he said. "We'd better get out of here before the king regains his senses."

Gently, he woke Isika. She wept, but after she whispered in Aria's ear and Gavi smoothed her hair with one hand, she tried to be brave, dashing tears away, though her mouth was set in an unhappy line.

He helped Isika onto Wind's back, then asked the horse for permission to sit behind her.

Do you have her permission? The horse asked in reply.

He does, Isika said.

Then it's fine with me. Someone needs to keep her from falling off. Though it could be her younger brother . . . . But while the horse was deliberating, Jabari was already swinging a leg over the horse behind Isika. She leaned back against him and he held the reins with one hand, tucking his other arm around her ribcage to keep her from falling off.

They went as quietly as they could. Jabari saw the cats and the Keerza using their powers, shimmering into sight and then out again. In the edges of his sight he also spotted transparent threads linking the Keerza to Isika.

What are those? he asked them.

We give her our strength, one of the Keerza replied.

Nevertheless, she was soon asleep in the saddle, her head bumping against Jabari's shoulder. He wished he could make the journey more comfortable for her.

Soon they were in the tunnels leading out of the city, and after what felt like forever but was not nearly that long, they were out, blinking in the sudden light.

Keethior found them there.

This way, he said. *Abbas is taking the captives to the Karee village and we must go that way also. Isika needs to see the healer.*

I thought so too, but is that the right thing? Nenyi said she needs to get back to Maween, Jabari said.

She won't make it, the bird said seriously, and Jabari heard the animals begin to panic. He looked down at Isika. Her face was turned in toward his neck, her eyelids fluttering. Her chest rose and fell shallowly, and her wound felt hot to the touch.

"Yes," he said aloud so that Ben could hear. "The Karee village. Let's see what this healer can do. But then we go home."

Chapter 36

For Isika, the journey passed in a haze, with a few clear moments that she would always remember. Waking up with her head bouncing on Jabari's shoulder. Camping at night, all four of the cats curled around her to keep her warm. The pain in her arm and leg that never left. Watching the Keerza run down a hillside, the sun flashing off their hides, the cats among them like sharp glints of silver. The long train of travelers, all of them tired and dirty, captives who walked the long miles back to the Karee camp. Isika wished she had the strength to talk to them. Occasionally, she caught sight of Abbas and his sister running ahead of the rest, the tall warriors gorgeous and strong.

Keethior refusing to stop bothering her.

Don't sleep, young one. You've slept too much.

Be quiet, Keethior, I'm tired.

She needs to try to get healing from the earth. We won't make it.

How can this poison be so strong? Isn't she the World

Whisperer? That was Jabari speaking. Isika smiled slightly. He had a nice voice, even in animal speech. She tried to tell him, but she couldn't make her voice work.

It is betrayal poison. The wound came from her sister. Put her in the stream.

She's freezing and shaking from fever. She'll die if I put her in the stream. Isika frowned. Jabari was angry. Why?

"What's going on?" That was Ben. Isika tried to open her eyes.

"The bird thinks we need to lay her in the stream to see if she can gain some healing from the earth. But she's shaking with cold and the stream is freezing."

"Could you try to heal her, Jabari?" Isika heard Brigid ask. *Brigid!*

"Me? I don't have a healing gift."

"I think you might, if you tried it. You can do many things that Isika can do. Why don't you try that forehead thing that she does. Draw the poison out through your body.

"It's better than nothing, Yab," Ivy said. "If it doesn't work, we should consider the stream."

"I'd rather try anything but the stream," Jabari said. "Here, Brigid, support her so she can sit up."

Isika felt her arms and legs being rearranged, and she smelled the orange bright scent that Brigid carried with her. She smiled again.

"What are you smiling about, dear one?" Jabari whispered from somewhere in front of her. "I'm going to put my forehead on yours and try an Isika-kind of healing, okay? Don't be startled."

After a moment, Isika felt the slight pressure of Jabari's head against her own, and smelled his skin and firewood smell. Then a rush of warmth as pain left her and her arm ceased its throbbing. After a few moments she opened her eyes, feeling curiously light and not as cold, but very sleepy. She smiled into Jabari's face as he leaned back to look at her.

"Brigid smells like oranges and you have a nice voice, all deep and growly," she said. "Did you remember to send the poison into the earth, where it can't hurt you?"

Jabari's eyes filled with sudden tears, and she put a hand up to his face.

"Don't cry," she told him. "You did it perfectly." But the world was growing foggy again and she fell into a deep sleep.

After that, Jabari spent time drawing poison out of her each evening. She faded in and out of sleep, sometimes having energy to talk, but usually not. It began to feel as though she and Jabari had traveled on Wind forever. She knew her horse was tired from having two riders, but he was trying to hide it out of concern for her.

She had dreams of Aria coming toward her with a sword, and she woke up from those dreams crying. It felt strange for everyone to be so worried about her. She was used to being worried about others.

Then they were thundering into the Karee camp and Jabari didn't stop to say hello, didn't stop galloping until he rode Wind directly to the healer's tent and jumped from the horse with Isika still in his arms. She noticed this vaguely from the strange place she had retreated to, a garden within her own mind.

The healer came. Isika heard him make a long hiss.

"Your whisperer is dying," he said.

"Do you think I don't know that?" Jabari asked in the

angry voice he seemed to be using a lot lately. "Can you save her?"

"She needs to get back to her lands," the healer replied. "She's tied to them and it's breaking her to try to heal so far away."

"She won't make it there."

"I can't do anything for her here."

Brigid started to weep. Isika heard Ben shouting.

"Please," Jabari asked, and he sounded broken. Isika had never heard his voice sound like that before. "There must be something."

"There is one thing, but you must know that it is very dangerous."

"Danger doesn't matter. She is dying."

"I can put her into a deep sleep so that her body barely takes any energy at all. She will not wake until she is back in your land and has recovered enough to break out of this sleep. But if she doesn't recover quickly, she may never wake again. It is a huge risk." He paused. From far away, Isika heard his next words. "But you are right, if I do nothing she will not live long enough to get home. She could die tonight."

From her far away place, Isika pondered dying. She would see Nenyi all the time. But Auntie would be sad. She heard Ben and Jabari coming near. Someone gripped her hand for a moment, whispering to her. It was Ben. Jabari put his face very near hers. Isika couldn't open her eyes to see him but she could hear him and smell his woodsmoke smell.

"Do you want to do this, dearest one? Did you hear?" Isika gave the tiniest nod, and Ben sighed.

"She hears and understands. I can tell by her music. Isika,

do you want to do this? Do you want the healer to put you to sleep?"

Isika nodded again.

Ben hugged her. "Get better, sister," he said. "I need you." Then he stood up and Isika heard his soft footsteps as he moved away. Beside her, Isika could still hear Jabari's shaky breath.

"I love you, Isika," he whispered. "I would give you my own breath if I could. Stay with me, okay? Don't leave me here alone. It took me so long to find you."

I love you, too, she told him, but the words couldn't reach him. And then there was nothing.

THE NEXT TIME she opened her eyes, she thought she might be dead. It was so bright and clean. No dust, no desert. But no, this was her room at Auntie Teru and Uncle Dawit's house. She smiled and closed her eyes again, falling back into sleep.

The next time she woke, she was being carried. She peeled her eyes open. It was Abbas.

"There you are, little one," he said. "We think you'll get better faster if you lie in the grass each day. The healers have been feeding you broth to sustain you, but you need to wake up more, eat good food. Come on, little one, Auntie is going crazy. So is Jerutha."

He lowered her gently to the grass, and Auntie tucked a blanket under her head. Isika ran her hands over the springy blades of grass, and they curled around her fingers like they had missed her. She felt so much happiness in the life song of

Maween that she could have cried, but instead she looked at Auntie and smiled. Auntie burst into tears.

Isika lay in Auntie's garden for hours, every moment that she could. As she grew stronger, she ate Auntie's soups and even bits of flatbread. She ran her hands over the grass just to see flowers spring up at her touch. Then she could sit, and later walk, but she hadn't left the house or seen anyone besides her family, including Jerutha and Abbas.

"Where is Jabari?" she asked one day. She remembered asking when she first woke up, but she couldn't remember the answer.

"Doing some recovery of his own," Auntie said. "He nearly killed himself trying to heal you as you traveled home."

"What?" Isika asked, terrified.

"Don't fret. It's why I didn't tell you earlier. He's doing much better now, walking and eating again, like you. But from what I understand, the palace servants have discovered him trying to leave the palace to come to you a few times, crawling down corridors when he is too weak to walk."

Isika grinned, but for some reason there were tears in her eyes.

"Auntie," she whispered, "he told me he loved me."

Auntie snorted. "He's a dimwit if he just now realized that. Do you love him too?"

Isika thought. "I think so," she said. "Remind me what that feels like again."

"Oh, no no, I'm not telling you that. You need to figure that out."

She thought, by the tears in her eyes and the way her

heart sped up, that she had already figured it out. She sent him a note.

"Do you feel like walking to the market tree? It might do us some good."

He came for her the next day, leaning on a cane. She was shocked by the sight of him, almost as shocked as she had been the first time she saw her own face in the mirror. The two of them were a sight, all angles and hollows now. Jabari even had a few silver hairs around his face. But he nearly took her breath away. He was so beautiful. She remembered him behind her on the horse, holding her all that time. She swallowed.

"Ready?" he asked.

He walked slowly, so she matched her pace to his and tucked her arm under his elbow.

She didn't know what to say. "I'm so sorry," she settled on finally. "I'm sorry that healing me made you so sick."

"It was an honor," he told her. "But the earth doesn't heal me the way it does you, so it's taking me a bit longer to get my strength back, even though your wounds were worse."

Isika glanced down at her shoulder and thigh reflexively. She bore scars in both places—thin silver lines that didn't seem like they would ever go away.

They walked in silence for a while. Isika tried to ignore the stares from the Maweel they passed.

"They are only worried about us," Jabari said, when she looped her ser over her head to gain more privacy.

"That's what I don't like," she told him. "I'm supposed to be queen someday, after all. It feels bad to have them see me like this."

They had reached the tree, and Jabari turned to look at her, his face drawn and exhausted.

"Betrayal poison kills people," he said, "with or without sword wounds. Betrayal of a family member is almost unthinkable. They are not thinking of you as weak. They are thinking that you are the most magical creature they could imagine and that they would do anything to offer themselves to you. So would I."

Isika smiled into his lovely, tired face. The line of his jaw, the deeper shadows under his eyes, his skin, the same dark, dark brown as the tall tree above them.

"Let's not climb," she said. "Let's just crawl into that seat right there." She pointed at a crook in the tree that was low to the ground.

"Thank you for pretending that not climbing is a choice for me right now," Jabari said, smiling. "But is there room there for two of us?"

"There is. We may have to sit close together. But we were on that horse all the way home."

"We were," he said. She couldn't look at him.

They did sit very close, legs and arms touching, and leaned their backs against the tree. It was just high enough that their legs were off the ground. Isika closed her eyes and felt the tree's life force flowing into her cells, buzzing and flickering behind her eyelids. She waited for the pictures she needed to see, and she wasn't disappointed. There they were —Herrith and Aria in the garden, sitting on a swing, Gavi hovering in the background. She couldn't hear them, but they were whole and well, and outside, not in a cell somewhere. She heard music and the sound of Nenyi's voice, and she may have drifted off to sleep, because when she opened her eyes, it seemed like a lot of time had passed. Jabari was staring at her. She smiled at him sleepily.

"You have such a nice growly voice," she said, and she put her hand on his face. His skin was warm beneath her fingers. He stared at her and then moved toward her and kissed her. His lips were warm and soft against hers. She sighed and leaned into him, kissing him back. Then she pulled away, but not too far.

"You told me something when I was very sick," she said, feeling shy. She looked down and caught his hands in hers. He wove his fingers between hers and held tight but still didn't speak. She went on. "I couldn't talk, so I couldn't answer."

She glanced up. His eyes.

"I want to answer now," she said. "I love you, too, Yab. I think I always have."

He grinned then, the huge white grin that split his face, transforming it. "Of course you do," he said. "Look at me. Who wouldn't?" And then he leaned forward and kissed her again.

Want to know about World Whisperer 5 as soon as it comes out? Sign up here.

~

What is the most important ingredient for a book's success? Besides, of course, the book itself?

It's what you, the Reader, says about it. Social proof. Reviews.

When people are out there, in the wilderness of the book jungle, looking for something to read, the main question they ask is, "Have other people read this? Did they like it?"

So if this book is your kind of book, and you think it might be someone else's kind of book, I will be over the moon if you leave a review on whatever site feeds you your books. Reviews can be the key to a book's success. Thank you!

~

ACKNOWLEDGMENTS

First of all, thank you to you, dear reader. Thank you for loving Isika and Benayeem and all the rest, for following their story and being so supportive along the way!

I'm lifted and loved by my family and community as I write these stories. Thank you Chinua. You are my one true love for life, and I am so thankful that you love me and this series.

Susan Offner, what an editor you are. Thank you!

Kai, Kenya, Leafy, Solo and Isaac, I love you more every day. Thank you for being my kids and friends.

Rowan and Mom, thanks for lending me your eyes and finding the mistakes. Mom and Dad, you are more supportive than I deserve. Thank you.

Tj and Mark Chapman, Diane Brodeur, Brittani Truby, Ami Thompson, Rowan Keyzer, Alicia Wiggin, Annie Laurie Nichols, and Jessie John, you are still magical creatures. People like you are the reason God made jellyfish. I pray that you will be surprised by sunsets and unexpected beauty. Thank you for being my rockstar patrons.

Journey Mama, readers, I love you so much. Thanks for being such a kind group of friends. I couldn't do this without you.

Shekina Community and Pai Community. I have found a home. Thank you for letting me live with you.

Invisible, blazing, loving Creator, you sustain each breath of mine. I am endlessly thankful.

ABOUT THE AUTHOR

Newsletter

If you want to join Rachel Devenish Ford's Newsletter and learn about books and new releases, sign up here. Your address will never be shared!

~

Bio

Rachel Devenish Ford is the wife of one Superstar Husband and the mother of five incredible children. Originally from British Columbia, Canada, she spent seven years working with street youth in California before moving to India to help start a meditation center in the Christian tradition. She can be found eating street food or smelling flowers in many cities in Asia. She currently lives in Northern Thailand, inhaling books, morning air, and seasonal fruit.

~

Works by Rachel Devenish Ford:

The Eve Tree

A Traveler's Guide to Belonging

Trees Tall As Mountains: The Journey Mama Writings-
Book One

Oceans Bright With Stars: The Journey Mama Writings-
Book Two

A Home as Wide as the Earth: The Journey Mama Writ-
ings: Book Three

World Whisperer : World Whisperer Book 1

Guardian of Dawn : World Whisperer Book 2

Shaper's Daughter: World Whisperer Book 3

Reviews

Recommendations and reviews are such an important part of
the success of a book. If you enjoyed this book, please take the
time to leave a review.

Don't be afraid of leaving a short review! Even a couple
lines will help and will overwhelm the author with waves of
gratitude.

Contact

Email: racheldevenishford@gmail.com
Blog: http://journeymama.com

Facebook: http://www.facebook.com/racheldevenishford
Twitter: http://www.twitter.com/journeymama
Instagram: http://instagram.com/journeymama

Want to know about World Whisperer 5 as soon as it comes out? Sign up here.

~

What is the most important ingredient for a book's success? Besides, of course, the book itself?

It's what you, the Reader, says about it. Social proof. Reviews.

When people are out there, in the wilderness of the book jungle, looking for something to read, the main question they ask is, "Have other people read this? Did they like it?"

So if this book is your kind of book, and you think it might be someone else's kind of book, I will be over the moon if you leave a review on whatever site feeds you your books. Reviews can be the key to a book's success. Thank you!

~